The Middle Ages

Also by Jennie Fields

Crossing Brooklyn Ferry
Lily Beach

The Middle Ages

Jennie Fields

wm

WILLIAM MORROW

An Imprint of HarperCollins*Publishers*

This is a work of fiction. The characters, incidents, and dialogues are products of the author's imagination and are not to be construed as real. Any resemblance to actual events or persons, living or dead, is entirely coincidental.

HarperCollins books may be purchased for educational, business, or sales promotional use. For information please write: Special Markets Department, HarperCollins Publishers Inc., 10 East 53rd Street, New York, NY 10022.

FIRST EDITION

Designed by Bernard Klein

Printed on acid-free paper

Library of Congress Cataloging-in-Publication Data

Fields, Jennie.
The middle ages / Jennie Fields.
p. cm.
ISBN 0-688-14590-6
I. Title.

PS3556.I4175 M53 2002
813'.54—dc21

2001044529

02 03 04 05 06   RRD   10 9 8 7 6 5 4 3 2 1

For Russ, whom I found again

Acknowledgments

I would like to thank my ever-wonderful agent, Lisa Bankoff, and my editor, Carolyn Marino, for their encouragement and suggestions. I would also like to thank Susan Spano for her insightful early reading, and Kate Hanenberg for accuracy about architecture. Personal thanks go to Russ Mason, Dora Capers, Steven Kroeter, and always to my beautiful daughter, Chloe.

The Middle Ages

One

———

Men used to follow me. They did. Honest to God. Right up out of the subway like rats following the Pied Piper. I know you're looking at me and wondering, What the hell is she talking about? She's ordinary. She's overweight. She's *old*! She's panting as she climbs the subway steps. Fifty-four. Fifty-five. Fifty-six. How many steps does it take to kill a middle-aged woman? Okay. In this ivory coat, I know I look like a jar of mayonnaise. I saw myself in a store window yesterday. I glanced fetchingly into the window and thought, What the *hell* is that?

It wasn't always like this. In the early eighties, construction workers used to annoy me with obscenities.

"Hey, baby, those forty Ds ya got?"

In the early eighties, I could sit between two fat people on the subway and still have room on either side. In the early eighties, I was twice mistaken for Andrea Marcovicci. Remember her? No.

Okay. I know you're saying, "Time passes. We get older every single second. Get used to it." Believe me. I'm trying.

Rising from the subway, I view the world above, and sigh. Another Times Square morning. The neon signs blink on and off and on again. Except they're not neon anymore. They're TVs the size of the Parthenon. And diodes and readouts. The sky above Manhattan is that shade of blue pink that smells of New Jersey. And here I am, yet again, on my way to my job as an architect.

I have been toiling at architecture for twenty-three years now. And lately, it's as if I've been pricked and all the juices have run out. It's 1999, and the architecture portion of my psyche is beginning to resemble beef jerky. Dried and cured. I design chains of banks, chains of supermarkets, chains of dry cleaners. I find myself telling my friends, "Well, I didn't *really* design that. Committee influence. You know." I have begun to think that if I ever was any good, I've lost touch with it. I worry that perhaps creativity is the exclusive domain of the young. (The majority of the people we hire these days were in diapers and banging their heads against the bars of their cribs in the early eighties.) Walking down Broadway, I try to refute the power of youth. *Great geniuses in later life* . . . ummm . . . (1) Georgia O'Keeffe; (2) Grandma Moses; (3) George Burns. There must be more . . .

They were no longer juicy. Nobody followed them. And yet, look at the impact they made, so late in life! Georgia O'Keeffe. Have you ever seen a picture of her in her later years? She was beautiful. Beautiful as driftwood tossed for years in the surf. Character. She had character like nobody's business. And George Burns. He still made movies till the end. He still made people laugh, into his nineties, for God's sake. And Grandma Moses. Well, I don't know much about her. She became famous for painting like a child. Maybe she shouldn't count.

A mother with two young girls is passing me in the opposite direction on Broadway. Oh, yes. I recognize her. That was me too. It's only nine-forty-five A.M. and the girls, all blond and flyaway, are already sticky with purple lollipops. Their dark-haired mother looks haggard, worried, miserable. The girls are yanking her forward, their tongues and faces slathered with goofy grape. For one brief second, she catches my eye. The look she gives me is complex and affecting. On one hand, she is screeching for help; on the other, she is smiling lopsidedly. "How funny that I should be at the mercy of all this," her look says. "Me, Elise Farcus, once beautiful, once desired. These wonderful little girls. These sticky little lollipops. This is my life."

Ah yes. I recognize her. Come the late eighties that was me. A woman with small children. Too tired to care that my breasts were nominally still pointing upward. Too involved with my twin daughters to feel sexual when men smiled at me, which they did less and less. Daniel, their father, never seemed to.

In my twenties, I was desirable but insecure. In my thirties, I was covered with spit up or had toddler bags of Cheerios edging out of my pockets, and living with a man who'd lost all interest in sex with me, let alone romance. In my forties, I'm free of all that: the toddlers are grown, the man is gone, but where the hell did my beauty go? On this ordinary morning, this strikes me as a cruel joke. I pull my ivory coat around me, cross Broadway to my office building, just avoiding getting run down by a bicycle messenger with a whistle and a yellow jacket. He is free, this bike messenger, and wild, and appears as though he doesn't care who he runs over. I, on the other hand, am an indentured servant. Indentured to my mortgage, my daughters' private school tuition.

I am about to walk up the steps to the plaza of my office building yet again, and then I stop. People pile up behind me, there in the middle of the sidewalk. I am shoved, cursed at. The crowd flows around me as if I were a rock in a stream. Still, I can't seem to move forward. It is a Thursday. An ordinary Thursday. Yet my office building looms like the monolith in 2001. Frightening, ominous. Must I go there? I have a bank drawing laid out on my computer like a patient on an operating table. But I simply can't move forward, or rather, I can't move forward up the stairs to Paramount Plaza.

"Lady. What the hell you doin'?"

"For Chrissake, move!"

It's rather exciting to be shouted at, to call any attention to myself at all. But I can't go in. I really can't. There's a force field in front of the building and I've lost the code to break through it. So instead of moving forward, I turn left. And then I spot the C train entrance on Fiftieth Street. It calls to me, "C'mon, Janie. I'm going up along Central Park West. Wanna come? We could have fun. Oh, come on!"

I can't believe I'm doing this. Nine forty-five on an ordinary morning, descending the crumbling steps down to the C train. It's been six months or more since I've been down here. The last time was when I took the C train to the dentist. My my. It must be time for another dental checkup, I think randomly.

The subway station, at the end of this hot summer, smells of urine and damp though this morning is cool. The ceilings are hanging with peeling paint, and tiny stalactites and stalagmites from a pipe that could well have been dripping for the last ten years. But there is a sense of fine expectation here. A good twenty people wait along the dark platform, sighing, shifting. It must have been a while since a train has come. I stand on the platform, excited, shivering. I'm playing hooky. HOOKY!

I haven't played hooky since third year of high school, when, in a fit of misery over my mother's failing marriage to Ed Butz, I hitchhiked to the movies in the middle of the day. I saw *Butch Cassidy and the Sundance Kid* twice, only leaving my seat once, to buy the biggest tub of buttery popcorn they sold. And best of all, I never got caught. That's one of my happiest adolescent memories—eating buttered popcorn and getting hot watching Butch and Sundance conquer their world with sarcastic blue-eyed glances. And here I am at forty-six reliving that stolen afternoon. I look at the others on the platform. A man in a suit, clearly late for an appointment. A girl in torn jeans and a sweatshirt studying a notebook. A young man with a Russian-language newspaper reading what appears to be an article about Howard Stern. You have no idea how strange Howard Stern's face looks in a sea of Russian letters. When the train comes, it is nearly empty. I haven't yet decided which stop I intend to get off at, or what exactly I plan to do when I get there. I take a piece of gum out of my purse and chew it. I feel like I'm sixteen. God, this is fun! The man with the Russian newspaper is now reading an article with a picture of Monica Lewinsky. She looks very odd dressed in Russian too. I feel the way I feel when I'm traveling. Pleased and contained, and ready to experience anything.

At Eighty-first Street, I am just debating where I should get out when the train pulls into the newly renovated station. Along the fresh tile walls, mosaics of whales and elephants and bats glow under the new lights. The American Museum of Natural History. Right at the front of the subway platform are the doors to the museum, with their frames of newly polished brass and clean windows revealing the pink glow of marble inside. With the same force that drew me to the C train, I step out onto the platform. I haven't set foot in the museum since when? It was 1990, 1991 at the latest. I held two identical little hands, and we wobbled our way through dioramas of polar bears and Native Americans.

The museum is cool and empty. A bored ticket seller sits tapping her fingers on the marble counter. I see I have entered the part of the museum nearest the new Rose Center for Earth and Space with its spherical planetarium. I have watched this new part of the building go up whenever I've visited friends or my dentist on the Upper West Side: a perfect globe set into a cube of glass. And now it's done.

"How much for the planetarium?" I ask her.

"Nineteen dollars."

"Nineteen dollars?" It's hard to imagine that the world has become this expensive.

"Like I said," she mutters. She looks down at her fingernails, which are false and an acid shade of orange overpainted with minuscule Chinese junks and sunsets.

I pull out a twenty-dollar bill. "When's the first show?"

"In twenty minutes."

"Can I get in?"

She laughs. "No. The entire city of New York is waiting. Can't you see?" She grabs the bill before I've offered it to her and spits a ticket out of her machine. "Take the stairs, through the doors, turn left." She hands me the hologrammed ticket that has a moving photograph of the planet earth as seen from space. "Here is your passport to the universe," she says in a voice that says she'd rather be cleaning toilets. "You can check your coat first, past the stairs to your right."

I am giddy. Maybe because I've just blown twenty bucks to look at fake stars. Maybe because I'm about to be rid of the terrible ivory coat. (Perhaps I should leave it here?) Probably because I'm not sitting at my desk designing the prototype for the Bank of Monmouth branches. And definitely because I'm forty-six years old and this is only the second time in my life that I've ever done anything the least bit unexpected.

Well, there aren't millions of people waiting for the sky show, but there are about thirty-five. Mostly tourists, I determine. Older people. A few families. Couples. Not many alone like me. Right there in the lobby, they run a video with Tom Hanks narrating and we crane our necks to watch the monitors that hang from the ceiling.

He tells us we are about to take a journey to outer space. And to think I only expected to go to work today. When the doors open to the theater, they announce, "Fill all the seats. Move to the middle. Leave no empty seats between you," which is completely absurd, since the theater must hold two or three hundred. But dutifully we move to the middles of the long, empty rows, sitting side by side as though expecting tour buses of hundreds to discharge their passengers any minute. An older gray-haired man sits down beside me. He is one of the few who also seems to be alone.

"Visiting New York?" he asks.

"No. I live here."

"First time here?" he says. Could he be trying to pick me up? Nah.

"Yes. To the planetarium. You?"

"Oh no." He smiles. "I come here every Thursday morning."

"Really?"

"I get such a kick out of it," he says. "You have no idea. Nobody gets it, why I'm so . . . obsessed." He has nice teeth. He must sixty or sixty-five. I'd like to ask him if he has a job, or if he's retired. He is wearing an expensive-looking pink polo shirt. I can't imagine spending nineteen dollars every Thursday morning for what can't be more than a half-hour show. Maybe he retired wealthy. Sold his company to a conglomerate or something. Possesses his own golf cart.

"I have forty-two of these," he says, holding up his passport to the universe.

"Really?"

"So this is forty-three. Oh good. They're beginning."

The lights lower and then go out completely. The room is pitch-black. Even the exit signs have gone nearly dark, down to a faint phosphorescent green.

"Oh, golly! I am so ready for this," the man says. I smile in the dark. I can't remember being in a place this dark. Not since I used to hide in my closet as a kid. And even my closet was lighter. I can't see anything. Not even my own hands. Something rises from the middle of the room. A voice tells us to stay in our seats no matter what. A claustrophobe would certainly be convulsing by now. But I, like the man next to me, am so ready. A vision of the earth begins to spin, traversing the screens that surround us. Then we pull out to see the planets. Pull out farther and stars appear. I lean back, letting Tom Hanks take me on a journey. We explore our galaxy, then leave it, move out into the vast universe. Our galaxy then becomes just a speck of dust. Our star cluster is rendered nearly invisible. We are nothing. We are smaller than small. We are meaningless molecules, atoms. Tinier than that.

I listen to the man beside me, and suddenly realize he is aroused. I mean not just excited by the vastness of the universe, or the unimportant size of even our Milky Way. He is excited in the way that got Pee-wee Herman arrested. I think I hear a zipper, then I can feel him moving in the seat beside me. I can hear his breathing, and as we collectively fly through a black hole back to planet earth, I hear him groan, "Oh. OH!" Others are making noise, too. We are flying thrillingly through a black hole. But I am quite certain he's journeyed even farther.

"Wow," he says, catching his breath. Zip zip.

And this is how I spend my first act of disobedience in years and years. Next to a man who has far outstripped me.

My name is Jane Larsen. I am lucky I kept my name when I married because the marriage didn't last, and I'd be wearing his name now like an outgrown dress. Larsen has always suited me fine. It's my mother's name. Here's a picture of my mother at nineteen. She was pregnant and not married the day she gave birth to me in 1953.

A child out of wedlock. I wonder who took the picture. She kept it because she told me it reminded her of her worst mistake and her best pregnancy. "I didn't throw up once with you." Except for the fact that she was pregnant, you can tell men certainly would have followed her.

For years, I couldn't talk about this at all. It was our secret. It was the stiff underwear under the soft-flowing dress. My mother, my gentle, quiet mother had sex before she had a real wedding ring. Marta Larsen from Dubuque, Iowa. Exiled from home. Dishwater-blond hair pulled into a bun, working as a waitress in a coffee shop in Chicago until I was born, and then after. Wearing a "wedding" ring she'd bought herself at Woolworth's. She once pulled it out of an old jewelry box to show it to me. It was plastic underneath a metallic glaze. It weighed nothing. It was like a charm from a Cracker Jack box.

"I cooked up this husband who was off in Korea," she told me. "Kenneth James Larsen." A sergeant, she told everyone. The people in the coffee shop asked her nearly every day what she'd heard from Ken. So she started to think about what he might look like, and what he wore when not in uniform, and how much he missed her, halfway around the world. It was a good thing I was her first baby because she barely showed until the end. People didn't approve of women working late in a pregnancy. Women just didn't do that back then. But what was she going to do? She couldn't go back to Dubuque. She needed money. She was all alone. I once asked her if she'd been afraid. "I didn't have time to be afraid," she said.

I've been to Dubuque. I know why my mother left. It is a tight and silent place. Not sure it has a right to be there. There's a sign on a railroad bridge as you come into town. It says DUBUQUE. A PLACE TO LIVE. "A Place to Live." Not a good place, a happy place, a lovely place? No. Just a place. It wasn't a place to live for my mother. Not after she slept with her married high school principal.

Sam Everhardt. I've often thought of his name but can never really *understand* that he was my father, because I never met him. He died when I was just a baby. Not once had he ever laid eyes on me. My mother told me that he never tried to find her, or to follow her or give her money. He never acknowledged the card she sent to his office with "Private" emblazoned on it. According to her, the card read:

```
I gave birth on August 2 to a baby daughter
named Jane. She's yours.
   Marta Larsen
```

And my mother was far too proud to pursue him, though he was an adult, and she was only a child, thrust into an unkind world alone. She made as much of a life for herself as she was able to. She worked at the coffee shop. She rented an apartment she furnished as well as she could with the three hundred dollars of baby-sitting money she had saved, and the money from her small salary. She bought a used crib and she told me she folded towels on an old chest she found on the street and used as a changing table. Her landlady gave her baby clothes outgrown by her grandchild, Anthony Junior. Boys' clothes, but my mother was happy to have them.

Here's a picture of me just hours after my birth. Ugly. Squinchy-faced. I was born in Michael Reese Hospital on the South Side of Chicago just as they were signing a peace treaty in some overlit room in Korea. The Korean War was over, and my life was just beginning.

"Guess your husband will be back soon," my mother's friends from the coffee shop told her when they visited her in the hospital with flowers and baby dresses.

"Gosh, I sure hope so," she told them. "It's no fun having a baby without Ken around. He's just a sucker for little babies."

She told them she named me Jane because it was Ken's mother's name. But she really chose it because it was simple. She wanted her life and everything in it to be simple. Jane Larsen.

Until the day she died, she would often call me both names, as though Larsen were my middle name, i.e., Mary Lou. "Jane Larsen, where are your shoes, young lady?" "Jane Larsen, if you get yourself pregnant, you will be very sorry indeed." Somehow, when she called me Jane Larsen I knew she loved me. I knew it meant that I was my mother's alone. It was her way of being affectionate, and possessive. My mother was a Larsen. I was a Larsen.

After I was born, my mother finally called home, and spoke to her eldest (and—another sin—divorced) sister, Aggie (no longer a Larsen; surname Canelli from her ex-husband). Aggie came immediately to Illinois on the train with a black patent-leather hatbox (that later became my doll box) and three cardboard suitcases. She took turns taking care of me and trading shifts at the coffee shop with my mother. Aunt Aggie and I were great friends, both members of the Marta Larsen Fan Club. Can you see her face in this photo? How patient she looks. How nonjudgmental. These are just a few of Aunt Aggie's fine qualities. Loving my mother was our greatest bond. But even with Aunt Aggie there, I never felt we were a real family. I pointed out fathers wherever we went. "There's a daddy. There's another. That's a really nice daddy there." Aunt Aggie said I counted fathers the way other people count license plates from Michigan.

But, we went on, the three of us, for quite a while together. Our apartment always smelled of Pond's cold cream and drawer sachets, while my friends' houses smelled of pipe smoke and leather briefcases. I liked to spend time at their houses and watch their fathers do things. Like one always put his handkerchiefs on the couch cushion before he took a nap. Another left the toilet seat up. I didn't even know toilet seats went up! I sometimes asked my friends if I could look in their fathers' closets. Fathers' closets were full of dark, shouldery suits and belts that looked evil. But I wanted a father in my house nonetheless.

Then, when I was five, I got a daddy of my very own. My mother married—wait. I have a photo here somewhere . . . yes! Ed Butz. God! He was handsome then.

I didn't take Ed Butz's last name. I wouldn't. But I was crazy about him despite his terrible name. (I used to stand in front of the mirror and say over and over, "Jane BUTZ, Jane BUTZ. Jane BUTZ," and worry it would become my name. My mother said, "Not if you don't want it to be.") Ed clearly loved not just my mother, but me as well. He told us what he wanted most was to give us a better life. To be a family. My mother, who'd been taking business courses at night since shortly after I was born, actually did achieve her degree. She proudly graduated before their wedding (I remember her shiny black gown and mortarboard. Five-year-olds adore costumes, and my mother let me try it on. Flowing in black rayon, I looked like a ghoul. I loved it, didn't want to take it off. I wish I had a picture of that). But despite my mother's degree, Ed didn't want her to have to work, and my mother didn't argue. Maybe someday, they both agreed, she could practice accounting— when her children were fully grown.

Then my mother had the opportunity to wear another costume. A wedding dress, voluminous and virginal, and wholly inappropriate for a woman with a school-age child, but she looked beautiful in it. Can you see? The color wasn't very good back then. Faded Kodachrome. But look. White gown, golden hair. Like a daffodil. (For the wedding, she eschewed dishwater for bottled butter blond and wore it that way until the day she died.) Look at the three of us. My mother in her wedding gown. Me in that funny lemon-yellow number with the crinoline petticoat. (It crunched and I *loved* it.) Ed in striped trousers and a cutaway. So formal! So happy.

My mother and Ed went off on a honeymoon. I stayed home with Aunt Aggie and we played eighty-seven games of old maid in just two weeks. (We thought about calling *The Guinness Book of Records*.) But then the honeymooners returned and Ed moved us to a Tudor house with a big backyard, in the suburbs. I had a room they painted lavender blue, and a cherry tree right outside my window, which turned deep pink every spring. Even Aunt Aggie moved in with us. She had the whole top floor to herself. She took a job in the suburbs as a doctor's receptionist, until later when she remarried—Barney Sells, the NBC weatherman, a wedding that ended up in the society column of the paper.

I was smitten with Ed. He was much more fun than my mother, who always felt it was her duty to be a leveling influence. Ed was kind and able. I felt safe when he held me in his lap. He had perfect teeth that were so openly spaced they looked like dentil molding (an architectural feature I've always loved). I don't know why I don't have any pictures of him smiling. He smiled all the time and told my mother and me and even Aggie that we were the prettiest girls in the world. He built a tree house, painted perfect evergreen-colored diamonds on the garage door, and taught me to waltz.

I was particularly proud of the fact that he was a product manager at Kraft Foods in charge of Velveeta. It seemed to me that the entire population of North America worshiped Velveeta. Every Thursday, the whole family, even Aunt Aggie if she didn't have a date, would watch Perry Como and listen to Ed Herlihy talk about Velveeta's meltability and feel proud. I was the daughter of Mr. Velveeta. In the summers, we'd have barbecues that included all the recipes Ed Herlihy described on TV—salads with orange sections, coconut, and Jet-Puffed miniature marshmallows; macaroni salads made with Miracle Whip. Rice casseroles blanketed in Velveeta. Chicken ruddy with Kraft barbecue sauce.

I finally had the family I'd always dreamed of. My mother was a happy woman with Ed. I assumed once you were happy, you'd stay that way forever. Ever after.

For eight years, it seemed we were as happy as a family could be. My mother had three more children: two boys, Charlie and Pete: and a girl, Bess. Here. Take a look at this. That's Bess a week after she was born. She was the daintiest thing. I wasn't jealous of my siblings, because my mother treated me as a partner, as the only one with good sense. I had a special place in the family and I cherished it. They got my hand-me-downs. I got the originals.

Aunt Aggie moved just blocks away with Barney Sells, "the Cheerful Weatherman," and would come over to help cook and eat dinner every Sunday. Some Sunday nights, I would look around the dining room table at this ever growing family and feel a fullness in my heart that made me feel positively faint with joy. How could things get any better? I often wondered.

Then when I was thirteen, a woman called our house at two in the morning. My mother answered. The woman said Ed Butz had gotten her daughter, a secretary at Kraft, pregnant, and he should stand up and be a man about it. That night Ed Butz confessed that the pregnant woman was one of his many flings. It was a terrible compulsion he had with younger women. He couldn't control himself. My mother, probably remembering the lack of response from her own older seducer, made Ed leave at once, barely gave him time to pack a suitcase. He was gone before we got up for school. My mother told Ed he had no choice: he *must* divorce her and marry the pregnant secretary.

Ed moved out and lived at the Y for a long time. All of us missed him. And when he did arrive to take us out for milk shakes or for walks in the park, he wasn't the same around us anymore. He had a hangdog air about him, his shoulders raised, his head lowered like a dog that's been swatted with a newspaper. Shortly after, Kraft fired him, and I've never been sure whether it had anything to do with the pregnant secretary, or whether the upheaval in his life made him less of a good captain for the fate of Velveeta.

My mother was miserable. She was a woman who'd lost all sense of direction. She'd be doing the dishes and stop with a dishcloth in one hand and a pot in the other and stare at the wall. She'd watch soap operas all day, even though she'd never been much interested in TV before. Yet she never cried. And then she went to bed. For four weeks, she just gave up. There are no pictures of any of us for a long time after that.

"I'm sorry, Mama. About Dad. About Ed," I corrected myself though I had called him Dad for years and years, just like the other children. I watched her lying there, staring up at the ceiling. My mother seemed as empty and hollow and scooped out as the melon boats Ed Herlihy taught the housewives of America to make in his Kraft commercials.

"You could get a job as an accountant," I suggested. "You always wanted to be an accountant."

"No," my mother said. "I couldn't. I'm too old. I have no real experience. I took accounting in school so many years ago, I don't remember a thing." She shook her head and closed her eyes. "You know," she said, "I never guessed. I never knew about Ed. I never had an inkling. I thought I was his one and only. And here I was, just part of a crowd. I never knew a thing. Don't let anyone do that to you, Jane. Make a fool of you. You're so trusting. I know that about you. You want to like people. But don't be like me. Don't trust a man who says he loves only you. Don't trust any man at all. Don't trust anything in your life that seems certain. All your happiness might be a lie."

Back on Broadway, nearly noon now, I ease through the gauntlet of smokers taking breaks at the door to my office building. I am debating whether I should say I had an emergency appointment at the dentist, or had to wait for the plumber. I imagine briefly announcing that I simply *had* to go to the sky show at the planetarium.

The dentist concept wins because, like the American Museum of Natural History, he's on the Upper West Side, so if anyone saw me—I can't imagine who would have—my excuse would be valid. I step into the tall, dark elevator lobby. My architectural firm designed this building in the fifties, and a number of years ago finally decided to make a statement by actually housing itself in one of its own buildings. The firm is now large enough to occupy two floors.

"Hey," Mattie the receptionist calls to me as soon as the elevator doors have opened, and waves two pink "While You Were Out" messages, one from a client, one from Rodney Paris, the only living architect whose name is on the door. Actually, it's his father's name but he pretends he is the great man.

No one gets pink message slips much anymore. Most people just leave voice mail. So when I get them, I usually experience a sinking feeling.

"Everyone seems to be looking for you," Mattie says.

Mattie has two pierces that allow a blue titanium spike to go entirely through her left ear, top to bottom. It makes me shudder. It's right up there with African tribeswomen who stretch their lips to accommodate colored disks. It's public knowledge that Mattie is sleeping with Rodney, even though she's twenty-two or -three and Rodney is at least fifty. I wonder what Rodney thinks of the spike. I wonder, Will Mattie tell Rodney I came in at noon?

I hang my coat in the entrance closet and wend my way to my space, saying hello to no one. I think somehow by not saying hello, I'm invisible and they won't notice how late I am. I sit down in my ergonomically correct chair and sigh. I hate this chair. I happen to know it cost $1,100, and it nevertheless makes my back ache, so I resent it for false advertising. It has a lumbar support you can move up or down, but most of the time it feels as if I'm leaning against a rock. Still, I'm lucky to have my space by the window. When I inherited this corner from my friend Lou, who left after a bout with colon cancer "to find some peace in life," I felt guilty to be taking his space, but inexpressibly relieved. I prize the natural light and how quiet it seems here compared to the middle of the room. All these years, I have hated the big, open room, the whole studio aura. I know most other people here thrive on it, find it exciting. But I am a person who recharges her batteries by being alone, and near the end of my day, I'm worn thin, and quieter than usual. I have never outgrown this, or gotten used to this endless communal time.

Last week, I got a letter from Lou, with photographs. He and his partner, Glenn, are living up in the Catskills in a little log house he's renovated. It showed up in *Country Home* magazine. Beautiful and beatific, just like Lou must be now. He's free of cancer. They've made a killing on the stock market. He's found real happiness. Ah, but hey! I have his corner. This desk, this computer, this drawing board. And this window overlooking half of Manhattan and a light-dancing metallic shard of the Hudson River. Now come on. Who's the lucky one? Jeez, I hate feeling sorry for myself. It's so inexcusable.

I lift the frame on my desk that holds a picture of my girls when they were only seven. Their little Bucky Beaver faces with those enormous new teeth. Their lanky, rosy hair catches the sun of that day in May like threaded gold. I stare at the vulnerability of their perfect faces. At the softness of their eyes. I think of the woman with the lollipop blondes, and recall the wonder and exhaustion of those years. Now my girls are described as exquisite, gorgeous, sexy, dangerous. And all their shirts are short enough to show their beautiful little belly buttons. God, they are knockouts. But they will never again be as beautiful to me as they were then, when they were funny-faced, and awkward, and needed me to sing them to sleep.

I set down the frame and pick up the one beside it. It's a picture of Daniel and me, early in our marriage. I suppose I should have taken it off my desk years ago. But it's the most beautiful picture anyone ever took of me, because I was so in love. My eyes are dark and glowing. My hair is long and nearly black and shining like a Prell model. Daniel's standing behind me, his arms around me, his face close to my neck. Holding me as tight as he can. And God, he's an Adonis. Strong and broad-shouldered, white-blond and blue-eyed. We look like one unit. We look as happy as a couple could possibly be. I close my eyes for a moment and try to remember how it felt.

"Hey, Jane," Dave Mann calls out from his space just feet from mine. "Did you see the paper?"

"No. What?"

"Article about Mr. Rodney 'I'm Richer Than You Are' Paris Jr." Dave hates Rodney. We all hate Rodney, really, but he owns our souls.

"What's it say?"

"It's about his apartment. His 'glorious marble-vaulted space.' " Then he leans forward with a hand by his mouth and stage whispers, "You'll puke." He hands me the folded up *Times*. We exchange evil smiles.

Dave is one of the few people here over forty. It seems the majority of people who now surround me have dyed black hair and outsize shoes and smell of nicotine. Baby geniuses. They barely know how to draw. They live for their computers. And they're good on them. Sometimes I think their computer technique far outstrips their ability to design. I guess I'm just jealous. They're young, hip, and computer literate far beyond my abilities.

"Where were you this morning, anyway?" Dave asks.

"You won't believe it," I say in a voice so low it makes Dave lean forward.

"Really? What won't I believe?"

"I played hooky."

"What? You? No."

"I went to the planetarium."

"Architectural field trip? It's a self-indulgent design if you ask me. That sphere in a square thing . . ."

"It was actually kind of neat. The metal supports are quite interesting. But I didn't go there for the architecture. I went there just to not come here for a morning. I felt like a kid cutting class."

I smile at him. Nancy Kangol, who sits next to him, has caught a piece of our conversation. Lately, I've been lunching with her, talking with her a lot about the business, about my philosophy of architecture, about the choices we make with each gesture. Helping her with her designs. She's one of the young girls I hate/admire, with a black China chop and cement shoes, but I like her better than the rest. Or maybe I simply know her better than the rest. She tells me about her boyfriend troubles. She listens intently to my advice. Sometimes I think she reminds me of myself when I was much younger. She has all these dreams. All this hope. She dreams of becoming a famous architect someday, of altering the world in some way. What I like about her is that she has the gall to tell me this and then blush and say, "I guess I'm an idiot. I just can't help dreaming." I envy her terribly.

"You just decided not to come in?" she whispers. She sounds amazed. I think she thinks of me as being as upright as her mother. I'm certainly in the same age group as her mother.

"I was coming to work," I tell her. "I walked right up to the building. I just couldn't bear to come in this morning . . . so I turned around and got on the C train."

"Good for you," Dave says.

"I did something like that last summer; I called in sick three days in a row and three days in a row went to Jones Beach," Nancy says. "I didn't even feel guilty. When I came back with a tan, Rodney said, 'You're looking awfully healthy for a sick girl.' I guess he knew, but he didn't give me a hard time about it."

"That's because you're young and beautiful," I say. "If he found out I went to the planetarium, he'd probably can me."

"Yeah, right," Dave says. "I don't think so." He smiles at me. He has lovely teeth. And he's as familiar to me as a favorite pillow.

I glance at the note to call Rodney. What could he want? Usually he doesn't pay much attention to me. For one thing, I'm a woman, and unless he's sleeping with them or wants to sleep with them, he doesn't seem to have much use for women. Once, many years ago, he came on to me. He was much more handsome in those days, good-looking, but even then in a reptilian way. We'd been to a client dinner, and he offered to take me home in his limo, then wondered if I wouldn't rather come to his place. "C'mon, Janie. It feels so right," he said. He tried to kiss me. He was a good kisser, a deep kisser. I'd had a few drinks too. He was between marriages. I was still deep into my marriage, however unhappy. And I had Cheerios in my pocket. I wasn't in the least bit interested in going to his place. His kiss hit a busy signal. "Oh," he said in a very deep voice. "I'll take you home." He was sulky for a few weeks after that, then began to treat me as he always had. The way you treat the wallpaper.

I dial Rodney's extension and his assistant answers.

"Is he there?" I ask.

"Jane? He's looking for you."

"Do you know why?"

"I don't know, but he was anxious to find you."

"Should I come down to his office?"

"Oh no, he's already left for the Rockford Building. He won't be back until two."

"Oh. Well, tell him I called," I say. My voice is annoyingly chirpy. I hang up, wonder what Rodney would possibly want. I turn to my computer and the nascent elevation of the Bank of Monmouth facade. Why do I feel so fed up just looking at it? I hate banks. I hate supermarkets. I hate chains of any kind.

It's been a year since I designed a house. Houses are what I still really love designing. They live, breathe, like people. But Rodney doesn't seem to be taking on jobs like that for us anymore. He only did them as favors to good clients, anyhow. Designing houses doesn't employ enough people, he says. There isn't enough margin. We've gotten too big. I miss houses, though, miss the thrill of creating the stage set for people's lives. I have designed dozens that have actually been built by now. Houses for clients, and sometimes for friends. Houses by the sea. Houses with sweeping purple views of the Catskill Mountains. Houses with butlers' pantries and bidets. Houses for people who have money enough never to think about money.

But my favorite house is my own, and I had nothing to do with designing it, at least not its initial design. It existed long before I was born. I bought it with my now ex-husband, Daniel, back in the early eighties before the real estate market really took off, a shabby brownstone in Brooklyn. After sixty-three years of housing the McElroy family, it had been mercilessly turned into six shoddy sixties apartments. When we bought it, dried-out pinkish-orange linoleum curled up like fried bologna from the floors in each of the four kitchens, and dropped ceilings and fluorescents lit the apartments with the glare of church basements. The pocket shutters had been nailed into the walls, the etched-glass pocket doors too. Daniel proclaimed we'd already spent too much on the purchase of the house to spend another penny, but how could we live in the midst of a ruin?

I employed the money I'd inherited from my mother's estate to resuscitate its wheezing beauty. We turned it back into a single-family house, tearing out the avocado kitchens, restoring exact replica moldings where they'd been removed, soaking paint off ceiling medallions, scraping more paint off the marble mantels and the pocket shutters now released from their prisons, and the pocket doors with their etched-glass birds and flowers. Of course it took me years, because I got pregnant shortly after we moved in, and for a long time had to avoid everything with fumes. Still, there I was with a big tummy, sanding, prying, washing. And later, with leaking breast pads, polishing the elegant cherry banisters and newel posts until I could see three inches into the wood.

Now the brownstone is worth two and a half times what we paid for it, and since the divorce settlement, it's become mine. Mine and the girls, of course. Daniel said he'd never liked the house anyway. I paid him the measly $25,000 he'd grudgingly put into it in the beginning as his share. He moved to an apartment with open rooms and big windows, taking the valuable Stickley furniture that had never fit in the narrow house anyway. Taking with him the mementos of a marriage gotten off track. Sometimes, walking among the dark, elegant woodwork and pocket shutters and marble mantels of my house, I feel as though I'm living on some sort of exquisite stage set, anxiously waiting for the best part of the play to commence.

Of course, there have been some fine moments all along. Some nights when I thought Daniel really loved me. (Deluded nights, but fine at the time.) There was, of course, the day we brought the twins home from the hospital into a world of avocado-green kitchens and peeling linoleum. As I crossed the threshold, I held one in each arm, as tiny as loaves of Wonder bread. I wept. I felt as though I'd won the lottery, though I'd brought them into a world that might best have been described as "early tenement." Daniel looked on numbly. We named them Abigail for his grandmother, and Caitlin just because we liked it.

That was fifteen years ago. Now they throw hairbrushes and clothes and insults at each other, but within a setting as beautiful as a jewel box. They are more sylphlike and silken than the russet beauties of Pre-Raphaelite paintings, and that is what these rooms are like: the backgrounds of Pre-Raphaelite paintings, painted and draped in colors like garnet and sapphire and gold. The twins are proud of the house, love to bring their friends over and show off their rooms, which have borrowed the same exotic colors of the rest of the house, but have gone a step further. With saris for curtains and temple bells and exotic incense holders, their rooms resemble caravansaries. You expect to step outside and find camels waiting. When the inhabitants of these lovely, exotic rooms are happy, the whole world seems happy. But now they sulk and argue and rage. They are teenagers.

One thing my house doesn't have is a man. Not anymore. I suppose it would be nice to have a man around the house, as the old song goes. I suppose I should want a daddy, for my girls, just as I wanted one for myself. And then, there are all the practical things men seem to excel at: remembering the last time the furnace was checked; replumbing the toilets when the chain gets unhooked, putting in the air conditioners in the fourth-floor windows come summer. But the truth is, we do have a man. We still have Daniel. He does all of those things for us even all these years later. He's still the girls' daddy. He still comes for Thanksgiving, Christmas, Easter, Memorial Day, Fourth of July, and Labor Day. And sometimes for no reason at all. He still gives me wonderful gifts for my birthday, even when he doesn't have the money. Some people think I'm hanging on to this long-over love for Daniel. And it's true that when he walks in the door I feel inordinately happy, despite everything that's gone on between us.

Daniel is the man I thought I'd never capture. I used to think he was my version of Ed Butz: a man who could rescue me from worry and loneliness and fill my life with Velveeta. And much better than Ed, he had a lovely last name: Atherton. "Jane Atherton" has always sounded to me like a romance heroine. Or an Agatha Christie sleuth—the younger one who helped out Miss Marple and was quietly pretty despite her sensible English suits and tie shoes. But I never did take the name. I was stopped by an unspoken obligation to keep "Jane Larsen." Every time I thought of changing my name, I felt I was betraying my mother.

Daniel didn't mind whether I took his name or not. He said he loved me and lavished impressive gifts on me. Small gifts were never enough for him. It was alway the grand gesture. The necklace from Tiffany's, the fourth-row-center seats for Broadway. He was strikingly handsome, tall and slender, thoughtful and very British looking. Women have a tendency to stare at him. If you meet him, you will no doubt think first, Here is a sexy man, and second, He's so confident. And third, This man doesn't reveal much. All in all, I still love Daniel. I just don't trust him anymore.

I've always been attracted to him, and my attraction hasn't changed. I suppose it should, knowing he cheated on me throughout my marriage. I suppose I should just see him as ugly, or evil now. Instead, I just see him as Daniel. Flawed. Human. Older. Men don't get uglier as they age. They gain patina. They look more interesting. And certainly, Daniel has. He has gray sideburns now, and sunrays at the edges of his eyes. And a thousand untold secrets behind those eyes.

I didn't set out to marry a secretive man, but then, since I did, perhaps I was somehow subconsciously drawn to his secretiveness. Daniel is a champion at secrets. His secrets are as lavish as his gifts, and dark and worrisome, and I, like my mother, was totally clueless. I used to lie in bed after he'd leave in the morning for work—he left a good hour before I did—and weep for missing him. I was smitten in the worst sort of way: loving him diminished me. Daniel may well have been horrified to discover he'd married a dishrag who lived for his smile, for he used to say early on that what drew him to me was my feistiness and self-certainty as much as anything else. Only, the minute I married him, my feistiness dissolved. That's because the second we began to live together, his desire for me disappeared. In the beginning, long before the wedding ring, we were passionate lovers, making love in the backseat of a car, in a unisex bathroom, by the side of a lake at night. Suddenly, it was gone. Gone. *Phsssst.* I'd initiate, he'd turn away. I wouldn't initiate and he wouldn't either. This had never happened to me before. Male desire was an ever-flowing faucet in my experience. What the hell was this about?

And why was he always so eager to leave me every morning? Why did he say he'd be home after work and not come back until eleven? Why did I discover matches from some "club" in his jacket after a business trip when he'd told me the meeting had ended early and he'd stayed in his hotel room all night watching TV?

I always asked, and he always had explanations. Calm, annoyed explanations, like how dare I doubt him! He picked up the matches in the hotel room. Someone had left them there. He was working on ideas for a challenging new product, and he needed "alone time" at his office. In truth, he was sleeping with prostitutes, an old girlfriend, a woman he picked up at a bar, and a blond graphic designer who wanted to leave her husband for him. He was also going to strip clubs and once engaged in a threesome with two women. (All this he told me one weepy confessional night, years later.) He was living this dark, rebellious, secret life because the minute he married me, he saw me as his overbearing mother, keeping him from all that beckoned to him, and there I was, Mrs. Blind-As-a-Bat, working out on a stationary bicycle to rid myself of the fat I'd gained during my difficult pregnancy, and doing the dishes and changing the twins' diapers and thinking we'd be together always. And yet lying at night beside him, I was more lonely than I'd ever been before or since. It was a raw, unhealable loneliness. Looking at this elegant, sleeping man beside me made me lonelier. Wanting him to love me again like he once had made me feel as helpless as I'd ever felt. I thought that somehow it was something I'd done wrong, and something it was my responsibility to fix.

Now, I berate myself for my idiocy. I don't have an IQ of twelve. Why couldn't I see it? Because Daniel was my dream come true and I didn't want to wake up. Or maybe I was just duplicating my mother's relationship with dear old Ed Butz.

Despite all that, I have never understood how you could spend years of your life with someone and ever feel that you hate him, like so many of my friends hate their former husbands. Something drew me to Daniel in the first place, I figure. And we have children together. How can I hate the one person with whom I share all that is worthwhile?

Especially because now, ten years after he moved out, so much of the tension is gone. I don't expect to sleep with him. I don't want to know with whom he's sleeping. He never seems to have a real relationship with anyone. He's never introduced a single one of his women friends to the twins. The twins say Daniel and I get along better with each other than any of their friends' parents get along, and they're all still married.

All and all, I've lost interest in marriage. I doubt relationships. I can't imagine trusting a man again, certainly not enough to let him see me vulnerable. It's one of those mistakes that if you are smart, you make only once.

Great couples I have personally known: (1) Jackie and Stan, my next-door neighbors; though they were once great together, now they're barely speaking. She's having an affair with her tennis instructor. He, who knows? (2) Cloris and Bob, my college roommate and her husband. Their wedding was fabulous. Everyone dancing. Kissing. Wild. Now he's passively miserable. She's always angry. Their son is a juvenile delinquent and I can't stand being with them. (3) Loni and Mike (Daniel's sister and brother-in-law). I always thought they were so happy. They held hands. He was solicitous of her. They kissed in the corner at parties. She always seemed so proud and supportive of him. Two months ago they announced they're splitting up and marrying other people. He's marrying a guy whose name is also Mike. (4) Daniel and Jane. We were madly in love. We were romantic. He was the man of my dreams. We had great sex. It was all a prelude to an empty lie.

Rodney Paris never does come back from the Rockford Building, and I spend the rest of the day fiddling with the facade of the bank I've now begun to loathe. I feel as if I'm in a time warp. Didn't I already design this bank prototype about a hundred times? While I play with the moldings, and doors, and fenestration, I remind myself that according to Tom Hanks, I am just a squeegy little bit of nothing on a planet no bigger than a speck. This for some reason amuses me no end. It means that nothing I do really matters in the scheme of the bigger picture. And what a big picture it is! So if I design this window above the door of the bank to look like the face of Goofy, what difference does it make? Or if I locate a bathroom where the ATM machines should be, the world won't come to an end. I imagine toilet paper coming out of the machines instead of money.

When I leave, I realize that it hasn't been an ordinary day after all, but one that years from now I'll remember. The day I played hooky. Unless, of course, I continue to play hooky on a regular basis. The possibility doesn't seem remote at all.

You know, you wake up one day and you find that you've made a series of compromises. None of them extraordinary. Merely realistic revisions of your original dream. But compiled, they become much more. They send you on a path away from the possible. You discover you're not who you wanted to be. You're not even who you can be. You're just ordinary. Your story is hardly worth telling.

You know, I've gotten so good at just doing what is set before me, I've forgotten how to wish or dream. I've forgotten how to count possibilities. You spend the first part of your life metamorphosing. And then one day, you realize, you've forgotten how to change.

Two

———

$\mathcal{F}$ull of this insidious restlessness, I take the subway home to my daughters. It's been just a week now since they returned from camp, where they were junior counselors. They are very present, indeed, in the house, especially after the silence of the summer, filling it with their voices, shoes, bras, wet towels, used feminine hygiene products, makeup, and moods. I love my daughters. But I've come to believe that teenagers at a certain age begin to give off some essence as impossible for adults to suffer as skunk. And I feel very sad to discover myself avoiding them in the week since they've returned.

Once we seemed as connected as a Möbius strip. We flowed into each other and back again. Where did I end and they begin? These days, though, they grumble when I walk in. They roll their eyes. Teenage hormones have lengthened their limbs, elongated their faces, and closed their hearts. Mirror images, as identical as two of God's creatures could be, they don't even seem to like each other anymore. And worst of all, they can't imagine that their mother has feelings. The sensitivity they had as children has vanished. They say whatever they want to me, and often it's hurtful.

"God, Mom. You've really got to diet."

"Yeah. Wide load."

"Mom, you know I can't stand salmon."

"Since when?"

"Since forever. You are clearly getting senile."

Parents love their children unconditionally, I think. How unfair that children don't feel the same way about their parents.

I can hear their voices even before I put the key in the downstairs gate—and they're arguing.

"If you tell him, I am definitely going to kill you."

"I think he should know."

"You fucking fart. You're totally dead. Dead. Rigor mortis."

When they returned from camp, their faces seemed reminted— their jaws longer, their eyes more defined—and their voices imitate new friends. The buzz words are new. "Fucking fart" is a fresh favorite. As is "Gawwwwd," a new form of "God" that's spoken with the mouth totally shut.

But, this year, in returning from Hidden Cove, they look beautiful, and oddly, weirdly grown-up. You could easily mistake them for twenty-year-olds. Each of their golden-brown heads of hair has darkened a shade, from honey to oak, though in summers past, their hair lightened in the sun while their skins darkened. Now their hair and skin tone match perfectly, as though they've been dipped in bronze. My beautiful daughters: bronzed, tall, sleek, and crabby.

Abigail is standing by the refrigerator, holding it open as wide as possible, or so it seems. Cait is at the kitchen table, peeling apart a beeswax candle. Of the twins, Cait has always been the emotional one, Abigail the wise one, the one who surprised me with her insight and maturity, but in recent months Cait has gotten even more emotional, weeping at MTV videos, and letters from camp friends, and Abigail has been hijacked by a sometimes giggly, sometimes sulky, seemingly less intelligent model who views me with not so much disdain as despair.

"Where were you?" she asks as I walk in. She looks pointedly at the kitchen clock.

"I'm right on time," I say.

"I'm starved. So's Cait. What are we having?"

"I made a meat loaf on Sunday."

"No." Cait waves her hand. "No way. Not meat loaf."

"Why?" I remember Cait as a too-tall little girl of twelve tucking into a plate of meat loaf with joy. It's the only kind of red meat in which either girl ever showed any interest.

"Zits. Fat. Yuck," Abigail says. "Gawwwwd."

"Zits, fat, yuck?" I ask. "What is that? Chinese?"

Cait snickers.

"It contains too much fat, which will definitely give me zits, and it disgusts me," Abby says this in a very prolonged, condescending way, as though I am slow-witted or deaf.

"Oh."

Food Cait and Abby now hate: (1) Anything that's easy to make. (2) Anything they've had often since childhood. (3) Anything I particularly like or particularly like to make. (4) Anything they once liked.

Foods they seem particularly fond of: arugula, oatmeal, soy-substitute candy bars, chicken Kiev spurting butter. Go figure.

"You guys aren't going to eat meat loaf?" I ask.

"No meat loaf for us . . . unless you feed us with funnels, like the geese in France," she says. She throws her head back and makes a gargling sound.

"I'll have to try that," I say.

I pull together a meal for the girls of feta cheese and tomato omelets and arugula salads. We sit down, me to my lone plate of perfectly delicious meat loaf.

"Arugula! Yes!" Cait cries. It's incomprehensible to me how anyone could love arugula this much.

"After dinner, you have to help me with my French," Abby says.

"You have to help me with my science," Cait says.

"Okay. You have to help me with the dishes," I say.

No comment.

"There's something else we wanted to talk about," Abby says.

"What?"

They look at each other, then down at the table, then at each other again, in a sequence as choreographed as a Broadway dance number.

"What?"

"These are good," Abby says, eating her omelet. "Yup, really good." She smiles in an evil sort of way.

"They are," Cait says, in collusion. "And the arugula's great."

"*What?*" I say.

Cait screws up her mouth, but shakes her head.

"We've been discussing it," Abby says, "and we would like to ask you . . ." She hesitates and screws up her mouth in the exact same way that Cait does. "Half our friends have already gotten . . ."

I wait, afraid to find out what.

"Tattoos," Abby whispers.

"Tattoos?" I say. My throat closes around the meat loaf like a hand grabbing the string of a balloon.

"Everyone has them," Cait says.

"They wouldn't need to be *big* ones . . . ," Abby says.

"And what would they *need* to be?"

"Unique," Cait says.

"Distinctive."

"There's a good word," I say, trying to level myself. Tattoos? On my beautiful daughters? "What do you have in mind? Mom in a big red heart on your biceps?"

"You're so sarcastic," Cait says, as though *she* isn't. "We're being serious."

What I probably should have said was, "I'll think about it, girls. Maybe." And stalled and stalled until they changed their minds. I know this. Rationally I'm all there. But instead I say, "Have you ever thought what your tattoos will look like when you're sixty-five years old and your skin is sagging and you're these two old, gray-haired ladies with stretched tattoos that used to say 'love' and now say 'looooooooooove'?"

"Very funny again," Abby says, sighing. "You are so amazingly funny tonight, Mom. It's exhausting."

"That's a million years from now, Mom," Cait said.

"So you think. Just wait."

"We just want small tattoos. I want one on my ankle with a 'C' on it and a little wreath of flowers around it and Abby wants—"

"I'll tell her myself. I want an open book on my butt cheek."

"You want what?"

"To stand for . . . my love of books, you know." This from my sensible Abigail?

"You need to tattoo your love of books on your butt?"

"So, could we?" Cait asks.

"*No.*"

"Mom!" They say this together in excruciating harmony.

"No. You are both fifteen years old. You don't need tattoos. You'll regret it later."

"You are so boring."

"You are so safe."

I set down my fork and take a deep breath. "Sorry," I say, "but the thought of tattoos on the two of you makes me want to throw up my meat loaf. On both of you."

"Thanks."

"Let's stop talking about it . . . ," I say.

"We wanted to get them before the dance. Dad will say yes."

"Sure, Dad always says yes," I agree. "But I'm going to tell him I don't approve. And if I don't approve, you can't do it. What dance?"

"Never mind."

"What dance?"

"What difference does it make?"

"Oh, I suppose you just *can't* go without tattoos. Especially on your butt. You'll look so *naked*."

"Right."

"Oh please." I shake my head at them. "You guys are doing the dishes," I say. "Alone."

"We will if we can get tattoos."

"I don't respond to blackmail."

"Neither do we. Besides, we have to study."

"Not until you do the dishes."

"Not until we study. You have to help me with my French."

"You have to help me with my science."

This, of course, means that I do the dishes at eleven-thirty P.M. Alone. I rather like doing dishes. I've gotten used to this.

My friend Peggy calls me Ostrich Girl. She says that I not only show no interest in finding a man, but that if any men are out there looking for me, I'd never see them because I've defiantly buried my head in the sand. Peggy, who's been married three times, and most recently to a man named (believe it or not) Suck Duck Dong, an Asian scientist whose name is by far his most interesting attribute, has nothing to teach me as far as I'm concerned. She's married, but she and her husband haven't a single thing in common. Peggy, who by Chinese law should be named Peggy Suck, since the first Chinese name is really the surname, goes by the name Peggy Dong. Frankly, I don't know if I would take either name. (My girls, behind her back, call her Ding Dong.) But she was already using her second husband Frankie DiBiasi's last name, so she couldn't go on using that. She calls her husband S.D. Because I have known Peggy for a good twenty years, I was maid of honor at two of her weddings, and many times have had Peggy and S.D. over for dinner. I'm not sure why. S.D. generally stares at his plate, answers many questions with shrugs or nods to Peggy when he thinks she can answer a question better than he can—which is nearly always.

"It's just nice to know someone loves you," Peggy tells me. "And S.D. clearly loves me. I'm not saying he says it . . ."

"Yeah?"

"He just shows it."

"How?"

"He puts his arms around me when we go to bed at night. He smiles at me in the morning."

"But aren't you lonely with him?"

"After Frankie, his silence is one of his finest traits. Besides, S.D.'s brilliant. He's going to contribute something incredible to the world. He's doing AIDS research, you know. He's going to save lives. I feel like being with him means I'm involved somehow."

I met Peggy just after I moved to New York. Daniel and I were newly in love. We lived in an apartment so small, we had to hang half our clothes on the shower rod because there wasn't enough room in the closet for our hangers—every morning, we put them on the bed so we could take a shower. We had to climb over the bed to get into the bedroom. Only one person could be in the kitchen at a time. Peggy lived next door with her first husband, Sam. We invited them over to dinner. I was in the kitchen, pulling together my first attempt at oven-fried chicken. Peggy stood just outside the kitchen and said, "I am so in love with Sam. He brings me flowers after work every night. He likes to play with my hair. He does my hairdo for me every morning." She turned 360 degrees and I admired her beautiful French braid. This was an unusual and useful attribute for any husband to have. "And he's amazing in bed." She giggled. "Oh, sorry if that makes you uncomfortable. It's just that I want to tell everyone. I suppose everyone feels that way about their husband, huh?" Of course, by this time, what Daniel did best in bed was turn away from me.

I looked at Peggy. She was beautiful in the most American way possible. Ginger-brown hair, freckles on her pert little nose, blue eyes as big and liquid and long-lashed as a child's. I liked her immediately, despite her overly familiar comments. Besides, this was New York. People always reveal too much in New York. Even if they're from Ohio, as Peggy is. Maybe I need to learn how to do that, I reflected. My Midwesternness made me polite and tastefully closemouthed. The thing that drew me to Peggy probably was that she was so in love. You can't help liking someone that much in love. It shows they have a big heart, and you want to be part of their happiness. When Sam up and left her for his fellow lawyer Denise—and no doubt Denise thought he was amazing in bed too—Peggy was angry, verbal, and included us all in her loss. She ranted. She raved. She told us if we ever spoke to Sam again she'd kill us. And then she went on to marry the odious Frankie DiBiasi, who was a loudmouthed, crass man with thick fingers and nose hair and whose greatest attribute was that his brother ran a deli and he could get any deli meat wholesale. And now she's stepped up to Suck Duck Dong. At least S.D. is not offensive. He's not much of anything. Still, I love Peg, because she is my friend. Because she and I knew each other before we became ourselves. Because she always challenges me to keep an open heart about men despite her questionable track record. I find her optimism foolhardy, yet endearing.

Tonight, she calls and tells me she's having a party Saturday night.

"I have someone for you to meet," she says. "Someone with your name on him."

"There is no such guy," I tell her.

"Uh-uh. There is. His name's Hank 'Jane Larsen should have me' Marsh and he owns an art gallery. S.D. and I just bought a painting there. I've known him for years, though. Sam's sister dated him. He's sweet, quiet, tall, just your type. He even sort of reminds me of Daniel."

"Uh-oh."

"He's divorced."

"He's probably gay."

"Why? Is Daniel gay?" she says dryly.

"Of course not."

"Well, I don't think Hank is either. I'm having this dinner party just for you, madam, so you better show."

"Okay," I say. It's not hard to fit things into my calendar. All that's been on it for a long, long time is "Daniel's Weekend," "My Weekend," "Daniel's Weekend," "My Weekend."

"I even planned the party for this weekend, knowing you don't have the girls, just in case Hank and you really hit it off, if you get my drift."

"What? What do you mean?"

"Oh, for God's sake, Jane. I mean in case you would like to spend the night together. What's wrong with you?"

"Peg, it's been so long since I've 'spent the night together' with anybody, it seems as long ago as sleepaway camp."

"Listen, kid. We've got to change things. It's not right for a woman to spend an entire life alone. I think it causes cancer."

"I'm not alone. I've got the girls. I've got Daniel."

"My point exactly. Daniel. Ptooey! Get over it."

"I'm really very happy the way I am," I tell her. And I am. I am. Is it wrong to be self-contained? Satisfied with yourself? Why does everybody have to poke and prod and make me different? I know I need to change. I know I'm stuck, but this is one part of me I don't really want to change.

"Look, Ostrich Girl, life is short. Short. Do something."

"Don't you read the papers?" I ask her. "More women want to be single than ever. *Want* to be."

"Bullshit," she says. "That's what they say when they can't find anybody. I remember saying that I didn't want to make the cheer-leading squad once upon a time. Let me clue you in. I would have killed to wear one of those nauseating pleated skirts."

"You're hopeless," I tell her.

"Baby. I'm married. You're hopeless. Just show up Saturday night, so we can end your reign of misery. And don't tell me you haven't been miserable. Don't you dare."

The next morning, I arrive at work, and there is another pink "While You Were Out" note from Rodney.

"Call immediately," it tells me.

Therefore, without even hanging up my coat, I call Rodney's office.

"Oh, Jane. He asked me if you were going to be in today," his assistant says.

"Did he? Is he there?"

"Well, he's here, but he's meeting with those assisted-living people from North Carolina. He's having lunch with them too."

"Do you have any idea what he wants to see me about? The Bank of Monmouth?"

"I don't know. He never tells me anything. I'm only the hired help. I just know he's anxious to see you."

Well, without Rodney to take up my time, I'm back face-to-face with the Bank of Monmouth. Maybe, I think hopefully, he's going to call to tell me that the job is suddenly canceled.

"I hate you," I say aloud. "I hate you. I hate you. I hate you."

"Guy troubles?" Dave Mann says.

I laugh. "No. Bank troubles. I want to blow up this bank even before the first one's built."

"Rodney was through here looking for you earlier," Dave says.

"Was he? What the hell do you think he wants with me?"

"He seemed very intent on finding you. 'Have you seen Jane Larsen. Have *you* seen Jane Larsen? Isn't she in yet?'" He says this, feigning the reptilian voice that's Rodney's alone.

"Was he annoyed? He hasn't paid any attention to me in years. I can't imagine why he wants to now."

Dave shrugs. "Don't let it go to your head. He probably wants you to design a park outhouse or something. Something *really* satisfying."

"Thanks."

While I wrestle the Bank of Monmouth to the ground, I think about how thrilled I used to be to come to work. For eighteen years, I have been at this same firm, and before that, one other. Until these last few months, I always felt as if I was meant to be an architect, that I was dumb lucky to have landed on the one thing I could be extraordinarily good at. When you're good at something, you don't have to question why you do it. You don't have to ask if your life is meaningful. You are easily contributing something that simply feels right. That satisfies you and others. And while you do it, it is so absorbing, so fulfilling, for hours at a time, you become what you are doing. Is there anything more pleasing on earth? You lose all sense of time. You lose all sense of yourself. You are swimming with the muses. You are lost and found all at once.

I especially feel that way when it comes to houses. They are so intimate a part of life. So integral to how we spend every day. I talk to my clients before I design for them. Really talk. It seems so important. It is where I begin: this body of knowledge. These sessions are like first dates. I'm getting to know them, to like them, to find consistencies between us, to detect differences. To understand how they really feel inside.

Some of the questions I ask are quite mundane. I ask them if they sit together in the same room at night, or apart. (It's frightening how many sit apart.) I ask if they like to read, and how many books they own. I ask them where they spent their childhood summers. I discovered years ago that people long to return to their childhood summers. This goes deeper than almost any other question. You'd be surprised how deep. If they spent August at a lake in a knotty-pine cabin, I create a room that's dark and woody, with beaded wood paneling the color of whiskey—and inevitably, it speaks to them. If they spent their summers on Cape Cod beneath silvery shingles, I create rooms with small-paned windows, lower ceilings, white paint. If they spent their summers in the city, where the nights were cool and magical after sticky, hot days, I design houses that glitter at night. A place where cabbage roses look cool and blowsy in vases, where mantels are chilled black marble and doors are heavy and click shut with a sigh. Some architects build houses that are all somewhat alike, that follow a theme, and are identifiable as that architect's. I build houses each as different as the clients I build them for.

I annoy people with questions. I ask if they do their own dishes. If they sit up in bed in the morning and take the time to look out. If they like flowers, or care about the garden. If they like fires at night. That tells me where to put the views and how to shape the rooms so the furniture sits usefully, and the fireplaces are set where they will actually be lit. I ask them if they've ever had a dream they never thought would come true. Ah, now here's where I hit real pay dirt. One man said he dreamed of opening an Italian restaurant and I designed a kitchen that looked like one. I oversaw the cabinet building myself. I inset the doors with screens of palest raffia, the counters were washed soapstone, the floors were flagstone. The designer painted the walls the color of hazelnuts. Later, the owner invited me for a meal there. The room was glowing, even though my client was a terrible cook.

One woman told me she wanted to be a ballerina when she was a child, and had been forced by her parents to turn down the chance to join a troupe when she was fourteen, so I built her a huge dressing room that the interior designer mirrored floor to ceiling. A maple floor was laid, and ballet bars were put up all around like a dainty belt 'round its middle. Working with the interior designer, I made sure the mirrors were then draped at the edges in tulle, like tutus. And in the corner, because this woman was rich enough not to mind the cost, she approved us putting in a big, black, glistening grand piano. A Steinway. It had to be done as part of the construction because you'd have to take a portion of the wall out to remove it. When the woman saw the final product, she wept. Honestly. She wept. No one in her house knew how to play the piano but it completed her dream. "Can you play, Jane?" she asked me. "Play it." I sat down and played her the one piece I still remember: a Chopin étude. She was sixty-one years old and forty pounds overweight, but she kicked off her shoes and danced as sweetly as a child, and then she asked me to play it again. That was a day when I felt blessed. A day when what I did mattered deeply to someone.

A day when I had Jack Crashin to thank. I suppose everyone has someone in their lives who's touched them, affected them, rerouted them. Jack was mine.

I've loved a lot of men since Jack. And of course, I married Daniel. Yet, decades later, the power of Jack Crashin's memory is so potent, I can close my eyes and still see his face, his beautiful, articulate hands; can envision how his long fingers looked so many years ago, in my dorm room, as he worked on his college design projects. A mechanical pencil in one hand, a T square in the other. Even smudged, those hands were beautiful enough to make me want to watch for hours. I would pretend to be studying, hide behind a book and drink in the beauty of his surety, revel in the quiet ease of his movements, of his face. For no one I've ever met before or since has been so at ease in his own bones as Jack Crashin always seemed to be. Thinking of him, I'm often reminded of Jimmy Stewart. There was a core of goodness in Jack, a certainty of what he was meant to do, to be. I always found great comfort in his virtue.

My memories of my relatively short time with Jack are an orgy of learning. I was eighteen, just two and a half years older than my girls are now. He was twenty-two. He had skin both milky and rich, like velvet. He had a smile that reduced me to silence. He had those hands, more beautiful than anyone's I've known since. He was an architecture major, I was an art major. He taught me everything I knew about architecture up to that point. We drove from Frank Lloyd Wright house to Frank Lloyd Wright house. We looked at books full of Greek Revival and Georgian and Federal style houses. We slept all night outside the University of Illinois English Building on the lawn with four hundred other kids—a protest led by Jack himself to protect that elegant Stanford White structure from being torn down and replaced with a window-less seventies box.

He walked me through the building that night, before the protest. It was still open. Professors were working late in their offices; a few night classes were still in session.

"This was built as a woman's dorm," he told me. I looked into his hazel eyes. In them, I could see intensity, vision—attributes I feared I'd never know. "The structure was changed in the thirties, I think, maybe the twenties. But there are clues to what it once was. C'mon. I'll show you." He led me upstairs, to the third, and then the fourth floor. I could feel his body heat near me, could breathe in the bleachy smell of his white button-down shirt that he wore hanging long over his soft, torn jeans. The scuffling sound of his thighs in those jeans drove me nearly mad with longing. Up on the third floor of the dorm, the halls were narrow, and the air was warmer, closer. He took my wrist between his fingers. His touch was damp and warm. And there was his personal smell, underneath the clean smell of his shirt: something very like the smell of crayons being clutched in a warm hand. Waxy, closed, semisweet. There were several teaching assistants in their offices. One teaching assistant jumped with fright as we passed. Few people must have ever walked those halls.

"Sorry to scare you," Jack said. "We're taking a look at the architecture up here. There's going to be a protest. In about twenty minutes. To save this building."

The teaching assistant shrugged. "Means nothing to me."

Jack smiled, shook his head, and we moved on down the hall. He pointed to small shelves attached to the walls every ten feet or so.

"For hurricane lamps or oil lamps. Can you imagine how soft the light would have been?" I can still remember the moldings in those narrow halls. Exquisite. Detailed. Inlays edged the floor. Gordian knots. Greek keys. I could easily imagine girls in these rooms, girls in long white nightgowns. Far from home. Smart girls who had made it to the state university, who had never slept away from their mothers for a single night, who would never even know a kiss until they were engaged to be married. Once, they felt at home in these halls.

I turned to Jack and touched his face. I looked into his eyes. They were filled with excitement, no doubt for the protest, not for me. He smiled and leaned me against the wall. Kissing him was like diving into a pool. Cool. Refreshing. Exhilarating. He slid his hand up under my shirt.

"Oh, baby," he said, pressing himself against me. "We're going to save this building."

"I know we will, Jack. I know we will." I would have made love to him on the floor. Or anywhere at that moment. But loving me was only a detour to where he wanted to go. He took my wrist and led me down to the main floor. My wrist, not my hand. We were not equals.

We stepped out of the building and into the growing numbers of students. Jack led me to the side of the stone steps, where he said I'd be safe, no matter what happened. (There'd been other protests on campus that spring, that terrible, wonderful spring, that led to riots. People had been hurt. Trampled. There was a war to protest. There were killings on other campuses. I had protested in other demonstrations. I was more deeply involved in them than Jack was. But this seemed much more personal, more real to me.) I watched Jack get up on a makeshift podium. I could still feel his kisses cooling on my lips.

"Are we going to let the university put another box in this spot? Another meaningless, window-less box? It's our university. Are we going to let them tear down the history we've inherited? I say NO." The crowd was as excited by Jack as I'd been. My heart pounded. How could I help but love him?

The protest was a success. Alumni and board members, being made aware of the imminent destruction of one of their favorite buildings, put pressure on the university to preserve it. Jack was as happy as a dog having marked a tree permanently. "I did it, Jane. I did it."

"You did," I said. I felt proud and bewildered. He was so full of jubilance, I couldn't help feeling bathed in his joy. Still, I felt hurt that he hadn't said, "We did it." And I felt oddly overshadowed by him. I wondered sorrowfully if he could ever feel for me what I felt for him. Still, he shared his victory in other ways.

"Let's take a trip," he said. "Let's celebrate, just you and me." I packed my old camp pack with another pair of jeans and a knit dress, underwear and a lipstick, and together we toured three towns in Iowa where Jack had heard there were perfect examples of Midwestern Italianate. Driving in his rusted-out Dartmouth-green Volkswagen weighing so little it shimmied on the highways and could be shoved into parking places, we listened again and again to Crosby, Stills and Nash on the radio—especially "Suite: Judy Blue Eyes." "I am yours, you are mine, you are what you are . . ." We sang along and drove reverently past square white houses with cupolas and elegant sofitts and flat roofs. We sighed perfectly harmonized sighs and pointed out the beauty of Italianate wedding-cake perfection. And then we saw a classic Greek Revival house. Like an elegant elderly woman in a crowd of overdressed people. A woman who stood alone in her simplicity.

"I've never seen a house so beautiful," Jack said, his voice so full of air and wonder, it lifted my heart. He was so right. I had never seen a house so simple, so beautiful, so perfect in its landscape. It made me want to cry. It actually made me feel sexually aroused That night, we stayed at a cheesy, balconied six-dollar-a-night motel and made love so sweet I opened myself like a candy box. I was in love with Jack and architecture all at once. And somehow, both of those loves have remained with me. The architecture actively. And Jack . . . well, it's hard for me to remember ever loving anyone so innocently and freely since.

"I am yours. You are mine. You are what you are . . ." Ah yes. He was what he was. And he moved away because it was time. We were kids and he was four years older than I was. He wanted to take a special graduate course at Yale. The East was far away from the University of Illinois. Not a word was spoken about staying faithful. But I remember lying in bed with him that last night. We often talked for hours in bed together. That night, I nestled against his shoulder. No one had ever made me feel so safe. Who can quantify what makes a woman feel safe with a man? He was no taller, no stronger, than other men.

"I can't believe you're going," I said.

"It isn't real to me yet," he said. "I know."

"Will you miss me?"

"Sure," he said. I didn't believe him. His world was opening up. Mine was merely flowing along, I thought.

"I'll never forget you," I said.

He was silent for a long time. He was often silent for endless periods when I said something that made him think. Unlike every other man I have known, he never spoke unless he was certain he had something to say.

"Why?" he said finally, very softly.

"You've given me architecture. You've . . . I don't know . . . grounded me, I guess."

"You didn't need grounding," he said.

"I needed something. You gave it to me." He didn't say anything after that. We fell asleep in what felt to me like mid-conversation. But in the night I woke and he was sitting up, staring out the window.

"What's wrong?" I asked him.

"I never paid enough attention to you," he said.

"You did."

"No. I didn't." I felt a rushing feeling, akin to being pulled down a river. My heart was beating hard. I wondered if I was dreaming. Was he having second thoughts? Was he thinking he shouldn't leave me?

I took his hand and kissed it. He turned and his beautiful, articulate hand stroked my face so gently it made me stop breathing. He pulled me to him tightly.

"Jane," he whispered. "Jane. Jane." I waited to hear more, but there was apparently nothing he wanted to say to me but my name.

Eventually, we slid back down under the covers and we fell asleep entangled.

We wrote at first. There was no particular passion in the letters. Just a friendship. Just a common memory of times past. But, he was only the second man I'd ever slept with. I couldn't imagine what more I could ask of him. I couldn't imagine committing to him in any way. Certainly not marrying him. Still, when he left, I felt an emptiness I sometimes wonder if I've ever filled.

I used to think, especially during the lonely nights of my marriage, that I would hire a private detective someday, just to see what had become of him, the man who long ago had changed the course of my life, and then left it. But twin daughters have a way of eating up energy and time and unhappiness. And my career kept me busy. And in the end, I've only thought of him, and done nothing about it.

So here I am baby-sitting the Bank of Monmouth. Nowhere with the design at all. Here I am, my love of architecture ebbing away from me for the first time in nearly thirty years. Here I am, thinking of this man who thrilled me with a love of houses and buildings and history and shelter. And that's when I do it. I click on the Internet and pull up a search engine.

A memo went out just last week asking that the staff no longer use the Internet for personal purposes. What did that mean? everyone wondered. You couldn't check the weather anymore? You'd be fired for bookmarking the home page of the *New York Times*? You couldn't write E-mail or buy yourself a book about architecture on company time? It seemed too harsh. The Internet was a lifeline. It was a bridge away from the loneliness, the tediousness of all of our jobs. Therefore, everyone I spoke to proclaimed that the memo must not be for *them*. It's for the assistants, Dave Mann proclaimed. You know, the people who get *paid by the hour,* he said in a naughty stage whisper, as though he were talking about hookers instead of people who answer the phones and dole out supplies. I knew the memo meant him and me and everyone else. It was just downright insulting. Why should Rodney and the rest of them care as long as we do our jobs well? As long as they get what they've paid for? It makes me squint my eyes and shake my head. Someday I'll be out of here, I think. Out of this minefield of mediocrity. I pull up the search engine and type eleven letters into the box marked "Search": Jack Crashin.

Yesterday, I went to the sky show. Today I search for Jack Crashin. I don't expect anything when I hit Return. But it comes up suddenly, an answer to a question I've been harboring for years: what has become of Jack Crashin? There it is. Right at the top of the list: Jack Crashin and Associates, Architects, Nashville, Tennessee. Of course it's him. I'm infused by a sensation both hot and cold. Almost nauseating. I don't click on the entry right away. After all these years, I've found him. I could have done this three years ago. I could have done this any day. The information I've wondered about so many nights in the dark is here before me.

I have to take a deep breath and look away for a moment. I stare out the window at the gauzy sky and the quickly moving clouds as though his name gives off a blinding light. I stare into the middle of the room, where it's a spinning whirl of activity. But a blue spot stains everything. My fear. My thrill. Blinding me for a moment like a flashbulb's afterburn. I breathe like someone who's just come up from too long underwater. At this very moment, on this very ordinary autumn day, all my nerve endings are covered with honey. No.

I could come up with metaphor after metaphor, but no string of words can describe what I feel this moment, finding Jack Crashin again.

I click to his website: Jack Crashin and Associates, Architects. Four names are listed after his, two men, two women. One named Maria Goldenclonner. He probably finds that name perfectly ordinary by now. Goldenclonner. And Dennis Hemphill and Charles Gore and Cynthia Jacobs Mott. But Jack's name is in larger letters. Gold with a black outline. His name is the title. I click on his name and a page just for him comes up. A picture. A picture after all these years.

It's Jack, all right. Though I can't figure out what could have made him move to Nashville, Tennessee. Still, there's no mistaking the open grin, the soft black-lashed hazel eyes that simultaneously twinkle and look sad because they go south at the corners. This isn't to say he isn't changed by nearly thirty years. The counterculture beard he sometimes had is gone, the long-banged glossy shoulder-length hair—how I luxuriated in that silky hair, as blue-black as Parker's ink. Like Native American hair. Or Polynesian hair. I remember once asking him to shake it over my bare belly. Now it's cropped short and starts somewhere near the crown of his head, giving him a high, not inelegant forehead. Still, he hasn't changed so very much. He's clearly the same Jack Crashin who had enough confidence at the age of twenty-two to make me feel safe in his arms. Who taught me to see the world in a whole new way. A way that changed who I became. Beneath his picture, it lists his credits, including a number of local awards. I always knew he'd be a success. Beneath that, it says, "In his spare time, Jack relishes spending time with his family."

Sitting at my screen, looking at his familiar yet changed face, I press the colored words WRITE US.

Hey, Jack, I write, then I change it to

Dear Jack,
Could this possibly be the same Jack Crashin I
knew so many years ago at the University of Illinois? That great defender of historic architecture? If it is, and you'd like to catch up,
please write to me at
jane.larsen@pariswashburngreen.com.
I'd love to know what's been happening in your
life.
Jane Larsen

I hit Send and stare at the screen for a while. Now it's up to him. I am useless for a long time after I send the letter. I can't think. I can't design. I feel the way I feel after a terrible scare, or a big presentation, when adrenaline has swept through me and left me weak.

In time, I come back to the present, and find that I have become part of the room, the energy that makes it pulse. Sometimes during the day, I have these moments when the lack of privacy, the noise actually do thrill me. Perhaps, I think, I've found Jack to remind me why I am here.

When I return from lunch, there is another note that Rodney is looking for me. I actually wander down to his office to see him, but again, he's not there.

"He went off with those North Carolina people," his assistant says, sighing. "I just can't keep up with him. And no, I don't know why he wants to see you. I asked him and he flat out wouldn't tell me."

I leave her office with an uneasy feeling. But knowing that Jack Crashin might write me back thrills me. Maybe when I come in Monday, his answer will be there.

I go after the Bank of Monmouth with renewed interest. I think of what I can do to this building that would make Jack Crashin proud. All afternoon, I hope for the little bell to sound that tells me I have E-mail. And when it does, of course it isn't a letter from Jack but a reminder of a client meeting, a note from HR telling us they'll pay us $2,000 if we introduce them to an architect they hire, and jokes from my neighbor Jackie, who sends jokes nearly every day to me and about forty-five other people she knows. Today's jokes are Jewish haikus that she labels "Oy-Kus." My favorite reads: "Now I am a man. Tomorrow I return to seventh grade." At five-thirty, I check for Jack's letter one last time. I'm furious that I've given him my work E-mail address and not my home address. Now I'll have to wait until Monday no matter what, even if he writes sooner.

The whole way home, I daydream about what it might say. "I've longed to hear from you night after night," I hear in Jack's voice. I laugh out loud on the subway when I concoct this. "Jane who?" seems more like it.

Three

On Saturday morning, Cait and Abby play loud but suddenly familiar music as they pack schoolbooks and a few personal things, to head over to Dan's for the weekend. I hear it as I climb the stairs to hurry them along, and the recognition goes right to my soul. It's "Suite: Judy Blue Eyes" by Crosby, Stills and Nash. "I am yours. You are mine. You are what you are . . ." I stand on the landing outside their rooms and listen, and for just a moment, I'm in that old VW bug with Jack, rolling down the hills of Iowa, looking for houses.

It shocks me that the girls' generation likes the music we liked. Cait and Abby have all the Beatles albums, the Rolling Stones. Cream. When they can actually get the old turntable to work, they play my old 33 records, even ridiculous stuff like Herman's Hermits and Gerry and the Pacemakers and love it all, go around the house singing it. I don't get it. We *hated* the music our parents liked. There was a gap as wide as the ocean between their generation and ours. We hated their clothes, their values, their sheeplike belief in government, authority figures, and the almighty dollar. But the new teenage generation holds a weird reverence for the late sixties, early seventies. The music, the clothes. One of Cait and Abby's favorite things to do is to go down to the cellar and come back up wearing my old hippie dresses or spiderweb shawls or crushed velvet hats or torn, darned, and embroidered jeans. Wearing these baubles from my past, they are transformed. For them, it's just dress-up. For us, it was rebellion. It was breaking out of the rigidity our parents imposed on us. It was protesting a war that threatened the lives of people we knew. Maybe we fooled ourselves, but we thought we stood for something. Peace. Love. We wanted to change the world. We were painfully serious.

Abby opens the door to her room. "What are you doing?" she asks, seeing me stone-still on the landing..

"I didn't know you had this album," I say, trying not to sound too moony.

"It's really good, isn't it?" she says.

"I've always loved it," I say.

"You know Crosby, Stills and Nash?" she asks.

"Of course."

She shrugs. "I didn't know anyone knew it. I thought it was . . . obs . . . obs . . ."

"Obscure?"

"Yeah."

"It's one of my favorites. You guys almost ready?" I ask her.

"I am."

"I'll go and watch for Daddy. Hurry down. You know he hates it when you take too long. He always double-parks."

All the way down the stairs, and even as I wait by the window, I hear the album playing, and softly I sing along, each song bringing up a memory like an old photo album.

Dan lives twelve blocks away in a fancy co-op he seems just

barely able to afford. After we decided to break up, it took months for him to find a place he felt was good enough for him. His standards are perfectly unmeetable.

He arrives at the house in his new, gleaming, navy blue BMW. The girls think the car is the most glamorous they've ever seen. They are proud to squeeze into its low frame, and love it when Daniel puts the leathery-golden top down. It's down today. He double-parks and comes to the door, rings the bell in the unique way that says it's him: two rings in a row. All this to drive them only twelve blocks.

"Daddy's here," I call to the girls.

When I open the door, I am struck, as I usually am, by his length, his grace and ease. A natural basketball player. He blinks his long, blond-lashed eyes, and takes off his baseball cap.

"Hey, Jujube," he says to me, a name he's called me from the very start. "They ready?" he asks.

"Nearly. Come on in."

He kisses me on both cheeks, a continental affectation he picked up when he went to France for three weeks the year we split up. Smelling of some sort of green cologne, he sighs and flops down on the sofa near the window so he can keep an eye on his pride and joy out on the street.

"And how are the princesses today?" he asks.

"Crabby."

"I'd better put on my armor."

"Good idea."

"And you? Are you crabby?"

"Me? I'm never crabby. I'm the happiest damn girl in town. How're you?"

"Jujube, I am solvent. So very, very solvent."

Daniel is alluding to the fact that for once he's making money. He's always been into crazy get-rich-quick schemes that never pay off. First he started a company that made kiosks which dispensed colognes. He put them in shopping malls. I think about three people actually ever paid to get a squirt of cologne. Then there was the peel-off-nail-polish company. He noticed that the twins (at the age of four) were enamored of Baby Twinkle Peel-Off Nail Polish in a vapid shade of hot pink which they peeled off whole and left sticking to furniture all around the house. Peel-off nail polish made a lot of sense for little girls for whom nail-polish remover was too harsh. He thought it was the perfect product for grown women. He had a chemist create bottles and bottles of Danello Peel-Off Polish. For months he walked around with various-colored nails himself, testing out the shades. He spent months more perfecting the packaging with its embossed label. The problem was, he put the product out right when Jet-Dry polishes appeared. Never thinking about the drying time of his polish, he hadn't really noticed that his polish took forever to dry, longer than regular polish. And if it was put on too thickly, it could be instantly dented or even impressed with fingerprints. It was like Silly Putty. Besides, women didn't want their nail polish to peel off. They wanted it to last longer. He found a distributor who sold it into the stores quite well. Then he held his breath. He continued to hold it for two or three months. There was a slight upturn of sales at first, and then nothing. No repeat buys at all, at which point every pharmacy that carried it wanted it off their shelves.

But now he's hit the big time with his line of hair mascara that changes with temperature. Mood Streaks has become an instant hit with teen girls. In the cold, the streak is blue. But if the wearer holds the streak in her hand, or if she's hot, the streak turns purple, then red. Our daughters are thrilled that Daniel has finally created something that doesn't embarrass them.

And Daniel immediately went out and celebrated by buying the little Blue Beamer, as the girls call it. I call it the Mood Streak. I thoroughly expect it to turn red, the faster it goes.

The girls come down the stairs together. To please Daniel—a rare desire—they have put Mood Streaks in their hair. It shows up quite winningly against their golden-brown locks.

"Hey, Poppo," Cait says.

"Hi, Daddy," Abigail says.

"Angel babies," he says, hugging them both at once. "The Mood Streak twins!"

Say what you will about Daniel, but he's a great dad. He'd do anything for the girls. He's never been one for discipline. He freezes when they talk about boys. He overreacts when they're unhappy. But God knows, he loves them. They are the very center of the earth for him and he lets them know it. For that moment when the four of us are together, when the girls are in decent moods and I can look into their faces and see both Daniel's and my features mingled into something mysteriously reminted and beautiful, I could almost fall in love with him again. I never quite lose the longing for an intact nuclear family, for that perfect foursquare we were meant to be. If Daniel hadn't cheated on me nearly from the start— well, no need to go into it again—I imagine we'd still be together. The girls each kiss me on both cheeks. Daniel does too, and then he stops.

"Is that Crosby, Stills and Nash I hear upstairs?" he asks.

"It's mine," Abby says. "Oops. I left it on continuous play."

"I'll turn it off," I tell her.

"Wasn't that our song? 'Suite: Judy Blue Eyes'?" Daniel asks.

Our song. I probably played it, remembering Jack, missing Jack. And Daniel thinks it's our song.

"Gosh," I tell him. "Was it? I don't know."

"Thought so. Yup it was," he says. "Have a great weekend. Don't do anything you can't tell us in total detail," he says before he closes the door. He should talk . . .

I am alone.

Alone.

This is something that they never tell you when you get divorced, a hidden advantage that you discover only later: divorced people have guilt-free adult time. These every-other-weekends with no children have for all these years after my divorce made me a much more patient mother when I do have the girls. And if my daughters don't like to go to the theater, or the country, it doesn't matter because I usually do all those things anyway on the weekends they spend with Dan. When they return Monday nights, I am thrilled to see them, renewed.

Initially though, I am lost. When they walk out the door and their presence no longer fills 89 percent of the space in the house, I find myself going through a decompression process, like a diver coming up from the deep. I wander around the house looking for things to do, things I want. It's almost as though I'm looking for me. Usually, I take the stairs up to the top floor, to my bedroom, and climb right back into bed. I suppose that could be viewed as the move of someone depressed. But it isn't, or doesn't feel that way, in any case. I climb into the silky, crumpled sheets looking for lost sleep and almost always find it. What delicious indulgence. I'm not responsible for anyone but me.

When they were small, I needed it more, of course. In those years when there was never time for a nap, or to catch up on the sleep I lost to their nightmares or their coughing fits or their raids on my bed in the middle of the night, I was ravenous for any sleep I could glean. Back then, they'd leave and I'd climb back into bed and crash for two, three hours into a sleep crammed with weird, nearly psychedelic dreams. Today, I lie down in bed but can't sleep. I feel restless in the same way I did on Thursday when I played hooky. I want to raise hell. I want to surprise myself.

If I were a different sort of person, I'd go get a tattoo myself—no mere book on my butt, mind you, but something deeply intellectual. Let's see: how about a heart with "Romeo and Juliet" engraved in it? Or a quote from Dylan Thomas's "Fern Hill" twining up my ankle. "Now as I was young and easy under the apple boughs/About the lilting house and happy as the grass was green . . ." As it reached my not-so-thin thigh, verses and verses could be added practically without twining at all. . . . Or perhaps up there I could add, "Do not go gentle into that good night," reaching its tendrils up into my pubic hair.

I sigh. I need some excitement. Instead, I refold the sweaters on the shelf in my closet, recup my bras in the drawer, wash my hair—two sudsings, copious rinsing, when I comb it out I lose at least a thousand hairs I can ill afford—and take another nap until it's time to get ready for Peggy's party.

I take a long, hot bath and look down at my body. I've never been very friendly with my body. Even in the years when I was, apparently, attractive, especially to men, I couldn't stand to look at pictures of myself. I hated to catch a glimpse of myself in the mirror. See, the problem is, I always think I actually look better than I do. I mean, when I was a size ten, I thought of myself as a size six. Now that I'm a size fourteen, I think I'm a size ten. I always have this perfectly lovely imaginary vision of myself that I simply don't live up to. It's like being in a bad relationship. You expect one thing and are constantly disappointed. I look down and say, Where the hell is my size-ten body? I am repulsed. My breasts no longer pass the pencil test; in fact, they could hold entire notebooks beneath them and never drop them. My belly these days looks like I'm four months' pregnant, and it won't go down. Who is this woman? I've dieted and lost and gained back so many times my skin's elasticity surely must resemble a ten-year-old rubber band. I try to think, I yam what I yam, but I always hear a small but powerful voice belt out, Which yamn't so good, right behind it. My girls tell me—when they're being charitable—that I'm still beautiful. Peggy tells me. Dave at the office once said when he and I went out to lunch that he was proud to be seen with such a beautiful woman.

"You must be thinking of the old me," I tell him.

"No. I mean you now. You've got something about you still . . ." He blushes. He's never expressed anything like this to me. He's happily married and he's just being kind. "I watch other guys look at you, Jane. You've got such gorgeous eyes. Lips. Your face . . . You must know. You've always been a knockout. And if you're a little heavy, it's sexy. You wear it well. Voluptuous. Is that the word? Honestly. I wouldn't say it if it wasn't true."

I look at stars like Delta Burke on TV and think she's pretty, but who would be attracted to her? I feel unattractive even when I'm dressed up; I can't help it. I want to be what I am no longer. And diet and exercise never seem to make enough difference. You have no idea how frustrating it all is.

Nevertheless, I make an effort for Peggy's party. I put on just the right makeup—soft, smudgy eyes, luminously defined lips. I slip into a peacock tank top and a sleek (as sleek as one can be in my size) black jacket and a long, tight skirt. I spray a light, citrusy perfume into the air and walk through it. I slide small gold bands into my earlobes.

I imagine that Hank Marsh will look something like Michael Landon. Age just makes him look more boyish. I imagine him in the white, diffused light of a chic art gallery stepping back to observe a completely white picture.

"George," I can hear him say, "this one is supposed to be hung *vertically*. My God, what if the artist saw it like this! Change it quickly. Everyone will be arriving soon." Yes, I imagine Hank Marsh will be unique and attractive. One thing I have to say for Peggy is that she knows an attractive man when she sees one. S.D., for instance. He's attractive. He just doesn't have a clue as to how to communicate.

Despite the fact that I have no urgent need for a man in my life, of course I'm interested in meeting attractive men. Who isn't? I even like dating. Well, the early part of dating, anyway. That heady exchange of like information, that quickening recognition that you have so much to share, so much in common. The thrill of the first kiss. And then, I'd like to end all relationships right there.

Well, actually I can pinpoint the moment that I want to get out. It's that moment when you realize that if the man you're crazy about doesn't call soon, you may just become a stroke victim . . . that's the moment I'd prefer never to see them again. The moment when you realize that you've put the guy's needs first and you can't imagine what yours were in the first place. That's when I wish someone would silently intervene and lead me away. I mean, I already have people in my life whose needs come before mine: Abby and Caitlin. Because the truth is, I'm a sucker for all that domestic stuff. I love to cook for people. I love to tend gardens for others to walk in. I love to make beds with gorgeous, sensual sheets for visiting friends. I love giving too much. But look at what all that giving has done for me. Look at what it did for my mother. I just can't see love as anything but a miserable loss of self. For what?

Hank Marsh looks nothing like Michael Landon. He does, however, vaguely look like Daniel, in that he's tall, fair, graceful, and wears inordinately large shoes.

"You know what they say about big feet," Peggy whispers to me.

"Jesus, Peg." I've never found that to be true, that saying about big feet. I once knew a man with smallish feet who outmeasured all the large-footed guys I ever knew. When I told him that, I think it made his life.

Clearly, Peggy has let Hank Marsh know that this party is her way of fixing up the two of us, because he is shy with me, and nervous. He must be forty-eight, fifty years old. I can tell by the crinkles around his eyes, the parenthetical lines around his mouth. But, as with all aging men, these, annoyingly, only add character.

"So you're Jane," he says, collecting carrot and celery sticks for his plate, dipping them one by one in the ranch dressing before he sets them side by side. He looks away. He looks around the room. He probably doesn't have a clue what he'll say next. "My sister's name is Jane."

Ah, there. At last. "Oh." I sip my drink. "Is Hank short for Henry?" I finally ask.

"No. It's short for a horribly snooty family name."

"Which is?"

"Hannaford." He whispers it.

"Hannaford?"

"Yes. Awful. Right? Hannaford Marsh. My parents are like that. Do you want some carrots, some celery?"

"Like what?" I'm intrigued.

"Insufferably . . ."

"Old money?" I ask, amused.

"Insufferably snooty." He laughs. "Do you? Want some carrots? Some celery?"

I nod. He smiles. He has nice teeth. He makes up a plate for me, giving me a generous handful. "Dip?" he asks.

"No thank you." And it's not because I want to appear healthy. It's because dip would surely end up dripping ceremoniously on my silk tank top, staining it for eternity.

We stare at each other, crunching for a while. He with his delicious-looking dip. Me with my dry, extraordinarily crunchy celery and carrots. It's like a love scene from Bugs Bunny.

"Peggy says you own an art gallery. What sort of gallery is it?" I ask him.

"My parents, the good folks who named me Hannaford, think if I own an art gallery, I ought to have triple-matted engravings of horses. Or represent artists who paint full-size portraits of people named Muffy and Tokey, you know, for above the maahhhhntel."

"And your art gallery has . . ."

"Not one horse or society portrait. Just things I like. Mostly representational. Some quirky. A modern guy named Adam Lentz who does amazing, almost medieval portraits of people holding birds in their outstretched hands. A woman who does photo-realistic still lifes of old toys. But I also represent a few of the still-living abstract expressionists. Do you know that movement?"

"Like Hans Hofmann, Robert Motherwell? Jack Tworkov?"

"I'm impressed," he says.

"I was an art major."

"Really? Do you paint?" he asks.

"I did. In a very unextraordinary way. Now I design houses. I'm an architect."

"An architect. Yes. Peggy said. I sometimes thought I'd become an architect," he says. "I actually care a lot about architecture."

So we begin. So much in common. So much to talk about. He even seems like he might be attracted to me. He's smiling. He's leaning toward me, though I can't imagine why. Right near us, filling her plate with celery and tons of dip, is a thirty-year-old with a body from a lingerie catalog. She's even exposing her belly button above her sarong skirt. Even my eye cannot help but pause there in envy. But the handsome fool is looking at me.

So here he is. Hank Marsh. You can just tell he's well mannered. He chews with his mouth closed. He probably knows how to walk around and open a car door, not to slouch deeply into his soup bowl when he eats soup, and surely puts his napkin in his lap before his food comes. He is a thoroughbred. I don't know why these things attract me, but they do.

Yet, while I'm suddenly noticing his flat stomach, his strong square chin, very soon after I'm imagining us five years down the road. There we are at the dinner table. He's wearing a red-and-black flannel shirt. Tight jeans. Maybe too tight, because after a few years of marriage he's sporting something of a tummy. Okay. I've learned to live with this. I have a tummy too. Maybe in five years, mine will resemble a six-months' pregnancy. But, in this little scenario, there we sit. He's looking at his plate, eating. I'm eating too. He doesn't look up. I don't look up. What does it matter that we have tummys? We don't see each other. We have nothing to say to each other either. The scene comes in as clearly as a cable channel. There we are. Yes. The Miserables at home. I'm annoyed because despite his quite sensitively attuned brain, he still hasn't grasped the pattern of how to put dishes in the dishwasher (do all men have dishlexia?) so, just like with the twins, with Hank Marsh I am the sole reliable dishwasher. He's annoyed because yesterday, when I just went out to get dishwashing liquid, I stopped at an antique store and bought a bedside table for $1,375 that I bargained down from $1,660. It's beautiful. Sheraton style. Cherry. With a clam-broth glass handle. It's the final piece to make our bedroom perfect. But he thinks we should be setting more aside for our retirement . . . what the hell was wrong with the wobbly old fiberboard table under the faded cloth? Besides, what do we care about the bedroom? We haven't made love there for months. We look up at each other briefly, then look down again at our meals. We've reached the point where we can barely stand each other, and yet we're yoked together like two oxen with an entire field to plow.

Okay. Stop the cameras. I have no intention of going there.

I look up, and there he is: still charming, still a stranger, biting on a piece of celery, then chewing every bit before he speaks. "Actually," he says, "I'm looking for an architect. I bought a piece of land upstate just recently. Near Rhinebeck. In a little town called Clinton. The mailing address is Clinton Corners."

"I know Rhinebeck," I say. "It's wonderful . . . "It's one of my favorite places."

"I want to build a house on this land. It's a great piece of property. Overlooking a pond. Very rolling. Stone retaining walls already in place. It was part of a farm."

"A house." Suddenly, I'm quickened to the core. "I design houses. What sort of house are you hoping to build?"

"Peggy told me you designed beautiful houses. She said I should look at samples of the things you've designed."

"Yes!"

"I don't know what I want. Something simple. Maintenance-free. Gorgeous."

"Do you intend to entertain, or is it a personal retreat?"

"Oh, I suppose entertain sometimes. Retreat, by all means."

"Are you drawn to a particular era?"

"Well, you know, my grandparents have a turn-of-the-century behemoth on the coast in Maine. I just love that house. Of course, theirs is much bigger than anything I intend to build. I always laugh when everyone refers to it as 'the cottage.' "

"You spent the summers there?"

"Oh yes. Always, as a kid. It has the most wonderful sleeping porch overlooking the water. With a stone fireplace right out there. My grandfather would stack up logs in it each evening. It was like sleeping around a campfire. If my cousin Lonny hadn't wet his bed around two A.M. every night, with five aunts rushing in to change the sheets, it would have been great."

"Sounds wonderful. Would you know if the house is shingle style?"

"Yes. That's what it is. Shingle style. Funny thing is, it's Lonny who's going to inherit it, we all suspect. I think he finally learned not to wet the sheets."

"Well, perhaps you would want a smaller version of a shingle-style house. A turret here. A balcony there. Interesting fenestration . . . a sleeping porch if you like. With a fireplace. That's a wonderful idea."

"Fenestration?"

"Windows. Shingle-style houses tend to have a variety of interesting windows. Eyebrow windows, arched bays."

"Yes. Would you take a look at photos of the Maine house?"

"I'd love to see photos of it. And I'd really like to show you my book of houses."

"Absolutely." He looks deeply in my eyes. Somehow, the thought of Hank Marsh as a client is more thrilling, or at least more easily accessible, than Hank Marsh as a lover. "When can we get together?" he asks. I look over at Peg and she's beaming like a fucking lighthouse.

Reasons not to get excited about meeting Hank Marsh:

1. He might be coming on to me because he wants me to lower my architectural fee.

2. He might not like my architecture, in which case, there's no point in having any interest in him at all.

3. He might be mean or insensitive in bed, penurious with his money, addicted to ESPN, wear ladies' underwear, have an overbearing mother who hates women, be overly religious, only love horsey-set women who wear headbands, expect to be waited on, not bathe enough . . .

4. He might be secretly gay.

Still, I go to bed Saturday night thinking about him and that glorious sleeping porch. And Sunday, again, I wonder when he'll call. God, it's started already. It's started.

On Monday, the thought of a possible letter from Jack Crashin lightens my reentry back to the workweek considerably. When I reach my office, I don't even give myself time to take my jacket off before I check my E-mail. And indeed, a letter is waiting for me. I sit down in my office chair, still wearing my coat, so eager to open it. And afraid.

I sit for a while staring at the notice of his letter: Jcrashin@crashin.com. Jack is at the other end of my mouse. After twenty-eight years, after so many nights wondering. I see him in my mind as he was then, with his long, black hair, those beautiful hands, his voice, his sweet, inspiring presence. But what if he doesn't remember me? What if he isn't happy I contacted him?

"Dear Jane," it begins.

As I mentioned before, after Jack and I split up, we wrote letters for two or three years. Twenty-one of his letters are tied in a green ribbon in a box in my basement. Yet not one of them begins "Dear Jane." They just launch into his message, usually something fairly self-involved, and having little to do with me. Will this one?

> Dear Jane,
> I was surprised and so happy to hear from you. When I saw your name on my E-mail inbox list, I could hardly believe it. And then, with every word I read, I heard your voice, as though you were right there in the room with me. There's so much to catch up on after twenty-five years, I wonder if it will take us twenty-five years to catch up! Well, starting at the beginning: so you

became an architect, just like you wanted to. I see your E-mail address is Paris, Washburn, and Green. Pretty impressive. Do you know, your enthusiasm for architecture back at the University of Illinois intimidated me? Or at least goaded me into being more serious about my work. Do you love architecture as you did then?

I guess, since you found my website, you know that I am still an architect, now living in the not-so-deep South. I can't say I'm wildly fond of Nashville. But it's fine. Friendly. My life is good enough here, and aside from my long-running fight with the zoning board trying to make it *more* strict, believe it or not, I rarely find reason to complain. I have my own firm. Which only means that the headaches come to my attention first, and that I'm the one who has to worry about the bottom line—and there's always something to worry about, believe me.

I have two sons: Clark, who's seventeen, Ned, who's fourteen. Clark is already interested in architecture. He worked on a project just last summer, to rehab a historic house that was practically in ruins, with my friend Abe, a guy who specializes in wrecks. Abe said he has real aptitude. Now every time Clark passes a tumbledown house, he talks about how he'd like to get his hands on it. I think I've spawned an architect. Or, God forbid, a contractor. Certainly a renovator. Clark is so much like I used to be, it's a little scary. Looks like me, even. You, in particular, might be amused to see him, since you probably remember me near his age.

On the other hand, Ned, my younger boy, is so far from who I was or now am, it's a mystery. Ned told me the other day that he'd like to grow up to be a minister. He reads serious books about religion and gets mad when we don't go to church. Or, in fact, the more accurate word would be "disappointed." He never loses his temper. It's rather like living with a stern, but forbearing, father. His teachers call him studious and consistent. Clark is working hard to loosen Ned up. This could be a full-time task.

But it's funny, as different as my boys are, I love them both equally and am so grateful for them. Their differences, their quirkiness, just make them seem more special to me. And then there is my daughter, Laine. My sweet daughter, Laine. It would take a whole letter to tell you about Laine, so I will save that for another time. Do you have children? I imagine you do. You always loved children. I remember that you used to point out every baby we passed.

A few years ago, I drove back to the University of Illinois all by myself. I stayed at the Union. I don't think it's been renovated since we were there, at least not when I saw it. And it still had that awful fluorescent lighting.

The Union hasn't changed, but unfortunately the English Building has. I walked wistfully around the outside of it, recalling our protest. We saved that building! But the sad news revealed itself when I went up to the top floor. Do you remember it? I recalled the little shelves that were there to hold lanterns, and the beautiful moldings. They're gone, I'm sorry to report. They've turned the whole floor into some kind of computer lab with no moldings, nothing special. And they've installed central air-conditioning. But in the process, even the glorious Gordian knot floors are gone. Very sad. When I saw the

```
tile with which they were replaced, I thought of
you, and felt glad you weren't there to see it.
I admit, it was partially because of you, that I
led that protest. My love of architecture in-
spired me, sure. But without question, I wanted
to impress you.
    Jane. I wonder what you have done with your
life. I wonder if you are married, have a fam-
ily, are satisfied with all that's happened to
you since I've seen you. Thank you so much for
finding me. I'll be watching my inbox. Jack.
```

He's changed, I think. There's a humility in his letter that touches me. And a kindness. I never imagined he led that protest to impress me. I can hardly believe it.

I feel as if I have no blood in my extremities. Like I've forgotten to breathe for too long. I read the letter through a second time, warmed by his journey back to the university, moved by his feelings for his children. Stirred by how honest he was about his reasons for the protest. It's amazing how I could find myself so overwhelmed with feeling for a man whom I haven't seen in nearly thirty years. I want to write him back instantly, to make this monologue a dialogue. I want to reach him the way his letter has reached me. Without even taking my coat off, I write.

```
Dear Jack,
It was wonderful to hear from you . . .
```

I launch into a long and detailed letter. It is delicious and indulgent to tell Jack about the girls, my brownstone, my time at Paris, Washburn, and Green. I realize that I'm proud of the life I've led. I want to paint a picture for him. Maybe my motivation is slightly more calculating. I want him to be sorry he hasn't spent his life with me. Sorry that we aren't partners now in this middle part of our lives. The dearest of old friends, the sweetest of lovers. All these years later. Of course, I ask questions about his sons, his work, his firm. I write

> Most of all, I should tell you that you are the one person of the thousands and thousands I have known who has most changed my life. Had I not met you, I'd probably be a rather miserable high school art teacher. Probably not even a very good one. With teenagers in the house these days, it's nearly impossible to imagine that once I thought I could bear daily contact with hundreds of them. You changed that for me. I'll always be grateful.
>
> I have loved architecture all these years. Loved taking buildings from vision to reality. Loved it all. Until recently. Maybe I'm just tired these days. Maybe I miss designing houses, which is what I love best. I have a dream that someday I will go out on my own. I'll leave behind the politics and the assignments I hate. No more colonial shopping malls. No more assisted-living facilities dictated by clueless clients. Somewhere outside New York City, up north a few hours, maybe—in the Berkshires, or the Hudson River Valley—I'll set up shop. I'll design only houses that are framed by hills. I'll find peace.
>
> Tell me all about your work, your days, what you've been doing for the last twenty-five years. Tell me all about your dreams. And of course, tell me all about the "exotic and Southern Suzanne" as you once called her.

In the last three letters he sent me before we lost touch, he talked about his then girlfriend in just those words: "The exotic and

Southern Suzanne," whom he'd met at Yale. "Suzanne and I are what is known as 'in love,' " he told me in the last letter. I hated her. I was brokenhearted. Jack never once said he loved me. It's what made me finally decide not to write him anymore.

But I did call him once, a few years later. He was still in New Haven, working at some small architectural firm. He told me that he and the exotic and Southern Suzanne were married. Still, I noted that he didn't sound too happy. That night, I remember crying in bed, and chewing on a whole spectrum of feelings for my lost Jack. Why had I let him go? Why hadn't I tried harder to hold on to him? But, as I lay there in the dark, I lay next to a guy named Dan, who sleepily put his arm around me and said, "Shhhh, it's okay," without asking me why I was crying. Dan, the substitute, who, in the end, I also loved far too well, became my life

And the exotic and Southern Suzanne, is she Jack Crashin's life still? Over the years, as I've tried to imagine what might have become of him, I've envisioned him living in New York in a co-op overlooking Central Park. Tasteful and spare. Little monkey-wood bowls on his dresser for emptying change from his pocket. Matching dark wooden hangers in his closet. On the walls, Chinese screens with gold-leafed backgrounds. Soft, down-filled leather armchairs the color of cognac. Thoroughly masculine. Oh, I could see it all so clearly. And just as clearly, I knew—*knew*—that Suzanne had long ago gone back down South. She hated New York, she and Jack fought continually. Jack was now contemplative, and happy at last to be alone.

I'd dreamed that we would run into each other on Central Park West one day. Jack would be wearing a mossy-green sweater that brought out the depth of his hazel eyes. He wouldn't look anything like the fifty-year-old he'd become. Still slim and refined and solid, he'd put his arms around me and make decades disappear in a single hug.

But when I read his bio on his web page last week, the image changed. First of all, there was Nashville. I certainly hadn't counted on that. And then there were the words "In his spare time, Jack relishes spending time with his family." Relishes. Ever since, I can't help seeing an outdoor barbecue with lots of noisy company, fat bottles of ketchup and mustard on the table and three skinny bruised-legged blond girls holding out hot dogs to be coated by Jack, in a silly chef's hat. Well, now I must replace those three girls with two boys and a girl. But I still see Suzanne there, sitting off to the side, smoking a cigarette, a vaguely sour look on her face as she gazes out of the corner of her eyes at her children and their hot dogs. She, I've always imagined so blond and slender she might disappear, her eyebrows plucked to pencil lines, her nose thin and pinched and her lips pale and pouty. She makes Jack's life hell, but it's a familiar hell he isn't ready to jettison.

"And how is the exotic and Southern Suzanne?" I write, sorry that once again, I must acknowledge my nemesis. Still, when I hit Send I realize I haven't been so excited about anything in a long, long time.

At two, I am finally called into Rodney's office. I am so full of Jack and his letter; it makes me feel vulnerable, distracted. No time to face Rodney. One must be armored to face Rodney. One must have one's weapons drawn. Rodney can intimidate anyone, when he chooses to. And he has the soul of Machiavelli. The stories about him could curl Tonto's hair. One story has it that Rodney slept with the wife of every junior partner in the firm, and even with Mrs. Washburn, who at the time was in her sixties, just to prove he could. He has stabbed his rivals in the back at every opportunity. I've heard him bad-mouthing other partners to clients. I've even heard him give another partner, Ken, the wrong address for a key meeting, and then complain to the client when Ken didn't show up.

And he does smaller things, shameless things, to flaunt his power. For instance, here's his perfect plan to ensure that he is doted on in the restaurant of his choice in front of clients: he visits the chosen restaurant three times in the same week. The first time, he goes with people he knows and purposely causes an unpleasant scene to call attention to himself.

Once, I witnessed this myself. A perfectly fine, though quiet waitperson named Joe was assigned to our table. "Hello, my name is Joe, I'll be your waitperson," he said in a somewhat monotone voice. Rodney said to him, "You don't seem happy. Are you happy, Joe?" The fellow, a tall, slender man with long fingers, frowned and paled. "I'm happy," he said, and left the table to put in the drinks order.

Well, happy wasn't good enough for Rodney. He smiled a perfectly evil smile and called over the maître d'. "I want a new waiter," he proclaimed. "This waiter is taciturn."

The maître d' wrinkled his brow, no doubt debating the meaning of the word "taciturn."

"We'll give you our best man, Paul, to wait on your table, sir. We are terribly, terribly sorry." He bowed his head in utter servitude. It was sickening.

Rodney thanked the maître d' and handed him his business card wrapped in a twenty. "Do tell me your name," he said. But finding out that the maître d's name was Carlos was not the point. The card that Rodney had passed to him said, "Rodney Paris, Chairman, Chief Architect, Paris, Washburn, and Green" on it, and Rodney wanted poor Carlos never to forget it. Rodney had made his first strike. He even watched to see if Carlos unwrapped the twenty and looked at the card.

Well, I wasn't involved with the rest of the plot. But I heard all about it. After making that initial scene, Rodney returned to the restaurant twice more that week. The first and second time, Paul, who was personable and professional, was assigned to Rodney's table; Paul and the maître d' got outrageous tips, and the third time, Rodney brought the client. Of course, by the third time, the Red Sea parted when Rodney entered the room. The poor, hapless, taciturn Joe stayed as far away from Rodney's table as possible, lowered, no doubt, in management's eyes. And Rodney got the attention he thinks he deserves. I've come to hate Rodney more and more as the years pass. More and more as he attempts not to age, with his spiked hair and his recent single ear pierce. More and more as he's come to think of himself as king.

I walk into his outer office and his secretary asks me to sit while he's on the phone. I can hear his gruff voice through the open door, can see one of his hairy arms in a rolled-up sleeve, picking up a paperweight, shuffling papers, slamming his palm down to make a point. But I don't want to know what he's saying, don't want to hear the machinations, the manipulations in which he is surely indulging.

When I hear he's hung up the phone, I feel the muscles tightening in my neck.

"Go ahead in, Jane," Sally, his secretary, says.

Rodney's office is appropriately grand. The furniture is Corbusier, leather and chrome from the thirties. There is a black vase on the coffee table, birds-of-paradise sprouting from it. And pictures of Rodney's six children (from three different marriages) stand in white marble frames like tombstones along the sleek black credenza. How would it be to have Rodney as a father? I remember Rodney's own father, a kind man, a good man. How has Rodney risen from this?

He has his back to me, but still manages to say, "Jane, sit down," as though he has eyes in the back of his head. Then, slowly, he turns, looking grim. I sit warily, noticing first the uncomfortable chair I have seated myself in. It leans back too far. Makes me feel trapped. Noticing second, the intensity of Rodney's look. "Well," he says. He clears his throat. He hates this, whatever it is.

I find it hard to resist my inclination to bolt.

"Despite the good economy, we haven't had a very good year," he says finally. Yeah, what's it to me? I wonder.

"No? Why do you think?" I answer dutifully.

"Various reasons. Too much staff, for one." He looks me in the eye. His own eyes are a cold gray, remind me of the ocean off Cape Cod where Daniel and I used to take the girls in the summer. Gray, nearly opaque. Cold water. The girls would scream when they waded in. Daniel and I would hold their hands, walking them in inch by inch. Eventually the water would feel fine, lukewarm even. Acceptable.

"I'm going to have to let you go," Rodney says.

I feel my mouth open slightly. I find it hard to take more than a shallow breath.

"Let me go?" I ask. "Why me?" My scalp prickles. Heat rises, makes my cheeks feel as if they've been slapped.

"Merely a matter of what you're on. And how expensive you've become. The Bank of Monmouth job is not so important to us. The client's easygoing. They won't mind if I change staff on them. I've got to cut back, Jane. It's not that I want to . . ."

He wants me to feel sorry for him, I realize. How long have I been here? I wonder. I begin to count in my mind. Eighteen years. I've held on to this job through recessions, through cutbacks. Through it all. I should have moved long ago. But inertia stayed me, held me in chains.

"You haven't seemed to care much, lately," Rodney says. "I have to say, Jane, we've known each other a long time, but you just haven't been . . . Jesus, I don't know . . . focusing. You resisted the computer for so long. I'm not even sure you use it much now."

"I do now."

"You can't resist change in this business. Seems like lately you resist everything. So now that I have to cut back, how can I not think of you?"

"I do good work," I say.

"What lately?"

"I—"

"I've seen virtually nothing on the bank so far, and have been disappointed in much of what you've worked on. Your work has been a little sloppy. And, frankly, you've gotten, raise by raise, quite expensive . . ."

"I'm in my forties," I say. "That's really the bottom line, isn't it?"

"That is not the bottom line. I'm letting six people go. They're all ages."

"All sexes, too?"

"Ummm." He's thinking. "Yeah."

I wonder. But what can I say? Even I haven't liked my own output lately.

"What sort of package are you giving me?" I ask.

"Human resources will tell you all about it."

"How many months' severance? I am getting severance, aren't I?"

"It's very generous. You're getting more than anybody else."

"I'm an associate," I say. "Who else is being let go?"

"I can't tell you that."

"Any other associates?"

"I can't tell you."

"What do you consider generous?" I ask.

"You're getting five and a half months' severance."

I blink. Five and a half months of pay. It's not so much, I guess, not after all these years. But it's five and a half months without having to work. Free time if I like. But I'm forty-six. How will I find another job? I've got two daughters who need to go to college. I've got a mortgage on my house to pay. My God, what if I have to give up my house? I see the moving truck, see myself weeping on the stoop. I see the sign: "Help me. I'm homeless. I have two daughters to feed. Any change will help . . ."

"Well," Rodney says. "If you have more questions, you can talk to human resources. IRA rollovers, that sort of thing. Penny Magnuson will take you through it all."

I want to say, "I'm the best house designer here. No one designs houses like I do." But what's the point? That skill means nothing to him, and everything to me. For a moment, there is silence. I look at his greased and spiked hair, the white stars at the corners of his eyes where the sun hasn't tanned his skin, and his taut, face-lifted (?) jaw.

"Well," he says. He wants me out of his office.

"I'd like references."

"Of course."

"Leads if you have any. Clients who want a house. You don't want to do them. You could do worse than give them to me."

"If I have something, I will. You'd do well to go out on your own. Do houses exclusively. Set up somewhere outside the city. You know. You always were into houses."

I think maybe he's insulting me. Or maybe not. It *is* what I should do. Go out on my own. Without any of the crap. The madness. But it's hard to get commissions. Impossible to begin. I get up from my chair. My knees ache. I'm forty-six years old and unemployed.

"When do you want me out of here?" I ask.

"Take your time. You're not an enemy of the people. Use your space for a while if you like, a place where people can contact you. A month. Two months. I don't care."

I know that's the last thing I want. To be skulking around the office with people gawking at me. Thinking to themselves, She wasn't any good. An associate fired. She must have deserved it . . . *I'm never going to get fired.*

None of it seems real. My head is light, as though it has filled with helium. The back of my knees are wet. My legs feel weak. I feel Lilliputian, wish I were invisible. People are looking at me as I walk back to my space. Laura Mackel, one of the few other older women at the firm, stops me.

"What's wrong?" she asks. "You sick?"

I'm mortified. Does it show so openly?

"Rodney just . . . I got . . . he let me go."

"Go where?"

"He fired me, Laura."

"No."

"Yes."

"Fired? I can't believe it. You're an associate, aren't you?" Laura blanches. She's wondering about herself. Wondering what it means that someone like me, who's been here so long, is vulnerable. "God, the bastard," she says. "I can't believe it."

I feel nothing at all. Just this heat around my ears, this weakness. This spiderweb-thin veil of shame.

I walk to my space, feeling Laura's eyes follow me. There are already packing boxes leaning against my drawing table. They wasted no time, despite Rodney's invitation to stay on as long as I need to. Marva, the office manager, must have been waiting to see me go into Rodney's office. I sit down in my miserable ergonomically correct chair and turn it toward the window so no one can see my face. My heart slams. Tears rise in my eyes and I swallow them before they fall.

Eighteen years of memories with this firm. Eighteen years of things to pack. Favorite reference books. Desk objects that have comforted me through pressured times. A black glass Lalique woman that Dan gave to me the year before we broke up. Small enough to fit in my palm, beautiful and cool and smooth, the woman is on her knees but hunched over, covering her head, her head pressed against her knees. Hiding her head. Oh, yes. That was a fine portrait of me back then when Dan gave her to me as a present. Seeing nothing I didn't want to see. I pick up the woman, drink in the cool smoothness on my palm and fingers as I have so many times before. Could I have seen this coming, if I'd really paid attention? Have I been hiding my head these last few months, ignoring the coolness in Rodney's greeting, ignoring the obvious as I did with Dan?

I feel the shock pulse through me, electricity that sucks the surety from my own skin. I have been at this firm since before my daughters were born. Since the first year of my marriage. I was pregnant here. Grew up here, really.

I start unfolding and punching the boxes into shape. I should call someone. Tell someone who matters what's happened. Cry on someone's shoulder. I should say something to Dave Mann, who works quietly next to me, ignoring me. I don't think he knows. Nothing in his body language says he's self-conscious in front of me. But if I tell him, I'll cry, I'll break down. I'll feel too much. Nancy Kangol? No, she thinks of me as older, wiser. How can I tell her? I should call my friends, Peggy maybe. Someone who would bear my shock, reflect back my outrage, so I could see it better, feel more than this electric numbness. But I don't want to. I don't want to feel too much. Besides, there's nowhere private to talk. I want to pack. I want to be out of here. To rid my life of this mockery of security.

I realize suddenly that people *are* beginning to watch me furtively, looking up from their computers, their drawing boards. I become aware that the room seems quieter than usual. The word has spread or they are all noting that I am packing. Still, no one has the courage to ask me, or chooses to commiserate with me. Into the boxes I place eighteen years of favorite books, yearly calendars scribbled cover to cover with appointments and phone numbers, my portfolio of houses. I should have left years ago, should have had the courage to walk out when I started to lose heart for the firm. I was a coward. Now I am burning with shame, with insult.

I need to go home. I need to sit in my beloved back parlor and curl up on the big, safe, flowered sofa. I need to lie on my bed with my favorite pillow, in the dark. I need to be home. Never before has the power of home seemed so clearly defined. This is why I build houses. To cradle. To protect bruised souls. To shelter uncertain lives. This is why. Leaving the boxes still not fully packed, I take my coat from the closet and put it on. Ivory wool. I feel old and fat and lost, but at least I'm going home.

And then I pause and send one more E-mail.

```
Dear Jack,
    Sorry, but please write me at my home E-mail
address rather than the office:
Architectgirl@answernet.com.
```

I think about writing more, explaining why. But I'm not ready yet to share it. Not ready for Jack to know something so negative about me so soon. When I hit Send, this time it's with regret.

Stepping out of the building, I am slapped by what has become a much warmer day than expected, miserably humid. Late-summer wet heat, the smells of sweat and garbage. How many years have I walked these same four blocks to and from the subway? Mornings, evenings. Back and forth. Drudgery sometimes. Often lately. But now, I'm free. Free in a way I can't remember feeling for years and years. FREE! Though I feel weak and worn, and shock still holds me in its narrow arms, the whole world seems incrementally more hopeful suddenly. My heart starts to drum. The gum-clotted, spit-strewn sidewalk glassphalt sparkles in the streetlight. How beautiful it is, I think. How infinite, like a sky full of stars.

Four

———

$\mathcal{I}$ have something to tell you," I say to the girls when I get home. "Something happened. Something not so great."

It is starting to rain. I've rushed in from the first of the raindrops. It's dark in the house, the light is silvery and eerie and no one has lit a single lamp. I walk around turning them all on. Will I have trouble paying the electric bill?

I look at their faces. Curious, mostly. I think if I just get it over with, I'll feel better. But it's funny how hard it is to be vulnerable with your own children. Especially with teenagers.

Cait looks at me, annoyed. "So, what? What happened?"

Abby flares her nostrils. And I'm supposed to tell them? She slams closed her math book. There is a moment of silence as dense and impassable as a wall of damp cement.

"What?" they say, shining the bright light of their annoyance into my eyes.

"I lost my job," I say. I try to sound easy, try to make my voice less hurt than I feel, try to sound as though it's just one of those things. I take off my coat and hang it on one of the Shaker pegs by the door.

"How did you lose it?" Abby asks. Her voice is soft and worried. I am comforted by that. And surprised.

"I don't know. It just happened."

"Did you do something bad?" Cait asks.

I smile. It isn't like going to the principal's office, I think. This is how they must imagine it, although Rodney certainly played the nasty, cold principal well.

"No," I say. "They had to lay off someone. They chose me." I sit down at the kitchen table, by Cait. I am glad to be in my kitchen. With the hand-painted fruit tiles I designed, with the curtains made from 1940s tablecloths. With the bead-board wainscoting that's been there since 1911. My house, my haven. I wish I never needed to leave it again. What a fine housewife I could be. I could learn to bake soufflés, make the back garden a paradise, knit a complex afghan as colorful as Joseph's coat.

"But you've been at Paris, Washburn, and Green forever," Abby says. She pulls out the chair on the other side of me and sits down. "Your mascara's a little runny."

I nod. "I cried a little. I *have* been there forever. Since before you guys even came along."

"Are there other jobs?" Cait asks. For a moment I see the little girl in her, the soft, vulnerable center beneath the annoyed facade. Like the soft center in a hard, hard candy.

"I probably have a lot of options," I say, wishing I felt as certain as I manage to sound.

"What options?" She pulls her chair closer to me, yanks on a tendril of her hair.

"Well, I could get another job. Or be my own boss."

"But if you're your own boss, who pays you?" Abby asks. I'm

touched and sobered that she's worried. Cait's always been the wor-rier, Abby the stiff-upper-lip girl. Still, they both want to know that their worlds won't tumble down. They just find different ways to tell me. How weighty a parent's job: to be honest and protective all at once.

"I'd have to find clients who want a house built, or an apartment redone. They'd pay me."

"That sounds good," Abby says.

"It might be. If there are clients out there."

"Are there clients out there?" Cait asks.

"I don't know. I'll have to find them. I met a guy, at Peggy's party Saturday, who might want me to build him a house. But I don't know for sure . . ."

"What happens if there aren't clients?" Cait asks.

"Then I suppose I could work for the city." I've heard all along that the city hires lots of architects. The pay isn't much different than the sort of pay I've been making. After all, Paris, Washburn, and Green never paid me all that much, mostly because I had never moved elsewhere to jack up my salary. And undoubtedly because I'm a woman.

"Don't work for the city," Abby says.

"What's wrong with the city?" I ask.

"It just sounds very . . . I dunno. Tacky."

I smile. "Don't be a snob," I tell her. "A job is a job. I have to see what's out there." But even I don't want to work for the city. There could be no more soulless building than a public building, a gov-ernment building, even government-subsidized housing. Every-thing, no doubt, chosen by committee. Everything homogenized for the "greater good."

"Are you worried?" Abby asks. I put my hand on her hand. Her fingers are longer than mine. Yesterday, they did each other's nails, alternating orange and blue—their school colors—on each of their fingers. They are just little girls, I think. But they are taller, more elegant, more beautiful than I have ever been. It is wonderful to give this to the world, this beauty, this miracle.

"Of course I'm worried," I say. "But it's only because I don't know what to expect. I think once I understand my options better, I won't be so worried."

"Mom," Cait says. She puts her hand on mine, so now we are a stack of hands. Her eyes are wide. She looks as if she wants to put her head in my lap.

"What, darlin'?" I say, in my sweetest, kindest, warmest tone.

"I'm sorry you lost your job, but I'm totally starving."

I laugh. "You guys okay with the leftover chicken from last night?"

"Sure," they both say. It's refreshing not to get any flak over the proposed menu. I take out the chicken and dumplings I cooked this weekend. This is what adulthood is: the pleasure of eating comfort food you've made yourself. Being your own mother.

"I think you should kill your boss," Cait says. "You could just go in, you know, nonchalantly, with a gun."

"You could go postal and wipe out the whole office," Abby says.

"You guys have to stop watching the news," I say. "It's more violent than the shows."

The warmed-up chicken and dumplings seems to soothe us all. We talk about school and various boys, and Dan, and their new teachers.

"Will you guys do the dishes?" I ask them, expecting full cooperation. But they've already forgotten that I'm the walking wounded. They get up sulkily.

"Do we have to?"

"Yes."

"After my French."

"After I write up my physics lab."

I sigh. "Okay."

What have I done wrong? I guess I didn't give them enough chores when they were growing up, so now they think of any little job as drudgery. And they've perfected the passive-aggressive thing. They simply don't do a very good job. That's how they manage to do so little around here. I always think, I can do this better myself. But, yes. I remember being the same way at their age. Until Ed left, that is.

I leave the sinkful of unattended dishes, and climb the stairs to my room thinking I'll call Aunt Aggie, or my sister, Bess. Instead, I lay down in the dark on my bed. I can see the lights of downtown Manhattan from my bed, the Woolworth Building, the Empire State Building lit in autumn colors. The night is as clear as I've seen it in a while. The city, a complex tangle of disappointments and possibility, looks so simple from here. Just a compilation of architects' dreams from long ago. Not one building in this whole blessed skyline is mine. All I've done for years and years are banks and supermarkets and assisted-living centers in Scottsdale.

It hurts to think about the impact of your life on the world. I suppose I get top points for my manipulative, tattoo-hungry daughters. And for my houses. My houses. I am happy to think that when I die, someone will be living in, and I hope *loving,* those walls. That long after I'm dust, someone will wake to a horizontal cottage window I chose, with six small panes instead of one modern ugly one and enjoy the way the light leaves a shadow of the muntins, like a ghost of a window, on a perpendicular wall; that someone will wash dishes while looking out over a long, pale-blue scarf of mountains; that someone will feel that they've found their pot of gold for having had their bid accepted for one of my now aged houses. Hubris, I guess. Longing for immortality in a mortal world. And yet, what else can we leave behind but our children, and long-forgotten hopes?

It crosses my mind to write to Jack, to tell him what happened. For some reason, it strikes me that he, of all people, might understand how I feel—he knows what architecture means to me. But I'll wait to hear from him. And then I'll tell him. How eerie, that of all times, I should bring him back into my life now.

I wake in the night, unable to breathe. I sit up in the close, brownish dark. I've lost my job. I'm unemployed. I might have to stand in line to collect unemployment insurance. Why is it so dark in here? Maybe the streetlight has gone out. Maybe the tree near it is sheathing the light in its black, leathery leaves. Maybe it's raining. The faintest tease of light moves softly against the wall. A single scolding finger of light. Saliva rushes to my mouth the way it does before I vomit. Swallowing it down, I close my eyes, lean against the headboard and feel weak with worry, lost. Tomorrow I needn't go to work. I needn't do anything. I could stay in bed for weeks the way my mother did after Ed moved out. I can imagine the girls coming in and out of my room with trays, worried. What would they put on them? Bowls of cereal? That's about all they can make in the kitchen by themselves. I, at least, made my mother eggs and bacon, pancakes, creamed spinach. She loved creamed spinach. She said I made it better than anyone. She ate it all and then lay back down on her bed and closed her eyes. I sat by her bed and watched her and cried for her. I was afraid to go to school. I was afraid to leave her. I was afraid to tell my friends what had happened. I know now that I could never do to the girls what my mother did to me.

I get up and brush my teeth. I brush hard, every tooth, just like my dentist taught me. I brush until my mouth is numb with the sting of mint. I splash my face with cold water. And then I walk to my favorite chair in the study and think about those days. It's funny how crisis recalls crisis. How pain brings up old pain.

I sit in my study remembering the day my mother and sister and brothers and I were forced to move from our beloved Tudor house. Ed Butz never found a job again that paid as well as the Velveeta job. He just couldn't afford the house anymore. Even the courts couldn't make him pay for it. He came over to help us move. My mother wouldn't look at him. He'd lost a lot of weight since he'd moved out. Even his socks didn't look like they fit him anymore. After months at the Y, he was living alone in some tiny room somewhere. Too small to have us stay with him or even visit very often. He couldn't cook. The girl he'd gotten pregnant either hadn't wanted to marry him or he hadn't asked. She was never heard from again. He stood in my room looking small and wary as I taped up my boxes.

"I'm sorry you're losing this room," he said very softly, his voice pressed with feeling.

"Me too," I said.

"You loved it, didn't you?"

"Yes." My voice was very small.

"I'm sorry I let you down," he said. "You especially."

I looked up at him. I was a teenager. I'd already begun to rebel against him before everything went haywire, which made his vulnerability that much more disconcerting now. And I'd always worried that somehow he didn't love me as much as the other kids because I wasn't really his.

"Why me especially?"

"Because you know what it's like not to have things you want. It meant a lot to you when we bought this house. I remember how happy you were. You have no idea how happy it made me to give it to you."

I nodded. I didn't know what to say. He had tears in his eyes, but it wasn't in my power to absolve him. I was a kid and my world was changing, was changed because of his mistakes. As I looked up into his tired eyes, I loved him that moment as much as I've ever loved anyone.

"Did you ever love Mom?" I asked him as he went out the door.

He turned and faced me. He grimaced. "Always," he said. "I've always loved your mother. I always will."

I felt very angry suddenly. I couldn't understand, in that light, what had happened to us. Couldn't make clear why we'd lost everything. When he walked out of my room that afternoon, for the first time in my life I realized that sometimes things didn't make sense. Sometimes things just weren't fair.

Now I sit in the pink chair and feel it all again. The surprise and disappointment. The lack of understanding. Only this time it isn't Ed Butz who's screwed up. This time, somehow, surely it's me. Or is it? I realize why I've awakened. I'm furious. I get up from the pink chair and want to do something that states my anger: kick a chair maybe or sweep all the things on my desk onto the floor. Or call Rodney at home and tell him what a lout he is.

Instead, I sit down at the computer and call up Jack's letter through my office E-mail link, and for a few sweet minutes in the shadowy dark of my study, in the middle of the night, nothing seems to matter but his renewed presence, his voice, and my memories.

Then I hear someone's footsteps on the stairs up to my study. Cait opens the door and comes in. She is wearing a pink nightgown and her hair is sticking straight out on one side.

"What's wrong, darling?"

It must be three in the morning. Or later.

"Mommy," she says. Without makeup and earrings, without her new confidence, she's just my little girl, the one who used to have buckteeth and freckles, the one who would clench her fists in her sleep sometimes. "You're up."

"I woke up."

"I'm afraid," she says. "I woke up too."

"Afraid of what?" Abigail will never admit when she's afraid. I always find Cait's ability to share her concerns with me touching.

"Are we going to lose our house?" she asks. "Are we going to have to sell our house?"

"Oh, no, darling. I don't think so." She is five foot eight and all legs, but she crawls into my lap and puts her arms around my neck. Her fingers are as soft as feathers against my skin. Her hair tickles my nose. She smells of shampoo and toothpaste and Clearasil, hours after she's used them.

"Abby said we might have to sell it."

"Well, I think it's very unlikely."

"But possible?"

"Not likely, no."

"But possible?"

"Caity, if you want to find trouble in the world, you can. I could sit around and worry too and think there are no jobs out there. But there are, and I'm sure I'll find them. I don't think it's something you have to worry about. Really." She nods and leans her head against my shoulder.

"I'm worried anyway."

"How's life?" I ask her. Sometimes it's good to get my daughters apart, to speak to each one individually. They are thoroughly identical, and yet so different.

"Did you ever think that nothing good would ever happen to you?" she asks in a wispy, sad voice.

"A thousand times. Is that how you feel?"

"All the time."

"It will pass. I used to worry just like you."

"Did you talk to your mom?"

"Not at your age. She had too many other things to worry about."

"Was that when your dad left?"

"Yes."

"Did you cry when he left?"

"All the time."

"Poor Mom," she says.

"But see, I survived," I say. "That's what you discover when you get older, that no matter what happens, you survive. It's a good feeling to know it . . . but no one can make you really believe it except when you get a chance to try it out."

All the next morning, I check my office voice mail for a call from Hank Marsh. (I gave him my Paris, Washburn, and Green business card, so surely, that's where he'll call me.) And I check my home E-mail, hoping to hear from Jack. Nothing from Hank, but when Jack's E-mail finally comes, I feel like a kid opening a present.

```
     Dear Jane,
     Thank you for writing me back. So generous of
you to say I've added so much to your life. I'll
take credit for stirring up your interest in ar-
chitecture. But for everything after that, you
are 100 percent responsible. You've made your
life what it is, and if you enjoy it, well, then,
you've made some wise and lucky choices.
     Creating my firm was something I did when I was
very young, before Laine even came along. I
didn't know what I was doing, and I learned by
my mistakes. It was serendipity. I was given a
handful of clients through various lucky coinci-
dences and I simply put my name on the door. When
we grew, I added more architects. I never planned
any it . . . it just happened. Our firm doesn't
build houses often, and when we do, my colleague
Cynthia is the one who designs them. She's quite
```

good at it. But you know, I'd put money on it
that you're better.

You said you were divorced, and you told me
about your daughters, but you didn't say whether
you've remarried, or what your present status is.
As for "the exotic and Southern Suzanne" (did I
ever really call her that?), I'm quite sure she's
fine, but I can't say firsthand because I haven't
seen her in nearly eight years. In fact, I can't
even tell you for sure where she now lives, mer-
cifully.

I sit for a moment with this news, wondering what it means. If
he sees his boys and daughter all the time, and he isn't even sure
where Suzanne lives, then has she ceded custody of her children
entirely to Jack? For eight years. How surprising this seems to me,
how sad. Children with no mother. This is far worse than my life,
a life with no father. Mothers seem to me essential, unbearable to
lose. No barbecues with Suzanne smoking on the sidelines, bored
and beautiful? No Suzanne at all?

I read on, hoping for clues, information, or the revelation of a
second wife, but the letter goes on to mention how he plays softball in a local league twice a week, the ringer on a team of doctors.
And about a project he's just begun, a new library for the blind outside Nashville. And how it's rained every day for a week so that
they've been very slow to begin construction. And the commute
back and forth to the construction site is nearly three hours a day,
making him late to dinner and upsetting his daughter, Laine, who
doesn't like any change in the status quo. At the end, he writes

Do your daughters look like you? Two girls with
long, dark hair and big, brown eyes. You were so
lithe and graceful. At least this is how I imagine them. How astonishing that we are so old we

have children not much younger than we were at
the time we met. And funny that, though I am
older than you, I have the youngest child, Laine,
who is just turning nine near Christmastime.

Nine. Laine is nine, which means that Suzanne disappeared
when Laine was only a year old. Sadder and more mysterious still.
How could any woman leave her children? I wonder. And to leave
a one-year-old . . . it astonishes me. No wonder Laine is sad when
Jack doesn't come home to dinner. He is clearly all she has.

I can't tell you how your letter has touched
me. I never imagined we'd speak again in any way.
I think I was very arrogant when you knew me.
Very self-involved. And I wonder how I treated
you. You seemed fragile to me. I remember you
talked about how your stepfather left your family. I remember you cried. T think I thought at
the time that you were too emotional, too break-
able, that you were better off without me in your
life. I would just make things worse. No. That's
not honest. I didn't think of you. I was selfish. I thought of me. The bottom line is, you
scared me, Jane.
But you have fared well, better than I have,
you will soon see. You sound strong. And sound.
How I wish I could have seen the future back
then. I think I would surely have acted very differently. Tell me more about you. More about your
houses. Everything. *Everything*. I'll be watching
the mail.
Jack

No "Love," but then I didn't expect it. I wonder what he means,
that I will soon see that I have fared better than he has. On the sur-

face, it surely doesn't seem so. He has his own firm, three children he adores, even if Suzanne has left him. How badly could he have fared?

He hasn't called," I tell Peggy. "And now that I've lost my job, I need his commission."

"I didn't introduce you to Hank to set up a business connection here," she says. "He's probably just busy. He said he liked you."

"He did?" I don't know if I trust her to tell me the truth.

"He offered it. I didn't ask him."

"I liked him too," I say, embarrassed.

"Yeah, how can you help it? He's a hunk. Let me tell you, if I didn't have the glorious S.D. in my life, I'd be all over him like white on rice. I'll call and tell him you said you like him. That should encourage him to call you."

"No. Don't do that! God, this is just like high school. Don't tell him I like him."

"Oh, for God's sake, Jane. Grow up. I mean, you should know by now that men over forty are even more tender than seventeen-year-olds. They're babies. They take rejection harder than anyone. They need encouragement."

"I just really sparked to his ideas for his house. He told me about a house in Maine his grandparents owned. He might like a house that reflects that style. It's right up my alley, and it's what I need. A commission to start me out."

"If I get him to call you, and all you do is try to finagle him into signing you up as his architect, I'll kill you. I am not playing pimp here. Matchmaker, yes. Pimp, no. If he calls you, it will be to ask you out."

"Fine. I'll go out with him."

"It's about time you get over Daniel, for God's sake. Opened up to someone else."

"I'm not in love with Daniel."

"You damn well are. It's time you admitted it. Why else do you avoid any relationship with a guy? Daniel doesn't deserve all this devotion."

"I am *not* in love with Daniel. I just don't see the point of having to have a man. Or being in love. It only leads to disaster."

"Well, look at me. I am *so* happy with S.D. Can't you tell?"

I haven't a thing to say to her. I certainly can't tell. If my relationship with Hank in any way comes to resemble her relationship with S.D., I'll be suicidal.

"I don't like your silence. S.D. and I are very happy. You can't tell from the outside what a relationship is like. S.D., it just so happens, fulfills me. Anyway, I'm calling Hank right now. I'll have him call you," she says.

"Thanks. You're a real friend," I say. "Really. I'm sorry I wasn't being supportive of you and S.D."

"You never are. I know I complain about him. Well, who doesn't complain about her husband? Do you know anyone?" No, I do not. She's right. That's why I don't want one. Although it's not just what Peggy says about S.D. that makes me think she and S.D. are miserable. I see it myself. Her disappointed eyes when he merely shrugs to answer a question. Her irritation when he leaves the room in the middle of dinner and doesn't come back. The cold, uninterested way he speaks to her. And after all, I remember how happy she was with Sam. How he lit her from within. That was love, even if it did end badly. I think of her with Sam. I think of my mother with Ed Butz.

"Anyway," she says, "let me know what happens when Hank calls."

I hang up, and try to imagine Hank Marsh's property of rolling hills stitched with stone walls. I think about that wonderful sleeping porch. I see two sets of arched many-paned windows peeking through a shingled facade. Eyebrow windows. A three-story turret. I'm itching to draw it all up, to stand in the living room, smell the fresh wood floor, run my hands over a newly milled windowsill, look out over a dark pond shimmering with late light. Wouldn't that take the sting right out of the ugliness at Paris, Washburn, and Green?

Dear Jack,

Have you wondered why I asked you to send your E-mail to my home address? That's because, as of yesterday, it's the only E-mail address I have. You see, my timing in contacting you really is eerie, because yesterday, Jack, I lost my job at Paris, Washburn, and Green. I've been there eighteen years. I've designed hundreds of houses and public buildings. I've felt (obviously) inappropriately secure there. And now I'm cast free. They've given severance (five and a half months') but now I must rethink everything. They say it's economic. That over the years I've gotten expensive. I don't know. Maybe it's me. Maybe I didn't try hard enough. I think I got stale. And tired of building assisted-living facilities. Maybe I deserved to lose my job . . . that's the hardest part, really, to think maybe I brought this on myself. Isn't that what being a grown-up is about? About taking responsibility for your own mistakes? It stinks, though. I have a lot more fun having delicious fantasies about torturing Rodney Paris. Tying him up and tickling his nose and feet with feathers. Locking him in a room, feeding him only bread and water, and making him design a thousand Colonial-style shopping malls.

I wish I had the courage to go out on my own, as you have. You say I seem strong and sound. I don't feel so sound now. I feel shaky. As if I'm

standing on the San Andreas fault, one leg on
each side. Now let's see, what kind of earthquake-
proof life can I construct for myself?
　　Love to you,
　　Jane

When I hit Send, I feel amazingly good for a woman who's just lost her job of eighteen years. To be in touch with Jack Crashin again, in any way at all, hardly seems real.

I know I should go to the office and gather my things, get out of there for good, but I can't seem to make myself dress in anything but jeans and a T-shirt, and I can't imagine riding into the city like that, walking into Paris, Washburn, and Green like that. Maybe tomorrow, I think, I'll be ready to close this very long chapter of my life.

I decide to make shrimp shish kebab for dinner, which I will grill on the barbecue. I haven't made it in years, it seems. But today, I have all day to fix it. I go to the fish store to buy the shrimp. And to the vegetable store to buy limes and ginger and garlic and corn on the cob. Once home, I throw myself into the recipe, mincing the fresh ginger, the garlic for the marinade. Squeezing the limes and enjoying the smell. Shelling the shrimp, and loving the crisp fragility of the split shell as I pull it off. I realize as I do this that I'm really enjoying myself. It's been a long time since I've had time to make a nice meal. To revel in the process of cooking. While I barbecue, I walk around my late-summer garden. The bee balm has dropped its daffy red petals. The black-eyed Susans' leaves are far too lacy, chewed by the giant slugs I should have captured long ago in tuna cans filled with beer. I used to do that, put out tuna cans every night, catching thirty or forty a night until there were no slugs left to abuse my flowers. But this year, I haven't seemed to have the time. I forgot to deadhead the roses in the spring too, and so they're not blooming now as they sometimes do come late August, early September. I haven't cut back the ivy or the holly in months, and the garden's beginning to look derelict. Somehow, the garden seems like a picture of my life these last few years. I've been too busy to care for it. And it's not as nice as it could be. It's bursting with missed potential.

And all the while I cook, and all the while I walk in the garden, I think about Jack. What would it be like to see him again? How could I bear to have him see me the way I am now? I wonder if he'd even recognize me. No. I don't want to see him. I'm happy to have a correspondence with him. It's perfect. It's intimate. It's revealing. I can open up a part of myself I haven't shared with anyone in a long time. And yet he can remember me as I used to be. Slender and long-haired. Carefree in my body. This is the perfect relationship for me, I think. Perfect.

At dinner, Abigail remarks that I am quiet.

"You okay, Mom?" she asks. They both seem to really appreciate the shrimp, the first time they've shown interest in my cooking in a long time.

"You know," I say, "I'm just really enjoying dinner tonight."

"And that's why you're quiet?" she asks. I look at her and see an adult beauty in her that stuns me.

"It was fun playing Martha Stewart all day. I really didn't mind not going to work. Of course, I'm going to start looking for a new job next week."

"I hope you find one," Cait says. "One that you really like. I don't think you ever really liked Paris, Washburn, and Green."

"Really?" I'm surprised to hear her say it.

"Yeah. You always looked tired and unhappy at the end of the day."

"Maybe I did."

I'm sure they can't remember the days when I loved my job. When I was designing houses that thrilled me. When I watched them rise on their sites like mirages: my drawings come to life.

"Did you tell Daddy yet you lost your job?"

"No, I'll tell him tonight."

"Oh, by the way, on to a *lighter* subject—lighter as in totally hysterical—Abigail's in love with Benjy Skrebneski," Cait says.

"Oh, please. I am not."

"She wrote 'Abigail Skrebneski' on her notebook."

"Shut up."

"Benjy Skrebneski is about as dumb as a rock. But Abigail doesn't seem to care, because he's a hottie—"

"I told you to shut up." Abigail colors gradually, from her neck to the top of her head. Just like a cartoon.

I smile at her. I remember writing "Jane Crashin" on my notebook many times when I was seeing Jack. "Jack and Jane Crashin." It was the perfect set of names to put on stationery. I remember blushing when anyone even mentioned his name. I remember feeling suffused with an unnameable, unstoppable hunger the minute he entered the room.

Dear Jane,

I can't imagine how you must feel, losing your job, but I doubt it's because you've gotten stale. You are far too able a woman to have let things get that bad. I'd put money on it that it's politics, or economics. Or fate. Maybe you were meant to pursue your dream early. I would love to see some of the houses you build.

I find myself rushing to work to read your E-mails. And thinking about you often. There is so much to tell you, and so much I hesitate to

```
tell you. You know, it's funny. I haven't trusted
anyone in a long time. But I have this feeling
that I can trust you. It feels so extraordinar-
ily good. I feel like I've been waiting a long
time to find you again. You still haven't told
me. Have you remarried?
```

The next day, I go into Paris, Washburn, and Green to finish packing and see the people in Human Resources, and then get the hell
out of there. As I walk up to the front of the building, I reflect that
I can rush right off to the planetarium if I want. I can play hooky
every day from now on—or at least for the next five months—and
no one will care.

Of course, by now, everybody knows that I've been let go. If I
weren't so stubbornly proud, I'd have been wise to come in after
hours to pack. Or meet with HR somewhere outside the office. I've
been there long enough, God knows. They might do that for me.
That way, I wouldn't have to meet the pitying or denying eyes of
everyone I see.

It's interesting how a situation like this tells you so much about
people. Some people greet me as though nothing's happened at all,
though surely they know by now. Others are all treacle and pity,
"*God,* I am *so* sorry." Still others won't meet my eyes at all. I can't
decide which of the three categories make things the easiest. Dave,
whom I most want to see, doesn't seem to be around. Nancy Kangol sits down in my extra chair while I punch out a fresh box and
begin to pack.

"I don't get it," she says. "I don't get why they'd choose you," she
says.

I shrug.

"I actually thought for a brief, stupid second you really *were* fired for playing hooky. Dave told me I was crazy. I went in and told Rodney I thought he was making a major mistake."

"You did?" I look at her. Her white, white skin, her dyed black hair cut in a bob like a child in a 1920s photograph, chopped short in back, sleek and longer in front. Her dark lips, the color of black hollyhocks. "Thank you."

"He sputtered off some bullshit about how he needed to 'trim things up a bit around here.' Or something that wasn't even English. I told him he was choosing the wrong person to cut. Michael Keller. Now there's a person who adds nothing. Of course, I didn't say anything to Rodney about that."

"That was brave of you to go in there. Thank you."

"Brave. No. Look, Jane. This isn't the only place in town to work. There are plenty of firms. You've got a great portfolio to show. I know you do."

"I was at only one place before this one, and I don't have a clue how to begin." This is hard for me to say to her. To admit my weakness. As with my children, I've always felt the need to sound so certain. Still, it's comforting to weaken a bit.

"You must know people at other firms you could call. I have a friend at Kohn Pederson Fox. Another at Stockman's. I can make calls for you." I had no clue that Nancy would turn out to be my ally. I hear in her voice the desire to truly help me. Nancy refreshingly fits none of the categories of response. She's not denying that I've been fired. She's not sickeningly sorry. She's certainly meeting my eyes, and more.

She reminds me eerily of myself, trying to draw my mother out of her depression.

"I'd welcome those calls," I say. "And I'd go on the interviews to see. I'm just not sure I want to go to a big firm right now." I am surprised to hear my own words.

"Well, sure. I can imagine you'd like a break."

"It's more than that," I say. "I think I need to figure out what I really want to do."

She nods. "You mean, you might not want to do architecture?"

"No. No. I definitely do. It's just *how* do I want to do architecture? I think it's lost its pleasure for me somewhere along the line. I think I need to reinvent it for myself. Do you enjoy it here?"

She smiles wryly and glances off sideways, thinking. "Oh yes. Every day. So much. You've made a big difference for me here, you know? You've taken so much time to teach me things."

"I have?"

"Are you kidding? You've been a mentor to me when no one else bothered."

"Thank you." I am warmed. I certainly hadn't expected this. "I want to learn to enjoy architecture again, the way I used to. The way you still do," I tell her. She can't understand. She's under thirty. She has dreams. Precious dreams I want again.

Dave, returning from some meeting, comes right up to me and hugs me.

"Jesus," he says. "I fucking *hate* this place."

"Nancy loves it."

"You don't," he says to her.

"Yeah, I do," she says. "But I hate Rodney for letting Jane go."

"Well, it's their loss," Dave says. "In a way, I'm jealous. Did they give you severance?"

"More than I expected. But probably not enough . . ."

"You could take time off, travel, anything."

"Or spend it looking for the right job," Nancy says.

"You'll find it," Dave says.

Nancy gets up, looking fretful. "I have a thousand things to do. I'd better do them. Come say good-bye when you leave."

"Sure."

Dave sits down in her chair. I notice his receding hairline, the soft, dark rings under his eyes. I've known him for a long time. Through two marriages. I've seen him age: I've noticed recently how he gets up stiffly after a day in his ergonomically correct chair, just like me.

"This is your chance, Jane," he says. "To shake the cobwebs out, to start over, you know?"

"Yeah. But you and I. We've been here so long."

"All the more reason. You could even move. Live anywhere."

"Nah. The girls need to be near Daniel."

"Right. But they'll be in college soon, though, won't they? This could be a big adventure."

A big adventure. I like that. I smile at him. I lean over and kiss his cheek. He even blushes. Jane's Big Adventure. He's given me a banner to wave.

Suddenly I feel a hush blanket the room and I look up. Rodney is walking through. He has his chest puffed out. He's wearing a too-tight electric-blue European shirt, which merely serves to point out his slight middle-aged belly. He's wearing a bracelet, I notice, fashioned from a bent silver nail. He's got some client trailing behind him. Gesturing in an affected manner Rodney says, "This is where the ideas are. This is the brain of the great beast."

"The great beast." Jesus. It suddenly seems an extraordinarily happy fact that I won't have to see him—maybe ever again.

When he's gone, Dave says, "God, I hope at the most inconvenient moment, he runs out of Viagra."

I go off to Penny Magnuson in Human Resources. She sits in her fitted green suit behind her too large desk and drums a pencil as she talks to me. A thousand times I've come to her for vacation slips, or to discuss my 401(k), and never before has her face been so tight, her back so straight. She reads me my future benefits like a cop reading the Miranda rights. She's not happy about this. Beneath the shield is a flood of emotions. I wonder if I should poke at it.

"How long have you known?" I ask her.

"Don't ask me, Jane."

"I'm asking," I say.

"Money's been very tight. You have no idea. We used to be much more profitable. Overhead is killing us." She sees in my face, perhaps, that I have no interest in what she's saying and she stops. "I'm sorry," she says. "I really am."

"Five months isn't much for all my years here," I tell her.

"There's a formula," she says. "One week per year. It's actually two weeks more than five months."

"And there's no bonus for putting up with Rodney for twenty years?"

"Jane." She shakes her head. Her lips are white.

"I could sue," I say. "Should I tell them about the time Rodney wanted to take me home to bed?"

"Look, I'm telling you this as an old friend. I really am. I wouldn't sue if I were you. You have the right to do so. But there's no state that sides with the employer more than New York. Your chance of winning would be extraordinarily low. You'd be spending your money . . . and right now . . . It wouldn't help you find another job, either."

"I deserve more money, Penny," I say.

"There isn't more money," she tells me. "It's just not there."

I watch her fingers grip the pencil. Tonight, she will go home and say she had a rough day. A miserable day. I shake my head at her. I stand. I want to go home.

I go back to my desk, and as I gather my things, my phone rings.

"Jane Larsen," I say wearily.

"Hi," a deep, quiet voice says. "It's Hank Marsh. I've been trying to reach you, but all I get is your voice mail."

"Oh! Why didn't you leave a message?"

He pauses. "I didn't want to be a pest."

I laugh. Who would interpret leaving me a message as being a pest? His voice is remarkably cheering to me.

"I'm so happy to hear from you," I say.

"Look, Jane. I really enjoyed talking to you about my grandparents' house. I'd love to show you pictures. I wondered if you'd have dinner with me tomorrow night."

"Tomorrow . . ."

"I probably should be giving you more notice."

"Oh, well, I can make tomorrow fine."

"Good. You want me to pick you up at your office?"

There's no need to tell him I've lost my job, I think, when here I am trying to impress him with what a fine architect I am.

"No. I'll be on-site," I say. "Tell me where you want to meet."

"Guastavino's. Under the Fifty-ninth Street Bridge?"

"I love that place. It's so . . . architectural." Once Daniel and the girls took me to Guastavino's for my birthday. Guastavino was the name of the engineer who designed the vaulting system, which makes the bridge unique. The restaurant has incorporated the exquisite soaring vaults into its design.

"That's why I picked it," he says. "It's the ceilings. Inspiring. Yet the place is soothing. After a long day, I'm ready to be soothed. Six-thirty too early?"

"It's perfect."

"Well, if you want to meet there, I'll meet you outside, at the entrance. No rain predicted. Don't forget to bring your portfolio."

"Don't worry," I tell him. "I very much want to show it to you."

So, I wonder, is it a date? Or is it meeting to interview me as an architect? What does Hank Marsh have in mind? I know Peg cares, but I sure don't. Going out with him would be nice. Building him a house, that would be a thrill.

> Dear Jack,
> I've packed up everything from Paris, Washburn, and Green today and brought it home. So much memorabilia, so much I simply threw out. I have joined the jobless. Amazingly, I'm almost looking forward to a little time to myself. I realize it's been so many years since I've had time in my life. Even when I took vacations, they were so scheduled. With two kids, there always *had* to be something amusing on the agenda for them to do. Now I have nothing to do whatsoever. How odd it feels.
> You know, I was really concerned when I read your letter before last. The way you said that I will soon see that you have not "fared so well." I thought you would tell me in your next letter, but since you didn't, I'll ask. Tell me what you meant by that. And how is it that Suzanne hasn't been around for eight years? Does that mean you've raised Laine alone since she was one year old? Or have you married again?
> To answer your question, I haven't married again. I don't think I ever want to marry again, really. I loved Dan like crazy for a long time, and he didn't honor that love. He broke my heart. I have gotten very good at being alone. It's not that I've learned to tolerate it. I actually enjoy it. And now, I'll have even more time to myself. I wonder, though, without a job, and the companionship of work, if I'll be lonely.
> Do you remember the trip we took to Iowa City, Jack? I can't think of a trip I ever enjoyed more. Not even to Paris when I was twenty, or to

Tuscany with my husband on our honeymoon. No trip, in fact, has ever seemed more romantic to me, more impactful than that single weekend we spent in Iowa. It was because of you, and because of how you handed architecture to me like a gift that weekend. I was so madly in love with you, every single thing you did seemed extraordinary and memorable. The way you folded Doublemint gum and chewed half at a time, the way you combed your beard, the funny way you ate ice cream so it wouldn't end up in your mustache. It all seemed so sophisticated to me, so manly. Ancient and wise. And there you were, all of twenty-two. You had so many dreams back then, Jack. Everything seemed possible.

But most of all what thrills me when I look back—and I can almost recapture the wonder of it—was how you made me look at houses and buildings in a whole new way. Iowa seemed magical that weekend. Around every corner was another wonder. The familiar took on promise. I have never looked at houses in the same way since. And I will never forget that it was you who gave that to me.

We had so many dreams then. Both of us. Tell me, Jack. Did you fulfill them? Do you have any new ones now? Write soon.

Love,
Jane

Dearest Jane,
I never knew you felt so much for me back then. I suppose I should have known. I always liked you so much. I mean really LIKED you. We had such a great time together. But I don't know if I was capable of love then. I was so into my own nonsense.

That weekend in Iowa, though, is photographically clear to me. I remember lying in bed after we made love in some nasty little motel, and holding you in my arms and thinking how lucky I was. I was 100 percent full of joy that night. You don't forget a feeling like that. It's been so long since I've felt anything close to that, I can barely imagine I'll ever feel it again. I remember having a twinge right before I went off to Yale. Wondering if there was any way to keep things going between us. But you seemed young to me. And I had so many plans . . .

Life changes you. It sounds like your relationship with Dan has changed you. And now, I have to tell you the hard part. I hope you won't judge me by this. Perhaps I am the one who judges myself most harshly.

Suzanne was a difficult person from the start. Odd, I guess you'd say. Remote. Beautiful. Not very swayed by my meager charms. I probably loved her for just these things. She was the hunt that never ended, the prey I could never capture. Even when we were married, even after the boys were born, I'd look over at her at the dinner table and see that she was very far away. She's always been into strange things: religious fads and such. In New Haven, she thought she was a Buddhist. She threw herself into it wildly. She practically lived at the Buddhist temple. She meditated constantly. Later, here in Nashville, she announced she was "born-again." I considered all that her quirkiness. I accepted it. And at one point, she got into drugs. I'm not sure of everything she tried. I know there was cocaine. I think she might even have shot heroin. I suppose you think that if a spouse of yours did all this, you would have taken action. You said that being a grown-up is about taking responsibility for your own mistakes. See, that's the hardest thing for me. I did nothing. I told her I didn't like it. But she was so willful. I can tell myself that I didn't know how to stop her. Very likely it wouldn't have been easy. But I have to live with the guilt that I did nothing. She got more and more remote. I think she might even have had other lovers. I don't know if she thought of leaving me. Our lives certainly diverged.

She said I lacked spirituality altogether. She said I was cold and unfeeling. Yet it was always me trying to draw her out. She never much liked my attempts at being affectionate. Sex was something she barely tolerated—at least with me. She sometimes smoked dope just to be able to stand going to bed with me.

But I thought marriage was forever, and we had children, and so, we went on. And then Laine came along. Laine was born with so many anomalies I couldn't list them all. And how can I not wonder if the drugs had anything to do with it? The valves in her heart leaked. She has webs between her toes. She has facial anomalies—her bone structure is unique to her. Most of all, she's moderately retarded. Even from the beginning, it was very clear. I never once said to Suzanne that I blamed her for what happened. But she blamed herself. And I blamed myself for not stepping in, for not trying to stop her behavior. Laine cried all the time for a while. She had seizures. The structure of her mouth was malformed and had to be rebuilt so she could nurse. And then, at one point, things got worse. She just lay there with no movement at all. So tiny and white and miserable-looking. They weren't even sure she would live. There were operations. There were

nights waiting up wondering if it was better if
she died . . .

That was the worst time in my life, Jane. I
felt so helpless. I'd helped to bring this baby
into the world only to suffer, it seemed. That
was when I learned to cry. I had never cried before, never let myself feel things. Suzanne
didn't cry. Something like this could have
brought us together. Should have. But instead,
she pulled away entirely. She could hardly bear
to go to the hospital. It was almost as though
she felt Laine had betrayed her.

It was like living with a ghost. I guess it
wouldn't have been surprising if she'd turned
back to drugs. Instead, in a way, something worse
happened. She got involved with the Church of
Some Souls. Basically, it was a cult. I find it
hard to even write about this. So much to test
us, and she just dissolved under it all. She
started doing all these weird rituals that they
taught her. She had a ritual knife she'd hold
over her heart and chant things. I once saw her
holding the knife over Laine and I really flipped
out. She wore garlic and cinnamon in bags around
her neck. She would only make love with her knees
facing upward. It was God's way, she told me. And
she started spending more and more time out. I
found I was always taking care of Laine, always
putting the boys to bed by myself. I'd sit in the
living room afterward and wonder why this was
happening. And it got to the point where she de-
monized me. I was her problem. I was the one
missing the point . . . Her friends from the
church would come over, and I heard their mali-
cious whispers about me. The phone calls where I
heard her say, "I can't talk about this. *He's*
here now." Well, they were chilling.

Finally, she left. She couldn't handle it, she said. For weeks, she'd said she could no longer parent with a person like me. Like me? Was I so terrible suddenly? I sat up night after night wondering what I had done. What I could have done differently. She said she didn't want custody. Not of Laine. Not of the boys. She said since I was the real problem, I should take the burden. She walked away. She went to some other location where the Church of Some Souls harbored her. I thought about getting one of those deprogrammers to go after her. But you know, I'm ashamed to say now, I wasn't sure I wanted her back. It would have just been a struggle to keep her, and for what? She really wasn't a fit mother. The boys had actually become afraid of her, because they didn't understand her moods, her rituals. And I began to realize that even if we brought her back in body, it seemed unlikely we would ever see her again in spirit.

It was hardest on Ned. He was just six years old. Unnerved as he was by Suzanne, he couldn't understand how she could have left him. Clark was nine. It was terrible for him too. Sometimes at night he would say, "Daddy, why did Mommy carry that knife and say those things? Daddy, why did Mommy tell me I had the spirit of an ox? Is that why she left?"

I almost lost my firm then. I found it hard to work. I barely managed to get things done at the office and then rush home to an ill baby and two sad boys. Clark started acting out. He got in trouble in school. He wouldn't do his homework. He had fistfights with everybody. Ned started doing all these ritualistic things like turning around three times before he got into bed. Or crossing his fingers twice before he'd touch a

doorknob. We employed a daytime baby-sitter before all this began, and thank God she stayed
with us. "They're just missing their mother," she
used to say. "It will all pass in time." She was
right. But it was hard to believe her then.

You know, you asked me about my dreams, Jane.
The truth is, I can't remember having any dreams.
Not for a long, long time. For these last eight
years, I've been too busy surviving to have any
dreams. Day to day has been all I could focus
on.

But I want to change that. The boys are doing
much better. And even Laine does pretty well now.
They've resolved the majority of her heart problem. She's learned to walk, and even talk quite
well, really. They totally reconstructed her
mouth. And recently, they've told she's far
less retarded than originally thought. She goes
to a special school where they're trying to teach
her to read. She's so sweet, so patient. She says
she is glad to be her. She actually told me that
the other day. "I'm glad I'm me, Daddy."

I asked her why. She said, "Because I live with
Clark and Ned and you and I have a goldfish named
Spitzy and we have a red car." I had to turn away
because I got tears in my eyes, and I didn't want
her to see. To think she feels lucky despite all
she's gone through. How can any of us rue our
luck after that?

Your letters are the first window I've had in
a long time, Jane. I don't want to overstate this
or scare you away. But I am so grateful you wrote
me. I hope telling you all this doesn't put you
off. I hope I'll hear from you again soon.

Love,
Jack

Jack's letter knocks the air right out of my lungs, and if there is a writer's equivalent of speechlessness, now I know it. While I have fared quite well—my beautiful daughters, my wonderful home, every one healthy, in one piece—Jack's faced the unthinkable. How much we take for granted. I want to write him back right away. To show that I'm not put off. But what can I say to him that isn't pure drivel?

    Dear Jack,

    Your letter brought me to tears. I wonder if
    there is any way to tell you how it made me feel.
    Perhaps there is nothing I can say to let you
    know how sad I am for what you've been through.
    Perhaps there's nothing anyone can say . . .

No. No. That's all wrong. Patronizing. Anyone could write it, and it certainly means nothing.

    Dear Jack,

    You must feel very angry inside for all you've
    had to go through. You must wonder, "Why me?" I
    can't even imagine how miserable you've surely
    been. To be forced to raise Laine all by your-
    self. The challenge seems unfathomably diffi-
    cult . . .

No. Too depressing. He'll feel suicidal after reading that. I'm not his psychiatrist. I'm his old lover. His friend. I put down the laptop. Get up and pace the study. It is night. Dark. Too quiet. The girls are asleep. I am alone with this. What can I tell him that comes just from me? I feel daunted. Intimidated by the task, I do something I never do. I go downstairs and pour myself a glass of wine. It was a bottle that was opened when I had Peggy and S.D. to dinner a few weeks ago. The wine is a soft ruby, splashing in the crystal glass. How oddly guilty I feel drinking it alone.

"To Jack," I say aloud before I begin to drink. It's a bitter wine. Dryer than dry. I wince as I drink it, but I drink it nonetheless. I think of Jack holding his poor malformed baby, bewildered by his wife's absence. When I finally climb the stairs to my study and sit down at my laptop again, twenty minutes have passed. I write:

> Dearest Jack,
> You've always had my heart. All these years. I've thought of you as the center of some sort of serenity. Some sort of joy we felt together long ago. When I conjured you up, during the worst moments of my life, I was always able to smile. You brought joy into the darkness for me. And to think, all these years, you've been so un-happy. The irony wounds me. I wish, somehow, I could have helped make your life lighter, just as you did mine.
> I think you must be a wonderful father, to have learned to so thoroughly love Laine for who she is. To have raised two boys with no mother to help. You know I had no father for the first five years of my life, and that was hard. But it was much, much harder to have lost one, having had him for a while. I can't imagine how hard it's been on your kids to lose their mother so young, so suddenly. You must be a saint to have been there so thoroughly for them, while reeling with your own losses. For they now sound very grounded, very healthy.
> All this, of course, makes me feel like a brat for whining about losing my job. How small that seems in the face of what you've experienced. As-

tonishing how things can be snapped right into perspective sometimes.

I guess what I want to ask you is, how can I make things better for you now? I have no idea even what this question means, other than that I wish I could make you happy, and any single thing you can think of to cheer you would be a gift to me.

But, I'll share some good news on my horizon. I have an appointment to meet someone tomorrow who might be interested in having me build him a house. I don't know what will happen, but just the possibility lifts my spirits incredibly.

Look, Jack, I am so happy my letters can be a "window" for you. My memory of you has always been a window for me. And these days, to be in touch again—how extraordinary it feels! I look forward to your E-mail more than you can imagine too. And just so you know, no matter what you tell me, you couldn't possibly scare me away.

Love from the depths of my heart,
Jane

If you ask me right at this moment, having just hit the Send button, my memory of his voice in my ears, imagining his face, his hands responding to the words I write, I would tell you that I'm in love with him. Nearly thirty years have passed, yet the thought of Jack Crashin still thrills me. That his story is so tragic only makes him seem more alive.

Five

$\mathcal{I}$ try on six different outfits for my dinner with Hank Marsh. Most things look acceptable from the front. Nothing looks good from the side. A select few look good from the back. I settle finally on the same black dress that I usually fall back on. It has a lovely low-cut front that amply shows up my two still-good features. (In the correct bra, they point upward just the way they're supposed to. And with them pointing skyward, my waist looks smaller.) Just as I'm about to leave, I get a call from Daniel.

"Hey, Jujube. I can't believe you didn't tell me."

"Didn't tell you what?"

"What happened at Paris, Washburn, and Green. I had to hear it from Cait."

"Oh, I meant to call you last night."

"How are you doing?"

"I'm fine. Really. I got all my stuff out of there yesterday. I just have to decide what's next."

"You know, worse comes to worse, life collapses or whatever, I'll support you, Juje, I will." Of course, this pleases Daniel no end, that for a change, with money, he thinks he can support me. God bless him.

"Thanks for saying so," I tell him. "I hope I never have to take you up on it. Listen. I'm awfully sorry, but I gotta run."

"Because?"

"Because I'm meeting someone."

"A date?" Daniel never seems jealous, exactly. But he does seem awfully curious about my love life—what little of it there is.

"Well, maybe. This guy asked me out for dinner. Guastavino's."

"Whoo. Guastavino's. He must be hot for you."

"I'm showing him my portfolio. He's got land. He wants to build a house."

"Wait a minute. Is this a date or business? I don't get it."

"Neither do I. But I've got to run, if I don't want to be late."

"So either he'll kiss you, or he'll hire you."

"Preferably both," I tell him.

He laughs uncomfortably. "Knock him dead," he says, It's funny, but sometimes, I still wish Daniel would show some jealousy.

Hank isn't there when I arrive, so I stand in the plaza outside the restaurant and crane my neck to see as much of the Fifty-ninth Street Bridge as I can. I daydream about Jack reading my letter. Will it reach out to him? I have a few random sexual thoughts of us together so many years ago. Mostly involving his hands touching that tender, impossibly ticklish hollow between my breasts and my armpits with a soft, sweeping motion that doesn't tickle me—just thrills me. I find myself getting sexually excited, so I shift from one leg to the other, and observe the new tiles they've put on the bridge vaults above the Terence Conran Shop with about as much focus as I can muster.

I hate waiting for people. There are so many stages you have to go through. First there's the "Phew, well at least I'm on time" stage. Then the "Jesus, where the hell is he?" stage. The "Am I in the right place? Maybe I'm not. Maybe he meant ANOTHER Guastavino's!" stage. And then—and this is the stage I hate the most—"Oh my God, he's been hit by a car/robbed/kidnapped/had a heart attack" stage. I fortunately have never reached the "That fucker stood me up" stage. Tonight, Hank arrives about midway through the "Am I in the right place? Maybe I'm not. Maybe he meant ANOTHER Guastavino's" stage.

He is all blush and stammer and pant and apology. "I am so, *so* sorry," he says. His hair is windblown. He has nice hair. Boyish. "I couldn't cross town. My taxi sat and sat and sat right near the Waldorf-Astoria. I think the goddamn President's here again. I mean, it's very nice he cares about our fair city, but I wish he'd stay out of it altogether! Or stay in a hotel in New Jersey."

I laugh. I've often said the same thing.

"I agree. But what can you do?" I say breezily. "I'm sure they've held our table." Hank escorts me in, lightly touching my arm. It must have been a while since a man touched my elbow, or maybe it's because I've been fantasizing about Jack. I feel a jolt of electricity like a short circuit at the Wiz. I shiver beneath his touch.

As I was standing waiting for him, in between worrying I'd wondered if Hank intended to take me to the less expensive Guastavino Restaurant or upstairs to the Club Guastavino, the quieter room with the more exclusive menu. I am surprised when we do indeed climb the stairs.

"I love it up here," he says. "I know it's an indulgence, but I want to be as close to the ceiling as possible." I look up at the cream-colored herringbone tiles and feel exultant. I don't care if we never speak again. Just coming here is wonderful.

The booth is a soft, comfortable gray. I sink down into it with pleasure. The arched French windows still gleam with the last reddish light of this nearly autumn day.

"I'm so glad you're not upset that I'm late," he says. "It was very gracious of you. I just can't stand it when people are late. My father was insane about promptness. It was beaten into me. God, I'll tell you, sometimes it was embarrassing. We'd always be the first to come to parties and have to drive round and round the block so as not to be arriving so early it was rude. Then when we finally rang the doorbell, the hostess would come out fastening her pearls, one shoe on and one shoe off."

I smile at him. "In New York, it's impossible not to be late sometimes."

"Yes. Everyone tells me that when I fret about being late. You look lovely tonight," he says. I wonder, Does he mean it, or is it part of his upbringing? Does this mean it's a date?

"Thank you," I say, thoroughly self-conscious. I tuck a lock of hair behind my ear. I look at my hands. I wonder what it would be like to be sitting here with Jack. I would look up at him. He would look back at me. A million sweet memories would fill our heads.

"I brought pictures of the house in Maine. Is it too early to bring them out?" Hank says.

"Oh no. I'd love to see them." I'm relieved he's getting right to the point. He pulls up a soft, doe-colored leather briefcase from the floor and sets it in his lap, then pulls out a manila folder. "Some of these pictures are very old," he says. "Probably around the era it was built."

From the folder, gorgeously subtle sepia photographs spill. And in them is depicted a house so gracious, so huge, so unique, it makes my heart palpitate.

"Wow," I say. I stare at the turrets with the intricate shingle patterns, the old and gracious striped awnings, the porte cochere with a carriage parked beneath. "Do you know what year? 1902, something like that?"

"Eighteen ninety-eight, I think my grandmother said. My great-great-grandfather built it so that the family could come up from Boston. It got too hot in the summer, even in Boston. They were very into fresh air, back then, getting away from the bad city vapors. Especially for the children. Granny's mother was the oldest."

"Were you born in Boston?" I ask.

"Oh no. Here in New York."

"I didn't think *anyone* was actually born in New York," I say.

"Yes. I'm a rarity. I've lived here all my life, except when I went to prep school, and to college."

"You don't have an accent."

"They didn't allow them at the schools where they sent me."

"Let me guess. Groton."

"Lawrenceville."

"And Harvard?"

"Princeton," he says. "You?"

I laugh. "Nothing so grand," I say. "New Trier High School. University of Illinois. It only cost three hundred dollars a semester. That made my divorced mother with four children very happy. I can see why you love this house. I'm in love already."

"There are some interior pictures in here as well," he says. He shuffles through the pile and pulls out photos of rooms furnished opulently but simply. Not as dark as one might expect for the era. Still, there are vases of peacock feathers. A shawl on the piano.

"Does it still look like this?" I ask.

"Yes. But much weeded out. Granny hates clutter. Yet I'd say most of the furniture is actually still there."

"You're so lucky," I tell him.

"No, Lonny's lucky. He gets to inherit the place. He's the eldest of us."

"Yes. The one who wet the bed."

"Great memory. If you ever meet him, you'll have to keep that in mind. He's a stuffy, self-important lawyer now who calls himself Lawrence Marsh the Third. It will amuse you no end to think of him crying, with soaking-wet pajama bottoms. It lightens *my* load."

"Why don't they just give the house to all the grandchildren?"

"Oh, it would be easier to divide Jerusalem. There are too many of us. And we all want it. Look. Here's the sleeping porch."

And there it is. An interior shot. The river-stone fireplace with charred logs in it. The neat little beds lined up against a wall of windows, all tightly wrapped with Beacon blankets.

"I'm in love," I tell him. "This is extraordinary. You should re-create this exactly. I've never known of a sleeping porch with a fireplace before. And look at the window hardware. And the wainscoting! You are the luckiest man on earth to have grown up with this. The luckiest!" I look up. He's beaming at me. If he doesn't give me this commission, I will definitely die.

"Show me your portfolio," he says gently.

"Well, this is an awfully hard act to follow," I tell him.

"Be brave," he says. I pick the portfolio up from the floor and unzip it. Of course, I am instantly critical of which picture I've put first, a more modern house, by a stream in Westchester, I built for a retired schoolteacher. I have things more or less in the shingle style. Why didn't I put them first? I'm an idiot.

"Show me," he says.

"Well, I don't think you'd say I have a style. I create each house to suit the owner's needs, dreams, really." As I take him through the portfolio, explaining why I did what, I try to read his face. He is smiling mildly, but is his smile derisive? Or is he truly interested, impressed? When I come to the three houses that most resemble the Maine house, his eyes light up.

"These are wonderful," he says. "Perfect. I love the way you put these columns here. These windows remind me so much of the 'cottage.' Yes. Look at this. You put a sleeping porch on the back."

"No fireplace on the porch, unfortunately. *That* really is a brilliant touch."

"Are you interested in designing my house?" he asks me.

"Are you joking? Absolutely. Passionately."

"Would you like to drive up this weekend and see the property?"

I have the girls this weekend. Damn. "Well, I guess I could drive up with you for the day."

"Oh, I'm sorry. You thought I was being too forward." He sits back in his chair.

"No. I didn't. I just have my girls this weekend."

"I didn't know you had children." It's funny that we never spoke of it. It's usually what people our age talk about. Our children. Perhaps he doesn't have any?

"Are they young?" he asks.

"It depends on who you are. If you're a lecherous old man, they're young. They're fifteen."

"Both?"

"Twins."

"Really? How impressive. You don't, by any chance, have a picture?"

I'm pleased he wants to see the girls. I take out my wallet and show him a recent photograph of them standing in the sunlight. Their hair looks as if it's caught fire. They have their arms around each other. You might believe they are the most compatible two girls in the world.

"Gorgeous," he says. "I mean, really gorgeous."

"Thank you. Do you have children?" I realize I know nothing about him. We got to talking about his house at the party and that precluded all else. I don't even know if he's ever been married. Nothing.

"Well, it pains me to sound so old, but my children are grown," he says. "Twenty-five and twenty-eight. Two boys. I never have had the pleasure of girls."

"What do they do?"

"One's a recording engineer. One's a perpetual student. Getting his doctorate in—brace yourself—philosophy."

"What *does* one do with philosophy, anyway?"

"I haven't a clue." Together we laugh. We look at each other shyly.

"Any pictures?"

"No. They're off the payroll. When the grandkids come, then maybe I'll carry pictures."

"Scary to think about grandchildren," I say. "It just seems like yesterday my girls were tiny. Just babies."

"For me too. In the old days, two hundred years ago, we'd be dead by now. Or in our dotage. Wearing shawls and rocking in rocking chairs and considered well over the hill," he says. "Toothless too." He says this with his lips wrapped around his teeth to simulate our loss. I have to laugh at him. He's charming. Maybe too charming. How can you trust someone so automatically likable?

"Listen, Jane. My land in Dutchess County is beautiful," he says. "The first time I saw it, I was won over. I had no intention of buying land. It was part of an ancient farm a friend of mine bought along with a million-dollar house. He intended to sell off fifty, sixty acres, and I was just along for the ride. The second I saw it, I had to have it. It's full of history. The stone walls are hundreds of years old. The farm's first deeds are from the 1600s. That early farm was called Springside because there's a stream and a pond fed by an ever-flowing spring. There's the foundation for an old barn built into the hill, so that there's an entrance above for grain, below for the cattle. If you walk through the woods, you see foundations for other buildings. Chicken coops? Sleeping quarters for farmhands?

Other lives. And all of it is on what was once a main road. A road that was moved. So now, it's set far back from the actual road."

"I can't wait to see it. Are you actually . . . I mean, am I jumping the gun thinking you're ready to give me this commission?"

"Done. I want you to do it."

"This is almost too good to be true. You sure you don't want to take a field trip to some of my houses and see them in person? Or speak to some of my past clients?"

"Don't unsell yourself. I think these houses tell me you're the one I've been looking for."

"This is so fortuitous. I've just been thinking of going out on my own. Exclusively designing houses. You see, it's the only thing I've ever really cared about. The timing's remarkable."

"I talked to Peggy last night. She said you lost your job."

"She told you?" I'm mortified. I hadn't wanted him to know. And now I seem foolish for having withheld the mention of it.

"It's okay," he says. "I don't think you should feel embarrassed about it. Look at your portfolio. It tells me what I need to know. Peggy says you were there a very long time. That it was probably politics."

"Yes, and boredom. Houses are what I really care about. For years, they had me designing banks and nursing homes. If I never designed another, I'd be happy."

"The good news is, you can focus on what you care about . . . houses. And on me."

"On you," I say.

"Well, on my house."

Our eyes meet. It'll be easy to focus on Hank Marsh, I think. Well, for a while anyway. As an architect, of course. It's funny, I feel guilty for the attraction I feel toward Hank. It's Jack Crashin I want most to think about. Jack, eight hundred miles away, sad, changed.

When Hank politely takes me home in a black limo, all the way to Park Slope, I probably should ask him in. Or lean over and kiss his cheek before I get out. But I open the car door quickly and am on the street before anything at all can happen. I haven't a clue as to what he wants from me. But I doubt it's me.

"Thank you for a lovely dinner. And a remarkable opportunity," I say.

"I'll call you Friday, to set up the weekend," he says.

"I'll look forward to it." I shut the door on him. I try to smile through the glass. He smiles back. He's way too cute to be interested in me, I think. But thank God he likes my houses.

The next night, I call my sister, Bess, to tell her I've lost my job. Bess is eleven years younger than I am and lives in Indiana. She's a schoolteacher in Indianapolis, married to a child named Corky who masquerades as a thirty-five-year-old man. He doesn't want children. He doesn't want to work. He never went to college. He collects beat-up old motorcycles and bar mirrors. He must have a collection of fifty liquor- and beer-labeled mirrors in the basement of their 1950s ranch house. "This Pabst sign is the ultimate prize. I won it at poker," he told me. He spends a lot of time in that basement with his toy trains and his Foosball game. When I asked Bess why she married him three years ago, she said, "I thought it was time to get married. He asked me. I just know at some point he'll agree to have kids." Bess was only four when Ed moved out. She's never been very good at discerning which men are worth spending time with.

When she answers the phone, she sounds dazed.

"Did I wake you up?" I ask her.

"Oh no. I was watching *ER*. I don't know why I watch it. It just makes me cry. Someone always dies and someone always learns a lesson. But I'm glad they killed that Lucy character off. I never liked her. She ruined everything. I still miss Doug, though. He made the show worth watching."

"How's life?" I ask her, aware that *ER* is as much her life as anything.

"Oh, well." I can tell she has to think hard, remove herself from her *ER* frame of mind and put herself back into her life. "Welllll . . . I hate my class this year. I don't know why I chose sixth grade. They're not kids and they're not teenagers, and they all have raging hormones and haven't learned to wear deodorant. You walk into the classroom and it just stinks. And you know what a sensitive nose I have. The girls like the boys and the boys hate the girls but they just can't seem to leave them alone. There were two fistfights between the boys this week alone and a fresh epidemic of lice, which is *very* upsetting to sixth-grade girls with long hair."

"Sounds like a wonderful year," I tell her.

"Yeah, right," she says.

"Has Corky been working?" I ask.

"Oh please, Jane. Don't start. It's like after Mom died, you took over."

"Sorry."

"Right now, he's out meeting his friends to trade players in his fantasy baseball league. It's his new passion. He's obsessed. He spends ten dollars every time he makes a trade, and he makes trades constantly. And he had to pay seventy-five dollars just to join. And last week he drank too much at one of their little get-togethers and he ran off the road and gave himself a bloody nose and a four-hundred-dollar dent in the car. So with all this wonderful stuff going on, of course he has no *time* to look for a job."

When Bess married Corky, he was working at a bowling alley, handing out shoes. He didn't bring home much, but at least it was a steady job, until he lost it because he'd found a way of knocking candy free from the vending machine, and he was stealing two or three Good & Plentys a day. He might have gotten away with that, but, one day, he decided to sell his found candy on the side to the customers when they rented the shoes. That's when they fired him. Still, the first time I saw him, I understood why she married him. He was too handsome to live, with narrow hips and huge blue eyes and a square jaw right out of a comic strip. It was Bess's version of marrying a dumb blond, I guess. But now she's paying.

Reasons to marry: (1) For beauty. (2) For great sex. (3) For companionship. (4) To become one with your soul mate. Bess married for number one. I married for number two. Peggy married for number three. I wonder if anybody ever gets all the way home.

"Why do you stay with him?" I ask her.

"What am I supposed to do, Janie? I'm thirty-four years old. Isn't there some fact that you're as likely to marry after thirty as you are to get hit by a bus?"

I laugh at her. "I think it's better odds than that. Besides, you're beautiful, sweetie." And she is. She looks more like Ed than any of the other kids. Tall and striking. Dark, thick hair. "And smart. And besides, you're the one with the money. If he won't have kids soon, you should think it over. After all, do you really want to have Corky as your partner in parenthood?" I've never talked to her so bluntly before, but God knows, she's been complaining about Corky for a year now, and every time we talk she sounds more unhappy.

"I'll tell you one thing. I could never go back to being Bess Butz. You know how hard it is having a name like that?"

"Have you seen Dad?" I ask her. When I speak to her, I never call him Ed. It feels easy to call him Dad. It feels good.

"Yes. Last month. I drove up to Chicago. He has trouble getting around now. He's getting pretty old."

I wonder what Bess means when she says Ed is having trouble getting around now. For a long while, he's used a cane, never complains, concentrating with each step. He's lived alone all these years in an apartment hotel on the Near North side of Chicago. He's had trouble holding a job ever since Kraft. It was as though losing Mother and us kids just fractured him. Lately, I am sure the problem is depression. I don't know, but he's never been able to put the pieces back together. I suppose Mother would be pleased. Poetic justice. But it's always broken my heart.

"I never really know what to say to him," Bess says. "I kind of babble at him like I do at my class when the school year starts and they're all nervous and unsettled. I feel like I should be giving him money, Jane, but with Corky out of work . . ."

"Why do you think he needs money?" I ask.

"I don't know. I have a feeling he's strapped. His clothes aren't so nice. I mean, I know he has trouble getting around to shop and everything. Once I took him to Marshall Field's, but he didn't seem very comfortable with me. I know I should do more for him. Bring him things. I'm the only one of us living within five hundred miles of him now. But I feel like I hardly know him, you know? I think you know him much better than I do. You were so much older when he left . . ."

"I should come out and see you," I say. "We should go visit him together. It would be nicer that way."

"Yes. That would be great. Perfect. Will you?"

"This year. I promise." I wonder what I will see. I can't imagine Ed any more fragile, for that is what he has become: terribly fragile. I too wish I could send him money, wish I could give something to him, the way he so generously gave to me when I was a child.

"So, how 'bout you? How are you?" she asks, clearly wanting to change the subject. The subject of Ed always pains her. It makes me sad.

I take a deep breath. Here goes. "I lost my job," I tell her.

"Oh my God. Oh . . . my . . . God! How? Why? Oh, Jane."

I expected this. Others' hysteria makes me feel very calm.

"It's not so bad," I say.

"Dad never got a decent job after he lost his job at Kraft. I don't mean to upset you . . . but it *could* be bad."

"He was depressed, that's why he couldn't find another. It's not the end of the world for me."

"God, if you lost the house, I don't know what any of us would do. Come Christmas, we'd be wandering the streets." Since my mother died, my house in Brooklyn is the center of my Midwest family. All the kids fly in at Thanksgiving, at Christmas. I carry padded Swedish cots up from the basement. Sleeping bags for the littlest kids. Each of my girls gives up a double bed. We manage. I love it. My family, together again. It reminds me of those nights around the dinner table in the Tudor house. I'm just as happy when they all sit around my table now. The family's grown. Pete's married and has two kids. Charlie's divorced and has two kids. I'm thrilled to be the one with the turkey and stuffing, the presents under the tree. They've all become my children. Even Ed comes sometimes, when I send him a ticket. Without Mother around, there's no reason to not have him join us.

Last year, even Aunt Aggie and Barney came. Now there's a couple who knows what love means. They live in Charleston, South Carolina, and take a long walk together each day. They take classes at a local university. They still hold hands. They laugh at each other's jokes. And they always have some exciting story to tell about something they saw or did together. Aunt Aggie deserves all that and more. Last Christmas, I raised a toast to Aunt Aggie. "She is who I want to grow up to be," I told everyone, and there was a great roar of approval.

"Don't worry. I'll have a new job soon. Besides, I already have a commission to design a house," I tell Bess in my most soothing voice. "And Christmas will be just like always."

"Sometimes I think the only thing certain in my life is you, Janie."

"Well, don't worry. Things will be fine."

"Good," she says. "Good. Listen, Janie, are you dating? Are you seeing anyone? Don't you think you'd like to marry again?"

"I went out last night with the man who wants me to design his house, but I don't know if it was to interview me or a date."

"Really? You don't know?"

"Well, honestly, what I cared most about was getting the commission, which I did."

"Why? Isn't he cute?"

"Oh, he's that all right. But, who needs to fall in love? Right now, I need work more."

"Mother once told me that after a certain age, people just don't fall in love anymore. She said that's why she never dated."

"She never dated because she just couldn't go through it all again. She was chicken. I've always thought anyone could fall in love at any age. But I don't know. Marriage again. Not unless I'm madly in love." I'm sad, I suddenly realize. I realize that I've probably given up on love altogether.

"I wrote to Jack Crashin," I say. "I don't suppose you remember him?"

"No."

"He was my college boyfriend. You were six or seven. But you met him a few times."

"College . . . you mean the blond with the buckteeth or the guy who looked like a Comanche?"

"The Comanche." I laugh. It's a perfect description of what Jack used to look like after he shaved his beard. He even sometimes wore a band over his brow. Ah, what an era it was.

"Wow. What made you write him?"

"He made me fall in love with architecture. I've always been grateful. I've thought of him over the years. I wanted to know what happened to him . . . so I E-mailed him."

"Yeah? So?"

"So he wrote me back. We're writing each other now. His life is so sad, Bess. He has three kids, including a retarded daughter. His wife left him and joined a cult."

"Boy. I thought that only happened in the movies."

"Apparently not. It made me feel so lucky. To have Cait and Abby and even Dan. With or without a job, it made me feel lucky."

"I guess you never know what's going to happen in life," Bess says.

"I guess not."

"That's why I hang on to Corky," she says. "And don't argue with me. That's why I hang on. I know all about Corky and his downsides. But I know what I have. He's a sure thing."

I don't know what to say after that. You can't tell a grown woman what to do. Not a friend. Certainly not a sister.

"I love you," I tell her.

"Let me know when you get a job," she says. "I'll be rooting for you."

"I'll be rooting for you," I say

Dear Jack,

I wonder what it must be like to be you. Your responsibilities are overwhelming. Do you never have time for you? What do you do that makes you happy, for instance? What do you do that you're going to remember in ten years?

This is what matters to me: I've been thinking of this all evening, ever since I talked to my sister, Bess. Do you remember me talking about my baby sister, Bess? She really was a baby then. Poor Bess. She's married to the world's biggest drip, and she lives to watch TV.

So here it is: I don't want to be a spectator. I want to be the main character in my own life.

I don't want to get old and sensible and watch the world go by. Do you know what I mean? I want to DO something. You were always an activist, Jack.

Maybe this is just middle-aged blather. Maybe this is why fifty-year-old guys buy red sports cars and sleep with twenty-year-olds.

But it's why I don't want to take just any job. Or do the same thing I've been doing for eons. Don't you ever just want to break the pattern?

Guess what! I got the commission to build that house I told you about. It's going to be wonderful. He wants something shingle style, and I can't wait to start designing it. I'm going to see the land this weekend. Tell me about your architecture. How would you describe the work you do? You were always espousing neoclassical architecture way back there in the 1970s when everyone was into those brutal brick buildings with no windows. Remember when they built the new Foreign Languages Building? We both wanted to spit on it. But what do you design these days?

I was trying to imagine you now, Jack. Trying to tell from that small picture on your web site what you really look like. Do you know what I remember most about you? Your hands. Your beautiful hands.

Love,

Jane

Dear Jane,

I often wonder what you look like now too. I imagine the same you with shorter dark hair. I remember you had only one dimple. I thought this was extraordinary—that you were asymmetrical!

And you had the tiniest teeth. Perfect little teeth. I told you how I'd had years and years of braces because my teeth stuck straight out when I was a kid, and you said, "Oh, I never had any braces." I just couldn't believe it. Your teeth were straight out of an Ultrabrite commercial. I hated you for that! You never had to know a mouthful of metal. You never had the lovely experience of accidentally swallowing those rubber bands!

Do you know what else I remember about you? You sighed with pleasure when we made love. As though it was delicious. Being an insecure sort of guy, I always found that reassuring. I told my roommate, "She sighs when we make love," and he laughed at me. "She must be bored or something." "No, it's not that kind of sighing," I told him. He said, "There's only one kind of sighing, Jack. And if she's sighing, I'd brush up on my technique!" He was a jerk. You know, I can't even remember his name. But, can you remember, Jane, why you were sighing?

Love,
Jack

Dear Jack,

I am quite sure that, if in bed with you, I sighed, that it must have been with pleasure. Otherwise, why would you have stayed so alive to me all these years? Too bad you don't know that guy's name, your old roommate. I could write and tell him so!

Today, I met with a man at Kohn Pederson Fox about a job. I got the lead through a very young woman I worked with at Paris, Washburn, and Green. The man looked at me and said, "How many years have you been there? You look very experienced." Translated: You look very, very old. I don't expect to hear from him again. But I don't care. It's easy for me to be nonchalant about plans now that I have five and a half months of severance. How free will I feel when it's gone?

It's raining today, that beautiful deep-smelling rain of autumn. The leaves are already starting to turn on some of the trees. The perennials are just beginning to die back in the gardens on my block. I'm so much happier when the days get moody, and dark early, and chilly. In the autumn, I come alive. Give me a pumpkin, a turkey, ankle-high golden autumn leaves and I'm in heaven. I guess it's warmer there in Nashville. Maybe it doesn't feel like autumn at all.

Jack, you said you wonder what I look like, and I guess I need to tell you that I've changed so much. I don't know if you'd find me attractive anymore. I'm not thin. I'm not pretty. I'm just a middle-aged unemployed woman with teenagers. I'm not that girl with the long hair and thin wrists and Alice in Wonderland shoes. I still have tiny teeth. I still have one dimple. Everything else is altered.

Aunt Aggie calls at four the next afternoon.

"Darling," she says. "Bessie told me about your job."

"Oh, yes."

"I hope you're not fretting."

"No. Didn't she tell you I'm fine? I'm fine. I'm just trying to figure out what to do next."

"I'd love it if you moved down here," Aunt Aggie says. "Charleston has an endless need for architects like you. You know, architects with respect for history. And of course, with our hurricanes, things are always needing to be rebuilt. Barney told me to tell you."

Aggie has always been my mainstay. When Dan left me, she was the first one I called. Maybe it's because she really knows how to listen, to never push too hard. Maybe it's because every word she speaks lets me know she's on my side.

"Well, I'm not going anywhere for a while, anyway," I tell her. "You know, the girls need to be near Dan. At least until they go to college."

"Oh yes, the girls and Dan. Well, college isn't so far off, though, is it?"

"Two years."

"Well, then maybe you'll consider it. Listen, Janie, I'm calling you for a reason, you know."

"You are?"

"I went to the doctor Tuesday. He did some tests."

"Uh-oh. Aggie, what kind of tests?"

"Oh, you know, one of those radio things. Ultrasound."

"Why?"

"Well, apparently I have a growth on my ovary. I have to go in and get it removed. And I never did a thing with that damn ovary. I never even took advantage of it! I joked about that with the doctor and he said that women who have never had children have more trouble. Imagine."

"Are they worried it could be . . . malignant?"

"They think it is, Janie. I thought you should know. Of course, they're not sure, but something looks suspect, I gather."

"Do you want me to come down there?" I ask. I feel dizzy, suddenly. I can't imagine Aggie ill. She never even catches colds. "I could sit with you in the hospital, be your nurse . . . ," I tell her. I would happily do that for Aggie. I would do anything for Aggie. "Dan could take the girls for a few days."

"There's no need. Barney will stay with me. I just thought you should know. And I didn't call you to make you worry. I'm hoping we're catching whatever it is early and that that will be the end of that. Listen, I want to pass along a compliment. The other day, Barney and I were talking about you. I told him about what Bess had told me about your job and everything, and Barney was a little bit worried. He said, 'You know, Aggie, I sometimes think Jane is the closest thing we have to a child of our own. I always just loved that girl.' Now isn't that the nicest thing? He meant it too."

"You know how I feel about both of you," I say. I am one inch away from bursting into tears. With Mother gone, I can't imagine life without Aggie. I imagine inviting Barney to Christmas dinner alone, and that's what does it. Three, four tears stream down my face.

"That's why we decided that you should be the executor of each of our estates, should something happen to the other one of us. Would you be? Would you allow us to name you?"

"Oh, Aggie. Of course. But God, I hate hearing you even talk about it."

"You know, if you're crying, you just stop that, Jane Larsen. I hear that whimpering. I want you to know, it doesn't bother me a bit, talking about death. Not one iota. I've had a perfectly lovely life, you know? I compare my life to Marta's and I feel lucky. A good part of your mother's life, she was just plain miserable. Everybody's got to go sometime. I could have gone ten years ago, and I still would have said I'd had a great life. I've done what I wanted to do, and I did it with whom I wanted to do it with. Barney and I have just had a plain old blast. You have someone in your life who makes you happy and you've won the horse race."

I laugh, loving her spirit, amused by her choice of words. A blast. A horse race. Wouldn't it be nice to go out, knowing that your life has been a blast, that the person you share your life with is the person who makes you happiest?

"I'll come down there in a second if you need me," I tell her.

"Do you remember, Jane, when your mother was getting married, you were, just what? Five, I guess. And you said to me, 'Aunt Aggie, even if Mama gets married, you and I will always be a family, right?'"

"Did I say that?"

"Sure did. And I told you that even if the world came to an end, you and I would still be a family." And then you burst into tears and said, 'Can it come to an end? I don't want it to come to an end.' And I had to explain it was just a figure of speech. The point of all this is, Jane, I always know you're right there. I expect you always will be. And it's a comfort to me. I love all you kids. You're the kids we never had, Barney and me. But, Jane, you're my special child, and as I face this small thing, it occurs to me that I should tell you."

I am speechless. When I lose Aunt Aggie, and surely that day will come one way or another, my world will come to an end for a while. "Aggie," I barely get out.

"Gotta go. Barney and I are going fishing. See, Barney's always wanted tropical fish and today we're going out to buy them. Angelfish, neon tetras, whatever my guy wants. And I want one of those silly little castles that sits at the bottom and spits out bubbles. We gotta go before the store closes. I'm coming, Peaches. I'll talk to you soon, Jane." And off she goes.

    Jane,
    I can't imagine any way that I wouldn't find you
    attractive. We are both middle-aged now. We are
    both very changed. After raising Laine, I don't
    think facades matter much to me anymore. I think
    connection means everything to me. And I'm begin-
    ning to feel so connected to you . . . . Your E-mails
    are like glasses of champagne. And I guess I've
    been thirsty for years and years. Since Suzanne,

there's been nobody I really cared for. I've dated, but so inconsequently. I'd rather stay home with the kids. I'd rather not risk my heart, you know?

I prefer the autumn too. I die in the summertime. Wilt like ten-day-old lettuce. Especially here. You have to stay in air-conditioning to survive, and it makes me feel so embalmed. You go from your air-conditioned house to your air-conditioned garage to your air-conditioned car to another air-conditioned garage to your air-conditioned office. And you could spend an entire summer with no real air at all. Or if you get any, you regret it. Clark was supposed to mow the lawn all last week, but didn't, so last night, I took out the mower and came close to a heart attack mowing it. It was about ninety degrees at about seven P.M. Scorching. My lungs said, "This is air? Can't you do better than this?" I swear, my whole left arm was numb, and I had this terrible ache up near my shoulder. I really thought, "Maybe it's my heart." And you know, that scared me. Especially when I think about the kids.

I came in and took a shower and was completely useless for the rest of the night. Laine said, "Daddy, you wake up so I can sleep." She wanted me to get up so I could put her to bed. Well, as soon as she was in bed, I crashed. Today, my arm feels fine. I probably just pulled it pushing the mower. But it made me want to take better care of myself. After all, Jane, I'm fifty years old. I can't quite believe it sometimes. I play softball and feel a mere thirty-six! I daydream about you and feel a mere twenty-two!

And of course, these days, I do daydream about you often. You had such magnetically dark eyes, Jane. I doubt those have changed either. I was attracted to you the minute I saw you, sitting there cross-legged on the quad. You were wearing a green dress. One of those long hippie ones that you used to wear. And I swear your hair was touching the grass. Remember how I came up to you and talked to you? You were sketching something. Another couple was sitting nearby, I think. The first thing you said to me was, "It's terrible." And I said, "I don't think it's terrible. I like it." And you said, "Thank you for being nice to me, but trust me, it's terrible." I thought that was so funny. You were arguing against yourself.

I told you before that I don't think I was capable of love back then. But I sure was capable of recognizing someone lovely and beautiful. That's how I remember you. What a fool I was to let you slip away. Although you were so young, I doubt you would have been really serious about me then, if it had come down to it. Besides, I think things turn out the way they're meant to turn out. And now is when I can feel most grateful you've come back into my life.

I'm not a religious man. I've never found a church that really spoke to me. I believe deeply in right and wrong, though. And I have a certain respect for fate. I have come to believe there is an order to the world. And when I think about how my life has unfolded, when I think of what's happened in these last ten years, I feel certain that you're back in my life for a reason. A reason we'll both soon know more about.

Hank Marsh calls me Friday during the day.

"I've been thinking about our dinner the other night. I want you to know, your designs were just the sort of thing I was hoping to see."

"I'm glad you feel that way. Thrilled, actually."

"So I thought we'd go up to Dutchess Sunday morning, if that's okay with you."

"Sure. My girls are so independent now, my schedule's pretty loose."

"I can pick you up about nine. Is that too early?"

"No."

"We can get up there about eleven, take time looking at the property, have lunch somewhere . . . no, we'll take a picnic."

"Are you expecting me to pack this repast? Homemade pie and all?"

"No." He laughs. "I'm not that sexist. And I don't cook. I'll buy it. Everything we need." He sounds excited in a pleasing, childish way.

"Okay. Well, I'll bring my camera, to take some photos. It helps me when I'm designing. And I'll bring a sketch pad, to try to map out the lay of the land. Do you have a place you've already decided will be the right place for the house?"

"Yes. I'd like you to see if I've chosen well, though."

"Sometimes I like to bring a ladder," I tell him. "Often I do. A very tall one. The kind that's a little frightening to climb."

"Why?"

"It's the only way to imagine what the views from the top floor will be like. It helps to site the house correctly."

"Wow. I never thought of that. I can borrow my brother's van, bring a telescoping ladder."

"That would be great."

"We can picnic by the pond. It will be a treat."

"It sounds like it." I'm surprised he's so set on this picnic. Maybe he's an old-fashioned romantic. Maybe he just likes to sit and look out over his holdings.

"And if it rains, we'll eat in the van." He laughs.

"I'd burst into the lyrics of 'Rain on the Roof' but I'll restrain myself."

"Only if you promise to sing it, if indeed we do end up sitting in the car," he says.

"It's a deal."

"Promise?"

"Promise."

"754 Seventh Street?"

"Right."

"I'll be there at nine. Good night, Jane."

"Good night."

I'm a little bit thrown by the warmth in his voice. I'm a little bit thrown by the whole thing.

Dear Jack,

I think of you so often, you are like my shadow now. I write letters to you in my head all day long. Everything I do, I narrate to myself, imagining how I will tell you about this or that.

I've gotten ready for bed now. I'm sitting here in my pink nightgown, my face scrubbed clean, barefoot. And as I've sat here, I've thought about how incredibly intimate E-mail is. You can read it naked and no one would know. You can get an answer back the very same day, sometimes even minutes later. But somehow, miraculously, it's more revealing than a phone call. More personal. More of a whisper in your ear. You can reread it when it reaches you, or scares you, or confuses you. There's no trace of it hanging around the house for others to read, and if you fear that your family is prying, you can lock the file. You don't need a stamp, you're not a helpless victim of an unreliable postal service. And this is what binds us. This intimate, sweet little thread of letters. And I can read both yours and mine again and again. Not like the letters we wrote to each other so long ago that I still have. With those, I can read only yours.

Do you know what I remembered last night as I lay in bed? I remember one night, we both took off our shirts and you held me against you, urging me to realize how amazing it was: your skin against my skin. My breasts, your strong chest. Do you remember that, Jack? It's an exquisite memory for me.

I have a question for you. At night when you lie in bed, Jack, do you ever think of me?

With growing love,
Jane

Dear Sweet Jane,

So there I was, sprawled out on my bed last night, just minding my own business, when you suddenly, out of the blue, crossed my mind! I know you probably think I'm just making this up, but I swear I'm not. Now mind you, I wouldn't want you to get the idea that this happens on a regular basis or anything. I mean, just 'cause I've been writing you *every* day for a few weeks, and just 'cause you've been playing a very wicked game of long-distance handball with my libido, and just because you are by far the sharpest, most compatible woman anywhere on my personal horizon, and just because I feel more comfortable talking to you than I've felt with any woman since I don't know when, and just because expecting that I'm going to hear from you helps get me out of bed in the morning, and just

because all of this has hit me from right out of
nowhere, you can't expect me to lie there seven
nights out of seven and have you constantly running through my head or anything. But I have to
admit, I kind of liked having you cross my mind
like that, and since you asked, I'll let you know
if you should happen to show up again tonight . . .

Six

Sunday morning, Hank comes to my door dressed in jeans and a sweater. His hair is perfect. His smile is charming. He looks like an aging Ken doll. Maybe a little too handsome, I think, as I grab my purse, my sunglasses, my camera. He makes me nervous. He stands in my vestibule, looking around. I visualize my childhood Ken doll, his wool hair partially eaten by moths, his plastic head patchwork and pathetic. I smile vaguely.

"This house is incredible," Hank says. "I didn't know houses in Brooklyn could look like this."

"That's because you're a snob," I tease him. "A lot of Park Slope looks like this. And Brooklyn Heights is earlier and even grander."

"I guess I was a snob. But I stand corrected. Maybe someday you'll show me the neighborhood. Where are your daughters?"

"Fast asleep. I'm sure they won't move a muscle until at least eleven or noon."

"My boys were like that when they were teenagers. Their aptitude for sleep exceeded all other talents." Hank smiles at me. He knows he's handsome. When he stands near me, I feel him. Like a force field pulling me out of myself. And he seems to want to stand near me. Maybe he just likes female admiration. His legs look great in jeans. Boyish and slim. And his stomach is flat. He looks too good for a fifty-something-year-old. I used to look at older men when I was young and wonder how anyone could want them. But now that I'm older, their appeal is too clear.

Hank's brother's van smells slightly of dog and has a baby seat in the back complete with a soiled-looking stuffed panda attached to the safety bar by its hangtag.

"Younger brother?" I ask him, pointing to the baby seat.

"Half brother," he says. "Much younger. He's only thirty-two, and they've just had their first baby."

"I didn't know your parents were divorced."

"It's not something that I think about much anymore. My own divorce is fresher in my mind. Your parents still married?"

"No. In fact, I never met my father. It's a long story."

"Whoa! Want to tell me about it? I'd like to hear." I think he really is interested.

"Well, maybe later."

The traffic is ugly getting to the Brooklyn-Queens Expressway, but Hank is a relaxed and confident driver. He tails a little too closely for my taste. And he changes lanes just a little too much. He's one of those men who has just enough overconfidence to be dangerous. Still, in this van that's so big and cushy, it feels like driving a living room down the road and I feel relatively safe. I relax into the pulse of the blacktop and the guardrails. The dance of the lane changes.

"I have a dilemma," he says to me, once we have finally gotten onto the Bronx River Parkway. We can go faster now, and the car seems to be sailing smoothly toward our picnic, toward this property I've been longing so much to see.

"What dilemma?" I ask.

"You."

"Me? I'm your dilemma?" I'm afraid this has something to do with the commission. He's not going to take it away now, is he?

"I really like you," he says. "I'd like to go out with you. But I can't read you at all. I'm not sure if you're interested in dating me, or if you're just interested in building my house. Which would be fine, by the way, if that's how you feel. Oh, and then I wonder if you think dating a client is maybe not okay . . ."

"I don't know," I say. "I wasn't sure you liked me that way."

"Why not?"

"Well, I'm not . . ." I look over at him, his strong jaw, chin, perfectly chiseled nose. "I'm not exactly cheesecake material," I say.

He laughs at me and reaches over for my hand. He squeezes it just for a moment, but his touch is just as electric to me as it was the other night when he touched my elbow. This is almost more than I can take. Part of me distrusts him. Part of me likes him. And I can't trust the fact that he seems to like me. I feel the way I used to in seventh grade with Stevie Bonneville, who tried to kiss me. I can't help wondering, What's wrong with him? Or is this some sort of joke? How can he possibly be attracted to me? And there's Jack. I don't know how to make any sense of this with Jack in the picture.

"I'm interested in you as an architect but also as a woman," he says. "I'm not that fond of cheesecake, anyway. You're soufflé."

I hope he doesn't mean I'm all puffed up. "Thanks," I say finally. "I guess I'll take that as a compliment."

"So?"

"So?"

"So are you interested in me? Or tell me the truth, is it the house?" Has any woman ever told him they weren't interested in him? Doubtful.

"Gee. I guess it's both," I say. "I don't really know you yet, of course. And I haven't let myself think you really liked me until now."

"Do you want to get to know me?" he asks.

"Well, sure," I say. I'm attracted to him against my will. I'd have to be dead or seriously post-menopausal not to feel his pull.

"So consider this our first date," he says. "I definitely want to get to know you."

"Quite the long-distance date."

"Perhaps we should burst into a harmonized duet of 'Getting to Know You'?" he offers.

"Perhaps not," I say. He laughs.

"Can you sing?"

"Only at gunpoint."

"See," he says. "I already know more about you."

The Taconic State Parkway gets more autumnal as we drive north. It's a remarkably beautiful road. Nothing on the roadside but the trees. No buildings at all. Only a single rest stop the whole way. No diners or commercial signs. A few times, I see deer peeking through the woods and some grazing right at the side of the road, and each time I have to warn Hank to slow down a little. There are deer warnings posted all along the way. In some spots, the road is so narrow, it doesn't seem possible two cars can drive side by side on the two lanes. The outdoor temperature monitor drops fifteen degrees on the minivan's dashboard. And I can feel it inside the car. I ask if I can turn off the air-conditioning altogether. The taste of autumn excites me. He hums as he drives. He seems pleased. Astonishingly, his humming doesn't annoy me. When Dan used to do that, I always felt murderous. For one thing, Hank actually stays on key.

"Here we go," Hank says. "We're close now."

We turn off at a sign that says "Bulls Head Road," and shortly after we turn up a long driveway, about a half mile long. It snakes through dark woods, then a hilly meadow. At the top we stop and park by an exquisite white Federal house.

"This is David's house, my friend I told you about. He said it would be fine if we parked here."

"He's not here this weekend?" I say, noting that there isn't another car around, although I spot a separate garage up the hill. I can see that once a public road ran in front of this house. Old trees line both sides of what is now just a fading path. Far down the hill is another house, now an abandoned, picturesque shell. Still farther along the road I see a barn, a shed. Houses were always built right at the sides of roads in a world before snowplows and four-wheel drives. How fortunate for Hank's friend that the road has been abandoned, and the house now stands on this secluded hilltop, where cars can't zoom by, or shine their lights in his twelve-over-twelve windows.

"David's in Europe. I wish he were here. I wish you could see this house. It's extraordinary. I'm sure one of these days, soon, I'll get to show it to you. I'm glad you wore pants and boots. It's a little bit of a hike. I'd drive the car down the old road, but it's so full of ruts. It might do something irreparable to my brother's van, and he'd kill me. Anyway, it's a nice walk."

Hank hoists a pretty old picnic basket out of the back of the van, and I take an old quilt, and a paper bag of things that must not have fit in the basket. The air is exquisitely cool and gives me a happy, intoxicated feeling. In the distance, I can see tall blue mountains.

"What mountains are those?" I ask.

"The Catskills. They're astonishingly large, aren't they? The Berkshires never look so impressive."

"They're beautiful."

We follow the crooked old road across a meadow and down through a thin, ancient forest and an orchard of gnarled apple trees.

In some places, there are actually patches of oil and stone paving on the road. In some places, the trees march along on both sides, acting as fences and road markers. Stone walls dominate the bucolic landscape, and old trellises, building foundations, and pathways seem to pop up like dandelions in the spring. The undulating hills remind me of the Lake District in England. All that are missing are flocks of drowsy sheep. I take my camera out of my bag and begin to snap photos of the property. An old stone wall covered in blue asters. An apple tree groaning to the ground with its load of dark, nearly purple apples.

"This is heaven," I tell Hank. He turns and looks at me. His face is dappled with sunlight and the shadows of leaves. His blond-red lashes glint in the sun. His smile gets right to me.

"I knew you'd love it. This is all mine," he says. "Everything from the orchard on." I photograph him too.

The road climbs another hill, and then I see it: the pond, the stream, the soft cupping hand of the earth. A perfect place to put a house. As we walk down into it, this great, soft valley, I am happy to find that even from the lowest point, you can still see the purple blue watercolors of the Catskills. I photograph them, and the place where the house simply must be sited. There's another old orchard up on the hill, with twisted branches heavy with spotty apples. At the edge of the pond, the trees are turning gold and russet and dark red. A willow bends right into the water. A curlew stands on one leg in the shallows. I take a picture, but I can hardly bear to speak and break the silence. Hank sets down the picnic basket and takes the blanket and bag from me.

"I can't imagine a more beautiful spot on earth," I tell him very softly. His smile is so genuinely childish, so pleased. He takes the old red-calico quilt, shakes it out, and spreads it on the grass by the pond. I see that the grass has been mown all around the pond and on a trail up the hill. On the far reaches of the mowing, purple loosestrife waves its graceful, invasive wands. Knapweed and chicory and butter'n eggs, the wildflowers from my childhood, color the tall grasses.

"Show me where you think the house should be," he says. "I want to see if we agree."

I walk over to the curve of the hill, face the pond, and stretch out my arms.

"Here," I say. "Right here."

"*No,*" he says. "You can't think that. I can't believe you wouldn't put it over here." His face takes on a bulldog determination.

"But to build it nearer the hill will give it context," I say. "And it's slightly higher, so the view of the pond will be more panoramic, and just as close." I too am surprised he doesn't agree with me. How can he not see it?

"No," he says. "I don't know . . ."

"It's perfect. The hill will frame the house. It will look more part of the land that way."

"Do you think? It's not what I was seeing."

I shrug. I'm used to having clients listen to my suggestions on siting. I honestly can't remember a time when I didn't win this important argument.

I remind him that we've forgotten to bring the ladder from the van, although, of course, we borrowed the van just to bring the ladder.

"Maybe once you see the views from the ladder," I say. "Then you'll change your mind."

Hank shakes his head. He digs his foot into the grass like a little boy.

"I can't believe you said there. I was sure you'd say here. It's just got to be here." He takes off his sunglasses and pushes his hair off his brow, looks down at the small hole he's transcribing in the grass with his toe.

His annoyance undoes the Ken-doll aura, puts a cloud on the moment.

"Of course, you've been living with this longer than I have. Maybe after the picnic, I'll see it differently," I say a little too brightly.

Hank nods rather gravely, but when he focuses on the picnic, the dark moment seems to move on. Out of the basket, Hank presents his feast to me: all sorts of little plastic containers of delicacies from Balducci's. Smoked salmon loaf, honey-baked chicken, dilled green beans, sweet corn with crushed gingersnaps. Out of the bag comes a loaf of French bread, a chilled and now sweating bottle of Chardonnay, and a bag of golden, blushing, Rainier cherries.

"I'm glad I brought my camera," I tell him as we fill the blue-and-white china plates from the basket. "This feast should be recorded."

Soon after we record it, however, it seems the food is well diminished, and we are dozy from the wine. Hank clears the quilt of food, packing everything up with purpose. I wonder why he seems in such a hurry, until he lies down and stretches out on the quilt.

"Take a nap with me?" he says, reaching up for my hand.

"Well, we've still got to go get the ladder."

"C'mon. It's just twelve forty-five. We have all the time in the world. Come lie down. Come put your head on my shoulder, Jane."

It's at this moment that it strikes me how little I know this man. And how long it's been since I've been near a man in any kind of romantic context. I can't imagine lying down with him and actually resting. I can't imagine being that close to him yet. I sit down on the quilt and feel so nervous, I can't imagine what to do next. He reaches out for me, and draws me down so my head rests on his shoulder. This should feel wonderful. A tall, comforting man, holding me in his arms in a beautiful meadow. Daniel and I once lay on a quilt in a meadow like this and made love in broad daylight. But I was twenty-seven and cellulite-free. And at that time, Daniel and I had been making love for months. Hank runs his hand down my back, exploring the base of my spine and the shape of my buttocks with far too much interest.

"I'm not ready for this," I say, sitting up suddenly.

"No?" he asks.

"It feels too much like a seduction."

"I think that's what it is," he says. "Although I would be happy to close my eyes for a minute before the actual seduction begins. All that wine, you know." His voice is tongue-in-cheek, but I can tell he's not really joking.

"I mean, I feel like . . . like I hardly know you." I hear myself sounding like a teenager. Surely Cait and Abby could have come up with a more sophisticated line.

He sits up and pushes a hand through his hair. He looks mildly annoyed. Clearly, he's a man who doesn't like his plans messed with. "I was trying to know you better," he says.

I don't know what to say to that, so we are sitting for a moment in silence. So different than the silence of the moment earlier with the curlew and the spell of this beautiful land. "You can't blame a guy for trying," he says.

"I just need some time. I haven't been with anyone new for a while . . . And what you said earlier, about not getting involved with a client. Maybe that was right."

He stands and straightens his pants legs. He doesn't look at me as he straightens his clothes, as he shakes off the stiffness of sitting on the ground. I feel like he's a dog shaking off a bad moment. "I'll go back to the car and get the ladder. You stay here." His voice is chilly.

I watch him cross the meadow and disappear over the hill, his head down, his mood thoroughly changed. I'm still feeling boozy from the Chardonnay. I feel terrible. I think of what I might say to make him feel better. I could tell him that I'm attracted to him. That a simple kiss might be a nice place to start. All of which is true. I begin to wonder what it might be like to feel his body pressed against mine again. To feel his hands on my skin again. Maybe if he just went slower. Maybe if he kissed me first . . . maybe if we talked a bit . . .

But when he returns, he's all business. He still doesn't look at me. Maybe Peggy was right about how delicate middle-aged men are. Less elastic. Less able to bounce back from rejection. His whole body speaks annoyance. His shoulders are hunched. His mouth is drawn. He keeps clenching and unclenching his hands. He puts the ladder down where he wants the house to be and climbs it while I hold on. It's a huge ladder and wobbly and I need to focus all my attention on keeping it steady.

"It's perfect here," he calls down to me. "I knew it would be." He climbs down and simply steps aside. He doesn't look at me. He doesn't say, "You go ahead."

I glance at him and begin to climb nervously. The little wine I had has gone to my head. And he seems distracted, so that I wonder if he's really holding on to the ladder very well. Still, I climb nearly to the top, as he did, looking out over the valley, and the old orchard, the forest fringe and the Catskills in the distance. It's an all-right view. But it lacks composition. It's a mistake to put the house here. I take a deep breath and sigh. I look down to see him looking off, paying no attention to me at all. When I climb down, I turn to him.

"Look, Hank," I say. "You seem upset. I . . . if it's about me, I just want to take it slow."

"Uh-huh," he says. I'm not sure he's really heard me. He moves away from me rather quickly. Or he doesn't want to hear me. My brother Charlie used to be like that when he didn't get his way.

Childish, sulky. I frown at him, but he's not engaged enough to notice.

He picks up the ladder and carries it closer to the hill.

"Where did you want it?" he asks. Venom. Annoyance. I know these tones in a man's voice. Just because I didn't kiss him? He really is insufferable. Before I've even gotten a good grip of the ladder, he climbs up. It's harder to hold the ladder here. It feels like a circus trick, holding him still. The ground is somewhat more sloping and will clearly need to be graded before the house can be built. He says nothing as he looks out in all directions. He climbs down and shrugs. It's a matter of winning and losing, him versus me. No way he's going to let me win now. Even if he could see that I was right. Still, I climb up to see. Ah yes. More varied, more secure, with the hill as an anchor. Breathtaking. The pond is a gleaming artist's-palette shape from up here. Because we are higher, I can see past the old orchard to a distant stone wall, and another deep-green bosomy meadow I haven't seen until now.

"No," he says as I climb down. "Good try. But it's better over there." He points to his original choice of spots. "I want the house there."

"Okay. Okay. But I just have to say this. Forgive me, but it's so much more interesting with the contrast of the vista on one side of the house, and the more intimate backyard of the hillside and trees. Besides, historically, that's how they built many houses back then. Against the hill for protection." When it comes to my houses, I'll wrestle down a dragon if necessary. I have a feeling wrestling Hank could exceed dragon wrestling in the useless-activity category.

"No." I hear one more ice cube hit his voice. I shrug, acknowledging his victory.

Of course there is nothing I can do. It's his land. I am only the hired help. I wonder if I'd made love with him on the quilt, would he have agreed to my location? Probably. I muse momentarily about whether it might have been worth it.

On the ride back, we are mostly silent.

"Look," I say after a while, "is there something I need to fix? Something I need to apologize for? I think you're being awfully rude."

"Am I? I suppose I'm overreacting. I'm just disappointed."

"Because I wouldn't lie with you on the blanket? Or because I preferred a different site for the house?"

"Both, I guess. I just had this so clear in my head, the way it would be. And it felt so right with you there. At first."

"I'm sorry I didn't read the script in advance," I say dryly.

"No need to get huffy," he says.

"Sorry. I would have said *you* were being huffy."

"Well, it would certainly be better if we were just client and architect," he says.

"Yes," I say. "Definitely."

"Good. It's a much cleaner situation that way." He grips the wheel at ten and two, and I notice his knuckles are a whiter shade of pale.

"I can't help wondering what sort of client relationship it will be," I say. "It hasn't exactly gotten off to a stellar start." I need this job. But not if it's going to be as combative as it seems right now.

"What are most of your client relationships like?" he asks.

"Most of my clients are still dear friends."

"Did you sleep with any of them?" he asks.

"No."

"Did you flirt with them?"

"No."

"Well, we need to make sure you keep your record clean."

"Right," I say.

I give up. I don't know what the man wants. No harmonizing of "Getting to Know You," that's for sure. All I know is that I want to go home. To my daughters. To my beautiful house. To my E-mail from Jack. To what I know. To what I trust. To the tiny, tiny place where I rule the world.

Reasons why I'm thrilled that Hank Marsh and I won't be lovers:

1. A romantic entanglement could easily influence his house-plan decisions in a negative way. Especially a guy like Hank.

2. I need this job more than I need this relationship.

3. He's a man who has to get his way all the time. Not a desirable trait in a lover.

4. He's too handsome. Handsome men are dangerous men.

You're home?" Abigail asks as I come in. She sounds absolutely panicked. "I didn't think you'd be here yet."

"I told you I'd be home late in the afternoon. Is there a reason it would be better if I wasn't?"

"No," she says, but clearly she's got something up her sleeve. For one thing, she's wearing quite an extraordinary amount of eye shadow, eyeliner, and mascara. They make her look like a cross-dresser.

"Where's Cait?" I ask.

"She went to Danielle's to study."

"And, are you expecting someone to come over, by any chance?"

"Um . . . Yes." She pushes a lock of her hair behind her ear.

"And that would be . . . let me see if I can remember his name . . . Benjy . . ."

"Skrebneski," she says softly, as though it's the most musical name in the world. Ah.

"Well, I'll be sure and hide myself away in my room when he comes. I'm sorry if you were hoping for privacy and now you won't have it totally. Although it would have been nice to tell me he was coming."

"I didn't know until this afternoon," she says. "Mom?"

"Huh?"

"If you like a guy and you let him know it, does that mean that after that, he'll just think you're easy and try to get all he can off you? That's what Lucy told me. Because Benjy heard from someone who heard from my asshole, loud-mouthed sister that I like him."

"And you know this because . . ."

"Because he told Lucy he knew I liked him. She says once a guy knows it, it's all over."

"I think that's kind of a blanket statement. It's true guys like the chase. But if he likes you too, he may just be flattered and even shy of you."

"Yeah?"

"Uh-huh. How did it come about that he's coming over here?"

"I asked him."

"Oh. And he wouldn't have learned from your invitation that you like him?"

"Well, I told him it was just to study."

"What time is he due?"

"He was supposed to be here at three."

"Oh." I look at my watch. It's 4:45. "This was a certain date?"

"Well, not a date."

"But I mean, a certain time? An agreement?"

"I thought it was. Should I call him? Should I see if he's coming or if he forgot?"

I put my arm around her and give her a loving squeeze.

"I wouldn't do anything," I tell her. "If he doesn't come, he's just not a very nice person."

"Well, what if he got hung up doing something else? Or maybe he got the time wrong. Or the day. Maybe he thought I said another day . . ." I hear myself in her words. These were just the sort of words I was chanting while waiting for Hank at Guastavino's.

"Abby, you think he could possibly have gotten it wrong?"

"No."

"Oh, honey. Guys your age . . ."

"Are pricks. I know."

"You can't always rely on them. But you shouldn't forgive him, either."

She looks disappointed. Her mouth quivers. There's nothing you can do to keep your kids from being brokenhearted. Life is heart-breaking and that's a fact. Still, it hurts to see them sad, to see the beginnings of what becomes cynical in all of us.

"Cait said he hated me. He thought I was stuck-up. She said she heard that. I just thought she was jealous . . ."

"It wasn't nice of her to tell you that. And it may not be true . . . still . . . don't count on seeing him today."

"I know," she says. She starts to cry and I hug her for a little while just like I did when she was much younger, playing with her hair, soothing her while she sobs. Then I fix her a piece of toast and cin-namon sugar while she goes to rescue her leaking makeup in the powder-room mirror.

"I hate Cait," she says later while she picks at her toast. "She made this all go wrong."

"I'm sure that wasn't her intention," I tell her.

"Oh, get over it, Mom. Of course it was."

"Why would she do that?"

"Because she doesn't have a boyfriend." Abby might be right, and yet I can't think of any way to defend Cait without talking to her first.

"I'll have a chat with her," I promise.

"She may have ruined my life," she says.

"Yup. Your only option now is to become a nun," I tell her.

"Shut up. It isn't funny."

"I know, baby. Just keep things in perspective."

"I don't think I need you to tell me that," she says in her most acid voice. There are times when my daughters each do a fine imitation of the Wicked Witch of the West.

"Sorry."

"You know," Abby says, "life would be a lot easier if girls didn't like boys. I mean a *lot* easier."

I laugh. "I certainly know what you mean," I tell her. "I've thought that myself many, many times." I've thought of that today, I think.

"I may never get married," she says. "I may never want to even live with a man."

"Oh, I suspect that you will. You just have to find the right guy."

"Is that how it works?" she asks.

"The right guy, the right timing. The right attitude. It all comes together at one point or another."

I wonder to myself, *Is* that how it works? I was crazy about Daniel. He broke my heart. But for one moment in my life, he was perfect in every way. If I knew all I know now, would I have still fallen in love with him? Yes. Oh, yes.

> Dear Jack,
> Today I went out to see the land where my new client wants to build his house and it was extraordinarily beautiful . . . I wish you could have been there with me . . .

I tell Jack about the wonder of coming upon the old gnarled orchards heavy with dark apples, and the smooth pond held in the cup of the valley, about the road that once was there and is now just a shadow, like a line erased on a child's drawing. And then I tell him that Hank was difficult and what a challenge it might be to build for him.

    The location is overall so gracious and hand-
    some, however, that I've decided I can make it
    look fine wherever he dictates I should put it.
    I think, unfortunately, that "dictate" is the key
    word. I hope we become friends again. It's hard
    to build for someone you feel angry with.

I think to myself that Jack will understand, that he will nod when he reads this, that he has surely had clients who have made him mad. But I realize that perhaps my telling him I'm angry with Hank takes away the smudge of guilt I feel for having found Hank so attractive.

    Speaking of anger, there's anger all around
    today. This afternoon, my girls were furious with
    each other. Abigail was certain it was all Cait's
    fault that a boy stood her up for a study date.
    Cait swears it wasn't she who tipped him off that
    Abby had a crush on him. There was a great deal
    of shouting and misery all around. And even when
    they went to bed, they refused to speak to each
    other. As I went to sit at the side of each of
    their beds to tuck them in—something they still
    begrudgingly allow me to do—I heard both sides
    of the story in tearful detail. The truth is,
    it's hard to be a sister, hard to be a teenager,
    hard to be a young woman, hard to be in love.
    Hard to realize that life has the power to might-
    ily disappoint. And the sad part is, with all my
    experience at all of this, there's nothing I can
    do but be empathetic. Sometimes life stinks. But

you've got to find out for yourself. How power-
less we are sometimes as parents to do much but
stand by and watch. At least with children this
age. The lessons are already taught. The values
are already instilled. All the rest is up to
them.

It's a great comfort to write to you. I think
coming to this point in our lives is extraordinarily lonely. Most, or at least many, people
have partners at our age. But even those who do
are often lonely in their relationships. I remember how lonely I was when I was married to
Dan. And so many of us have been too busy raising kids to have the kind of friendships that
really nurture us. My friend Peggy and I rarely
get together. And we don't speak as often as we
should. I would never, for instance, think to
burden her with small life stories like the mon-
umental fight between Abby and Cait, and yet how
nice it is to share it with you. I hope it
doesn't bore you. I somehow imagine you experience many similar scenes with your kids. I hope
you'll share them with me.

I was so happy to read that I crossed your mind
last night. Wish I could have been there for
real. I try to imagine what your bedroom is like,
what your house is like, what your life is like.

Dear Jane,

I'm pleased that writing to me eases you. Yes,
of course, my kids fight, sometimes bitterly, although I think having no mother has the effect
of making them more of a bloc than ordinary
brothers would be. And of course, they're very
protective of Laine.

You asked about the house we live in, and just

like the shoemaker's children having no shoes, well, it's not much to speak of. I built it when Suzanne and I only had Clark, and there were just three of us to shelter. It's a small, low ranch with jutting eaves and trellised arches front and back. I loved it at the time I built it, but I didn't have much money, and I had to keep it minimal, to say the least. Now, I confess, I hate it. It's cluttered with the lives of four people. And very, very worn. I haven't maintained it as I should. The expenses involved with taking care of Laine have been phenomenal. And the amount of energy it takes has kept me from growing my firm more to make more money, and from fixing things around here that need fixing. The trellises haven't had vines on them since Suzanne left. They are like the spines of dead animals, I sometimes think, left on the desert sand after the flesh has been eaten way.

I have often thought of selling the house, moving anywhere else at all, because no question, it's haunted with memories of Suzanne. I kept it at first because I thought it was the consistency the kids needed. But now, I think it's perhaps the misery hanging on. I don't really have the money to build a house right now, unless I did a lot of the work myself. And the thought of moving is so daunting.

You make me wish I had more wonderful things to show of myself, to share with you. I wish I was proud of where my life is right now. But I think I may have been a little depressed for a long time. I mean, a low-level, functional depression that's just stood in the way of enjoying my life more. Your letters have lifted me up, given me a wonderful reason to care, to change

things. I wonder if you will be disappointed in
who I am now. I guess I'm just not the Jack you
once knew. I hope that someday soon I can be
again.

W hat the hell did you do to Hank?" Peggy calls and asks me.

"Nothing. What do you mean?"

"Well, I asked how things were going with you and he said, 'Mur-
derously.' "

"That's a bit of an overstatement."

"He said that he thinks you don't like him at all, that you're just
tolerating him in order to build his house, which he kept saying is
fine. It's just *fine!*"

"That's absurd. I just told him I want to go slow. Just because I
didn't want to make love with him right there on the picnic blanket
doesn't mean I'm not interested. Jesus. What's his problem, Peg?
Are women just falling down at the first proposition these days, and
I'm behind the times?"

"I told you. Guys that age are insecure."

"That's not insecurity. That's pathological misinterpretation."

Peggy laughs. "Well, I'll tell him you said that."

"Yeah? I don't think so."

"Well, I'll tell him something."

"How are you, anyway?" I ask her.

"Oh—you know. S.D. works all the time. He's got that Asian
workaholic thing going . . . I hate it. I hate spending my nights
alone."

"And your kids?"

"I don't know. Mandy doesn't write or call. I guess she's liking
Vassar, but she keeps it to herself. Jake's definitely smoking, but I'm
not sure what. He's going to get kicked out of high school, I'm

afraid. He flunked three subjects last semester. He's absolutely never home. And I have to admit, sometimes I prefer it that way."

"Jeez. You okay with all this?"

"No. It sucks. But I'm breathing . . ."

"When was the last time I saw you? Oh, the party. But besides that . . ."

"Oh . . . I don't know. Two months ago?"

"You want to get together?" I ask.

"Well, sure, but I can't imagine when. One of these days. Dinner or something . . . I kind of hoped the four of us would get together— you, me, S.D., and Hank, but S.D. never seems to be free."

"You just want to hang out with Hank," I tease her.

"Yeah. Maybe I do. *I* would have fucked him right there on the picnic blanket, no questions asked." She laughs. But I happen to know she means it.

Barney calls. I can't believe I forgot Aggie was going to have surgery today. I feel terrible. I keep thinking as he speaks, I should have flown down there. I should be there with him, and by Aunt Aggie's bed.

"Aggie has cancer," he says very flatly. I can hear his breathing through the telephone. Each breath sounds labored and exhausted. "Just as the doctor said she did. I would have been okay if that was all. If it was just a tumor and he removed it. But it's worse than he thought, Jane. He says it's spread. Into the abdominal wall. He says he thinks it will show up somewhere else. I think he called it . . . met . . . metastasized."

"Oh God" is all I can manage to say. Aggie. My Aunt Aggie.

"I'm in a phone booth at the hospital. I don't know what to do. I guess she should know. I guess we should tell her. I don't know . . ."

"She'd hate it if you didn't tell her," I say. "She hates things that are dishonest or withheld. You have to tell her, Barney. She'd want to know. She'd want to know so she could fight it."

"She would too, wouldn't she?" he says hopefully. "She's a fighter, isn't she?"

"Always."

"Jane, I never thought . . . not Aggie."

"Listen, Barney. I'm coming down there. I'll call for tickets now. I'll be there tomorrow . . ."

But it's as though Barney hasn't heard me. His voice is distant and whispery. "Jane, the last few days I've tried to imagine what my life would be like without Aggie. We both thought they'd find cancer. I guess we never thought it would be this bad. But still, I tried to imagine what I'd do if something happened to her. And I can't imagine it. I just can't. It's like my brain stops dead. Kaput. I can't imagine. Immediately, I think about the Cubs. I mean of all things, the Cubs! The biggest losers of all time."

"Don't try to think about it, Barney. There are a lot of drugs now that they didn't have before. You never know. I hear stories all the time about people they said had just two months to live and ten years later they're still around." I say this all so cheerfully that I almost believe it. But I saw my mother die. I believe in the seduction of death. I saw each day as she was enticed more and more by the notion—"It's just easier to die . . ." Aggie has more fight in her, though. Much more.

"Aggie will make me think about death, you know?" Barney says. "She's like that. She likes facing facts."

"Maybe she can help you," I say. "Help you imagine how things will be."

"Maybe she can help me stop thinking about Sammy Sosa," he says. We both laugh. I hear the tension released when he laughs.

"I'm coming down there, Barney," I tell him again.

"No," he says. His voice is certain. It stings me. "Aggie's weak now. She won't want you to fuss. When she's back on her feet maybe . . ."

"I could help you take care of her. I took care of my mother when she was ill."

"Please don't come now, Jane. I guess . . ." He is silent for a moment, then takes a deep breath. "I guess I want to be alone with her at first. I need to share this with her alone." I feel lost, perplexed.

"We'll talk," he says. "Or Aggie will call soon. Tell the other children what's happened." I agree that I will. "And, Jane?"

"Yes."

"Thank God for you."

"I'm here for you. Let me know when I can come . . ." I hang up before I start to cry. I think about Barney, all alone in that hospital in South Carolina. Worried. Momentarily partnerless while she lies unconscious. How empty it must feel for him. He's so used to Aggie's advice and counsel. All these years.

They were in their late thirties when they met, handsome, healthy people. I have often thought they were the luckiest people I know. Because, you know, even now that they've grown old and imperfect, they still look at each other as though they've won the lottery of love. If I were to ever love again, if I were to ever decide it was worth it, that's how I would have to feel. Blessed. Overwhelmingly blessed.

```
Dear Jack,
    I found out today that my Aunt Aggie, whom I've
loved like a second mother all my life, has can-
cer. Aunt Aggie is the happiest person I know.
So grounded, so sure of herself. So in love. With
my mother gone, Aggie just assumed her role as
the matriarch in the family. I can't imagine life
without her. I guess when she's gone, then I have
```

to be the matriarch. Oh God. I'm certainly not
ready for that. A big part of me still wants to
be a child. Is it just me? Do you ever feel this
way? Is it time I grew up?

> Dear Jane,
> I am sorry about your Aunt Aggie. Really sorry.
> I remember you telling me about her. I remember
> you telling me what she meant to you. I think,
> however, when the time comes, you will make a
> fine matriarch. You have the soul of a matriarch.
> And it wouldn't surprise me at all if your whole
> family sees you that way right now. Good. Steady.
> Comforting. Loving.

I call each of my siblings and tell them about Aggie. It's funny.
It's like none of them really hears me. They say, Jeez, that's awful,
poor Barney. But there's no real hurt in their voices. There's no real
understanding. Illness, death, are elusive things. Like dreams, you
can't remember in the morning. Too painful to really own unless
you live with them every day. Even I keep forgetting in the next few
days why I should feel sad. And by the weekend, I can forget whole
stretches of the day. My mind says, "Aggie will live forever. She's
the type of person who will get better. No one's more of a fighter
than Aggie." I call Barney at home, and don't get him. I call him at
the hospital and he has to whisper when we talk, because Aggie's
sleeping. There's no real news. She's recovering. We all have to
wait.

Hank and I arrange to get together so I can further interview him
about the house. I invite him over on Friday night, when the girls
are at Dan's. I dread the meeting, of course, aware that I'm going to
have to juggle my attraction to him and my dislike of him. So ex-

hausting. The only good news is that we've decided to keep the relationship professional. And of course there's Jack. I don't know
how Jack should figure into all of this. He'll probably never be in
my life again, really. His life is played out on a distant stage, in a
world I have no access to. Still, it nags at me. I am often moved by
the vulnerability in his letters. His eagerness to communicate. I
can't help feeling that even being attracted to Hank is cheating on
Jack.

Hank arrives right on time: eight-thirty. I told him that he should
eat and then come over, that I just wanted to ask him a hundred
questions about his dreams for the house. He's dressed in khakis
and a polo shirt. He looks shy when I open the door.

"I like this neighborhood," he says again when he comes in. "I got
here too early and walked around. I just can't get over how beautiful your house is."

"Thank you." So he's starting by making nice-nice. Okay. That's
better than the opposite.

"It's heartening to see that your taste is so appealing to me," he
says. "All the things you chose here, I think I'd choose on my own."

"Thanks." I can't help looking at him: his golden-tan skin, the
blond hairs on his arms, his beautiful Ebel wristwatch, slightly big
on his refined wrist. The decided taper from his shoulders to his
hips.

"Look. I'm pretty lousy at apologies, but I'm sorry about last
time," he says.

"Are you?" I ask.

"I was a jerk. Peggy says so anyway."

"You didn't think you were until Peggy told you?" I ask.

"No. I knew I was being a jerk. I don't know what got into me . . .
I've never really brought anyone to the property before. Just David,
of course. I had expectations. It got me in trouble. I'm sorry."

"And I'm sorry you misinterpreted my withdrawal," I say, politely, but with no conviction. "I just needed to go slower. You shouldn't have taken it personally."

"Yes. I thought about it later and couldn't understand why I didn't see that at the time. You were pretty clear about it. Still, I think what I said, about us just being client and architect . . . well, at least until the house is built, might be a good idea."

"That's what I thought. The more I thought about it, the more sensible it seemed."

"Oh, it's sensible to wait," he says. And his blue eyes take on a devilish gleam. "I'm not sure I *can*, however." He smiles. "I can't seem to get you off my mind."

Jesus. There he goes again. Why does he say things like that? He needs to make sure I'm attracted to him.

"Was it me on your mind or the house?" I ask.

"You. Miss Cheesecake." I'm embarrassed. "I keep hearing your voice in my head. Some of the funny things you said to me."

I said funny things to him?

"Did that alter ego of mine that's haunting you tell you that you should move the house toward the hill?" I ask.

He laughs. "No," he says. "She didn't say a word about that."

"It's a shame," I say. "Well, come on. Let's talk about the house."

I usher him into the back parlor where I gesture to the larger sofa and he sits down. He's still looking around eagerly, taking it all in. I sit in the love seat, far enough away to keep things kosher. Close enough to really see him.

"You know the funny thing is, you're not really my type," he says.

Oh thanks, I think. I really need to hear this.

"What is your type?" I ask him. I'm afraid to discover what he'll say. A twenty-year-old blonde with a twenty-four-inch waist?

"Oh, someone more outdoorsy, tomboyish," he finally says after struggling for a moment. "My ex-wife was like that. She never read books. She liked to hike, kayak, ski."

"Is that what you like?" I ask. Since I hate all those things, I would be pleased to hear him say yes. Then I'll have less reason to be drawn to him.

"I hate it. Always have. And I'm bad. *Really* bad at all those things. I don't know why I'm drawn to hiker/camper/canoers. I could trace it back to a crush I once had on a girl counselor at camp."

I laugh. "Did you go with her on her pursuits? Your ex-wife, I mean. Not the counselor."

"Oh, I would have followed that counselor anywhere. I remember being fixated on the fact that she had a bra strap. I once reached out and touched it. She turned and said to me, 'What the hell are you doing, Hannaford? You don't go touching strange women.' That bothered me so much. I thought she'd called herself strange!"

"Your wife?" I ask impatiently. "Did you do sporty things with her?"

"My wife, well, sure. In the beginning, I let her drag me on trips down the rapids and hikes up in the Poconos that ended in ratty little inns with heart-shaped bathtubs. I hated being dirty. I hated risking my life over rocks. You know how you want to please someone, so you bend yourself a little. But then you start trying to reclaim yourself and the person who loves you is so baffled. You're not who she thought you were. 'What do you mean, you want to stay home and *cook* together. Ugh!'"

He picks up each little item on the coffee table, turning them over in his hands: it's my collection of match safes, including a cobalt-blue glass beauty with a ribbed barrel for striking.

"I love the stuff you have here."

"Do you?"

He nods enthusiastically.

"You're a domestic kind of guy?" I ask.

"Oh yes. It's embarrassing. I'd stay home for weeks with the right woman. I even garden. And I'm straight, honest to God." He raises his eyebrows. Again, I think he's cute. Damn.

"Is that why your marriage didn't work out? You wanted to stay home, she didn't?" I ask.

"That was a big part of it. You're very domestic too, aren't you?" he asks.

"I've often said I could be the perfect nineteenth-century housewife. I like to cook, sew, garden, watercolor, raise children, nurture. Jobs, politics, I could live without. Except for designing houses. Of course, that's what matters most to me."

"What kind of questions do you want to ask me about the house?" he says.

"Oh, sorry. You're in a hurry."

"No. Just excited about the process. Curious."

"Do you want beer or wine before we start?"

"No. Maybe that's what got me in trouble last time. Go ahead. Just ask the questions."

"So, do you see yourself living in this house alone or with someone?"

"With someone, definitely. I'm an optimist."

"Do you expect to entertain other people as well?"

"As often as possible. Sara hated that. Entertaining. She just didn't see the point."

"Sara was your wife?"

He nods. "Anne hated it too. Hated it."

"Anne is . . ."

"Well, stupidly, shortly after I broke up with Sara, I entered another relationship. With Anne. She was a carbon copy of Sara. Another nature girl. It was ugly after a while too. Uglier than with Sara in some ways, because we didn't have the kids to draw us together. You'd think that would have made it harder, having the kids, but it was the neutral point for Sara and me. Our place to agree."

"So how many bedrooms do you see wanting in this house? I mean, you've got your kids to think of, maybe . . . grandkids some-day."

"Four. Do you think that's too many?"

"No. Houses sell better with four bedrooms. Especially quality houses. And baths?"

"What do you think?"

"Two and a half. A powder room on the first floor, a master bath, and a bath for the other bedrooms."

"That sounds good."

"I take it kitchens matter to you?"

"Very much."

We talk so easily, in such an absorbed way, that when I finally come up for air, I realize it's nearly midnight. We're leaning toward each other on our separate continents of sofas. The pages of my sketchbook are filled with his answers, with starred passages. I feel like I know him quite well now, at least as a client. But I am surprised when he stands and holds out his hands to help me stand up too.

"Can I kiss you?" he asks. "I'm asking, because this way you won't be surprised, or put off."

No one has actually *asked* me to kiss him since eighth grade.

"I thought we were going to try and wait." Go away. Go away, I think.

"Well, gosh, I'm trying to wait. And we did wait. Hours." He takes my face in his hands. "Look. You're not committing yourself. It could be just one kiss and then that's it. We get to taste it, and then we wait. Or . . ."

"Or . . ."

"Come here." He excites me. I can't help it. And his kiss is sensual and hungry and very, very sexual. There are chaste kisses. I've certainly had my share. Hank has never kissed chastely in his life.

This I can tell immediately. I'm pulsing like a mambo band by the time he pulls away.

We're both speechless. I'm thinking, Okay, let's go to bed. I can't help it. You can't help it. Let's act like irresponsible teenagers. But the rogue puts his hands in his pockets and impishly shrugs.

"Okay. I'm going. But that was nice, wasn't it?"

"You're going?"

"You don't want me to?"

"Well, I wouldn't mind trying that again," I say.

"Nope. I just wanted to taste the wine. We can save the bottle for later. One more kiss and we're in trouble."

What a tease! Where did he learn this stuff? I walk him to the door. I'm awkward and downright unsteady.

"No kiss good night?" I say. *What* is wrong with me? Did that really come out of my mouth?

"Not a chance," he says. He smiles like the devil himself. The man's got me by the ovaries.

When the door is closed and he's on his way down the streets of Park Slope, I lean against the wall and realize I'm on fire.

When, as an adult, you don't have sex on a regular basis, you acclimate. You put a cap on it. You deep-six it. You cryogenically freeze it like Walt Disney's corpse. At least that's what I've done. These past few years, I've been very comfortable thinking sexually once every 100 days. Three times a year, I'm hungry for a man—and pretty mildly hungry at that.

I guess I could blame it on the fact that the more I wanted Dan, the more he pushed me away. When you feel undesirable, you feel undesiring. What I didn't realize was that underneath, buried so deep it never warned me with a soft, fluent heat, or a flicker of light, underneath, the pilot light was still on. Now, *VROOM*. I haven't felt like this in so long, I hardly know what to do with my-self. Get the asbestos blanket. If I were a man, this would translate to a three-week hard-on that would end up in the record books and quite possibly kill me. And all this from one sneaky, manipulative kiss.

Seven

I can't believe that I've let Hank throw me for such a loop. I've lost my appetite. I didn't sleep well last night. I can't stop thinking of his touch, the way he looked at me, that wild kiss. And he hasn't even called. I thought for sure that he'd call when he got home last night to tease me further. To whisper good night to me. Or at least today to keep the connection going. I haven't done this in so long, I don't know the rules. Maybe I shouldn't expect to hear from him.

The good news is, I'm just bursting with ideas about his house. I've been sketching and taking notes for his house all day. That's the one thing that's helped me make it through the day. I want to call Peggy and tell her what happened last night, even though I'm mortified to feel so excited by a single impetuous kiss. Ridiculous. Like a schoolgirl with the giggles. Peggy, who's been through it all so many times with Sam and Frankie DiBiasi and S.D., will surely laugh at me. Although at least she won't call me

Ostrich Girl. For once, I'm not hiding my head in the sand. I want Hank. I've decided that. Despite the fact that he's a client. Despite the fact that I can't imagine why he likes me. Despite Jack.

Peggy answers on the first ring, as though she's been waiting by the phone. She sounds breathless.

"Hey," I say.

"Jane. Oh. I thought . . . never mind. How ya doing?"

"Exploding," I tell her.

"Yeah?" She sounds distracted. "Why are you exploding?"

"Hank."

"Oh?"

"He came over last night, and teased the pants right off me."

"You mean you . . . he . . ."

"No. He kissed me. He made me crazy, and then he left."

"Oh. Um . . . How are you feeling about this? He kissed you?"

You never know with Peggy what's really going on. Once, after a particularly disjointed conversation in which there were nothing but non sequiturs, she told me the next day that she and S.D. were "doing the nasty" while we spoke. And when I asked why she even answered the phone, she said S.D. dared her to, that he thought it would be fun. It excited him. I found that offensive, but I try not to be judgmental about my friends. Especially about friends as long-standing as Peggy.

"How am I feeling? I feel crazed. I can't figure him out, Peg. I mean, when he wants me, he wants me point-blank. Now that I'm open to him, he's like a fucking politician. He wants to control the whole thing. I mean, is he a control freak or something?"

"I don't know," she says flatly.

"Are you okay?" I ask her.

"Never better." She couldn't have said those two words with a greater sense of irony.

"What's going on?"

"Nothing's going on. Why does something always have to be going on, Jane? Maybe I'm having a premenopausal moment. What the hell does it matter?"

"Peggy?"

"Okay. I just had a fight with S.D., okay? A big fight. Your timing stinks. It was so bad, he got in the car and left. I thought he'd call me. You know, on the cell phone. I thought you were him. I gotta go. In case he calls."

"Don't you have call waiting?"

"Yeah. But I gotta go. Just say good-bye, Jane. I'll call you tomorrow or something."

"Okay."

I hang up and feel confused as hell. I don't get Peggy sometimes. Sometimes girlfriends are harder than lovers. They don't have to be nice to you. They don't have to make up with you. Because they have no intention of sleeping with you later. You just have to wait until they want to be nice again.

Dear dear Jane,

What a day I've had. We've had a spike in the temperature, and I've had to spend a rare Sunday outside all day at a new site, so my brain is fried, my skin is bright red, and my spirits are as flat as that Illinois cornfield behind where your dorm sat. Laine is furious with me for working on the weekend. The boys aren't happy, because they've had to amuse Laine. All in all, everyone's upset, hot despite the air-conditioning, and ready for the real autumn to begin.

And me, well, somehow, not hearing from you all day yesterday really took a bite out of my mood. And I see that you haven't written today either. I'm sure you've just been busy or distracted. But

it worries me how much I look forward to hearing
from you. You know, when you've been married to
someone unpredictable like Suzanne, you can't
help feeling skittish about the unexpected. Is
there something I've said or done that's put you
off? Please be honest with me.

Maybe hearing that I've been depressed made
you want to back away, and I can't blame you.
Maybe I shouldn't have told you. But I think
that, lately, I've really rallied. And not just
because of you. I think in the last year, I've
realized that my life for too long has just been
about marking time. About keeping my head above
water. And one day I woke up and realized I'm
nearly fifty years old. Fifty. And if I have
twenty-five, thirty more years to live, I'll
feel lucky. I want to use those years better
than I've used the last twenty. I want to taste,
see, feel my life in a way I've forgotten.
Please write and let me know what's going on.
I'd sure like our relationship to be part of
what makes the future a damn sight better than
the past.

Even worse than my terrible phone call with Peggy is that I
haven't written Jack. I feel as if I've betrayed him in being so
drawn to Hank. I feel guilty and confused. And at the same time,
so distracted, longing to see Hank again. I guess E-mail can be extraordinarily intimate, but it just can't stand up to the touch,
smell, taste of another human being. Virtual is just that. Not
quite. Not enough. Almost like . . . And now I stare at his letter.
I've hurt him by not writing. I have to write him. I realize when I
read his next-to-last E-mail, where he confessed how depressed
he's been for so long, how very vulnerable his letters have be-

come. I should be protective of him. Kinder. What's wrong with me?

Dear Sweet Jack,

I'm so sorry I haven't written. I got caught up in my life, but it's no excuse. I'm sorry if I upset you. I met with my client last night to discuss the house and what he wants it to be. It was exciting talking through the hundred questions I posed, hearing his answers, and right on the spot imagining the solutions. I haven't felt this excited about a project in a long time. I have so many ideas, I've had to jot things down all day, so as not to lose them. I don't know about you, but creative ideas are like dreams to me. They are so elusive, so easily forgotten. By putting them on paper, they become real.

It's cooler here, so it's hard to imagine a heat wave there. It just makes me realize how far away you are, and that you live in a different world. Why on earth did you have to go to a site on Sunday?

Your telling me that you've been depressed didn't put me off. I thought it was very brave of you to admit it. Well, even to see it, really. I think so many of us walk around numbed by depression and never know it. I think I was depressed for a while by my breakup with Dan. Sometimes, I think I still am. I realize how I've tamped down whole parts of me that haven't had a chance to breathe. My sense of romance, my sexuality. It's easy to hide all that away. It's easy to forget that it's part of you.

Maybe you should start dating. Maybe if you

just got out, that would make you feel better. I was thinking recently that that might be good for me too. To get back into life, you know?

Dear Jane,

Your letter told me so much less than I want to know. Something clearly is going on with you, but you're not saying. All your previous letters have been seductive, and now you're telling me to date. Pardon me for finding this confusing.

Laine isn't feeling well today and I'm worried about her. She has a headache that's making her nauseous. All she can do is lie in bed and moan. Or sit up and moan. She said the room is moving. The doctor thinks it's just the flu, but it's almost like a migraine. Or an inner-ear infection. And she's gotten worse since this afternoon when we saw the doctor. I feel so helpless when she's in pain. She, of all my children, is most surprised when her body betrays her. She has often said when she had the flu, "Why am I sick?" She just can't understand. Nor can I. I'd so much rather it was me. I can't write for long. I think I'd better go to her.

Jane, tell me, please. What's going on?

Dear Jack,

I hope Laine is feeling better. I was worried when I read your letter. I told you that I think dating would be good for you because it's not like we can see each other. We're what? Eight hundred or more miles apart. And nothing in this world can bring Nashville and Brooklyn any closer together. (Imagine how terrible the accents would be!) I love the closeness our letters have given us after all these years. And this lovely con-

nection we've forged from so far away. But how
could anything go beyond that? So please let me
know how Laine is, and what exactly I've done
wrong for just wanting you to be happy since I
can't be there to make you happy.

Peggy actually shows up at my house the next day about five
minutes after I stop working on Hank's house and start cooking dinner. She never does that—comes over with no warning. It's not the
best time. The girls are hungry, and it's the one chance I have all
day to talk to them—while I cook, while we eat dinner.

"Sorry about our call yesterday," she says, standing at the downstairs gate.

"You . . . you want to come in . . . ?"

"Hoped you'd ask." She sets her backpack down on the entrance-
hall bench, sits down and takes off her shoes.

"Jake isn't coming home for dinner tonight?" I ask her. I wander
into the kitchen and she follows me. I resume washing the arugula
by dunking it in a bowl of cold water, scrubbing the leaves with my
fingers, then laying them on paper towels.

"I'm starving," Abby calls down from upstairs. "Are we close?"

"Come down and help me." I grab a chunk of Parmesan and start
to grate.

"Who rang the doorbell?"

"Aunt Peggy."

"Hey, Peggy," Abby shouts. "I'll be down in a minute."

"Jake?" I remind her.

"Oh, yeah. He's on one of those overnight nature field trips. They
always get one in before it's too cold. He goes out to the woods with
his class and probably rolls joints for everyone."

I could get into talking about Jake with Peggy, but frankly, I don't
have the energy. It upsets me that she just accepts his drug issues.
I find myself grating the Parmesan wildly. I look up at her. She has

maintained the illusion of youth. She looks a good ten years younger than I. She's still willowy, still freckled. Still long-lashed, a trait she plays up with plenty of eye shadow. Her big blue eyes entreat loyalty. Against my will, she's always reminded me of Ginger on *Gilligan's Island*. She looks especially good today in a chic lime-green suit that looks as though it was painted on her.

"Did you come over for a reason?" I ask her. I want her to feel at home. I love her company usually. I wish I weren't so tired and focused. Wish I didn't want to much to be alone.

"Yeah. I came to apologize," she says. "I was absolutely frizzed out last night. Thought it might have bothered you."

I nod. To say the least, I think. "Did you and S.D. make up?"

"Yes. We . . . well . . ." She laughs nervously.

"Don't strain to tell me. I don't want to know. I actually wondered at first when you sounded so strange if you and he weren't in flagrante delicto."

She laughs. "No. Nothing like that. It made you so mad, we've changed our evil ways. Now we just call one of those 900 numbers and tell the girl just what we're doing. S.D. loves it. He usually puts us on speakerphone, and the girl is paid to listen. Don't worry. You're safe from us from now on. Not that S.D. has any interest in sex at all lately. So old Hank's left you hanging, huh?"

"Yeah. He hasn't called. He's a mystery."

"Sorry about that. Guys. You can't ever really know what's going on in their heads. I started thinking that as we all get older, men become more like women. Sensitive and all that. But truthfully, well, they're men and we're women and we'll never really understand them. And it's what makes them different that turns us on anyway."

"Is there a male name for a 'prick tease'?" I ask her.

"A pussy tease?"

"Well, that's what Hank is. A pussy tease."

"What?" Caitlin asks, coming down the stairs. "I heard that."

"Never mind," I say.

"I heard it and I'd love to know exactly what you and Peggy were talking about. I know you're not discussing catnip. Hi, Peggy." Caitlin kisses Peggy on each cheek the way that Daniel kisses me. She's known Peg since the day she was born. Abby says Peggy reminds her of beatniks she's seen in old movies. Or Audrey Hepburn in *Breakfast at Tiffany's*. She says Peggy's kooky. Madcap. Something anachronistic, I think she means. Cait says Peggy brings out the weirdo in me. She says when I'm with Peggy, I am sincerely embarrassing. "Peggy's disciple," she once said. I resented that. I certainly have never thought of myself as letting Peggy lead me anywhere.

"Anyway," Peggy says, "maybe you and Hank aren't such a good match. I mean, he's already made you crazy. And it's been clear from the start that you'd rather design his house than go out with him."

"I didn't tell you that."

"Well, you've certainly implied it."

"Look. I admit I have mixed feelings about him. I don't want to be attracted to him. I just can't help it. And now that I want him . . ."

Peggy rolls her eyes. "He's a tease. Always has been. A flirt. His first wife left him because he cheated on her. And he cheated on Anne too, I hear."

"So what the hell were you doing setting me up with him in the first place, Peg? Some friend you are." I want to say, After all you know I went through with Daniel, how could you expose me to more of the same? But of course, I can't say that in front of Caitlin. In fact, I'm a little annoyed with Peggy talking about Hank at all in front of her.

"I thought it would get you out of your doldrums," Peggy says. She grabs a small chunk of the Parmesan and eats it.

"I am not in the doldrums."

"Mom was born in the doldrums," Cait says, setting the table.

"But I probably made a bad choice choosing him for you. It's just that he's single now. And he's so damn cute. He is cute, isn't he?"

"You won't hear me arguing . . ."

"I'll look for someone else for you."

"I didn't pay my matchmaking fee. Don't bother."

"Got enough for an extra for dinner? I hate eating alone."

I nod. "Sure," I say. I feel bad that I didn't ask her myself.

"Oh good. What are we having besides . . . what is that green stuff, anyway?"

"Arugula," Cait says.

"Is it edible?" Peggy asks.

"We're having arugula?" Abby says, coming down the steps. "Oh, man! Great!"

"What are you guys, rabbits?" Peggy says. "Give me a steak and potatoes any old day."

Today, I call Barney and am happy and relieved to discover that Aunt Aggie is finally scheduled to come home.

"She's looking pretty good, considering," he says. "She's thrilled to be getting out of there. You know Aggie. She doesn't like to be reliant on anyone."

"Can you take care of her okay by yourself?" I ask.

"I think so. She's just weak," he says. "She's actually lost a lot of weight in the last few months. You know, before the operation."

"Has she?" How out of touch with her I feel. When I think of her, I still see her face as it was when I was a child. Lately, every time we get together, I'm stunned by how age has changed her face, how tiny she's become.

"She's so light these days, it's not hard to help her get around," he says.

"I want to come down there soon," I say. "Spend some time with you guys. Maybe I'll bring the girls. They miss you."

"When she's settled and starting to get her strength back," Barney says. "Otherwise, she'll just be frustrated that she can't do things with you. Or she'll try to do things before she's ready."

"We'll wait."

"I don't care what the doctor says," Barney declares. "I think she's going to get better. She's got the right attitude. She's got me."

"That's right," I tell him. "You hear stories all the time of people told they have a few months to live, who live for years and years, or people whose cases are declared hopeless, then go into remission a month later." Have I said this to him before? No doubt I have. And how many other people have told him and told him. Still, I want to believe it too. And the light, joyful sound of Barney's voice makes me think it's possible.

"Thanks. Look, Janie, I'd better go," he says. "I want to get flowers for the kitchen table. Irises, even though they're out of season. She loves them. And I promised her I'd fix the toilet in the powder room. It's been running for a month."

"I wonder which gesture she'll appreciate more," I say.

"The toilet," Barney says. "I found out long ago that nice extras get you points, but doing your daily 'job' gets you love." He laughs. He sounds young again. I feel happy when we say good-bye. "Okay," I say out loud. "Okay. She's going to be all right. If anyone can do it, Aggie can."

I don't hear from Hank until Tuesday. He wonders when he should expect to see the first sketches of my design, and whether I need to go out to the property again.

"Look," he says, "you're free to go by yourself."

"Well, thank you."

"Here. Take down the directions just in case you feel like you need to go." I hear in his voice a disturbing distance.

"I don't know if I really need to go out again until I've got some ideas on paper," I tell him. "Details rely on the landscape more than the overall design does."

"Well, I just wanted to be a good client," he says. He is businesslike. Chilly.

"So, how are you?" I ask, lamely. I want our conversation to become personal and I can't think of a single way to do it gracefully. I hate what Peggy said about his being an unreliable cheat, but hearing his voice reminds me of his kiss. Of the way my heart started beating, and my head starting swimming when he held me in his arms.

"Oh, fine. Very busy. We're planning an opening for next Friday night. An important opening of an artist from Kosovo. It's extraordinary that we've been able to get the art here intact. You wouldn't believe the madness we've gone through trying to ship the work here. And the artist himself was, of course, scheduled to be here by Friday, but now he tells us he's afraid to leave Kosovo. For personal reasons. I guess there are still a lot of tensions there and he's concerned about his family. He feels that he needs to stay and protect them. We've just been stymied at every turn. Jesus. Sometimes it makes you say, 'God Bless America,' you know?"

"Yes."

"He's extraordinary as an artist, but of course, even more extraordinary because of the difficulties he's faced. He's made his own pigments from all sorts of things—plants, dirt, even cow's blood, he tells me."

"What's the work like?"

"The work of someone who's experienced war. Brutal sort of

stuff. But just the sort of thing that will get us press, put us on the map. Already, I've got the art columnists champing at the bit to see the stuff. A line outside the door, so to speak."

I never realized before that art galleries, like any other business, could be about politics too. I find it disturbing. But I guess, when I ponder it, what isn't about politics, or selling oneself, or image, or surface? It's an unsettling reality I should be accepting at my age. Still, it curdles that small bit of innocence I carry around like Zuzu's petals, in my pocket. That hope that things will turn out all right.

"Well, I've got to run," he says. "Let me know as soon as you're ready to show me anything. Even the most rudimentary sketches. I'm so anxious to see what you have in mind."

"So I won't see you until I've produced the goods, then?" I ask.

"No. Listen. Please drop by Friday. The opening. Seven P.M., 65 Spring Street. But don't expect to meet the artist."

"Oh, thanks, I'll see if I can come."

I'm glad the girls aren't here. I sit in my pink chair and stare at the wall. I feel like a jerk for still liking him. Turned on by a meaningless come-on. My seesaw feelings for Hank Marsh are only exceeded by my desire to build him the most incredible house I've ever designed.

Jane,

I took Laine to the hospital and there is something wrong. A hematoma has formed on her brain. There's no telling why, but they've got her in the pediatric ward for now on IV medication. I'm with her almost all the time and I have to admit, I'm really worried, although they say that since we caught it early, they can control it now. It's the randomness of this that frightens me. Laine's teacher thinks she actually may have hit her head on the playground and somehow didn't think she should tell us. Now she says she doesn't remember, although her memory isn't like yours or mine. She sometimes can't tell the difference between yesterday and weeks ago.

Oh, Jane, it's times like these that I'm so angry with Suzanne that she isn't here. I have no one to spell me. No one to care as much as I do. Laine is afraid when I'm not around. I've tried to help her bond with one of the nurses so she feels more sure when I'm not here. The nurse, Claire, is a very soft-spoken, gentle woman and she makes Laine smile. She makes me smile too. I guess that pegs her as the perfect pediatric nurse—she doesn't stop at the children, she makes us all feel better.

I'm writing this, sitting by Laine's side, while she sleeps, but I won't be able to send it until later when I get home. I knew that otherwise I wouldn't be able to write.

I hope that you're still so excited about your project. And that you forgive my earlier impatience.

Love,
Jack

I lie in bed and think about Jack. I think about how easily I was distracted from him. This makes me sad. If we lived in the same city, surely we'd be seeing each other by now. Maybe in love again. It's easy to imagine being in love with Jack. It's easy to imagine rolling over and finding him asleep, peaceful. I remember watching him sleep when we were younger. Even in sleep, he was confident. I remember noting that his lips always settled in a satisfied smile.

But Jack, the confident, above-it-all guy I fell in love with nearly thirty years ago, has changed. He seems so much more able to be vulnerable. I wonder how much I've changed in comparison with him. Have I changed at all? Once he wondered if he could ever feel safe getting close to me, because he thought I was too vulnerable. But you know, the funny thing is, after Daniel hurt me, I think I've become less accessible, less vulnerable. I wonder if I could let anyone in at all. A kiss, yes. Even a short affair. But love? I'm not so sure.

I wake in the night and hear sobbing downstairs. I get out of bed and go to the third-floor hall to listen, to determine who's crying. It's Abby. I knock softly on the door.

"Abby?"

"Go away."

"What's wrong, sweetheart?"

"Are you deaf?" she asks. I take a deep breath. Being the mother of a teenage daughter is akin to being the clown who's dunked at the carnival. *Dunk.* I, nevertheless, walk in.

"Maybe you'd feel better if you told me what's wrong. Is it Benjy?"

"I hate him," Abby says. "I hate Cait. I hate you. I hate everyone."

"What did Benjy do?"

"He fucked Xena Hanson, that's what he did."

"Oh . . ." I sit gingerly down on the edge of her bed. I can't even remotely imagine having ever said something like this to my mother. She would have up and fainted from the language, let alone the content.

"And you know this because . . ."

"Because Xena told Cait. Who, of course, told me."

My instinct is to say, And you trust that Cait is telling you the truth? But this would be disloyal to the other half of my womb's issue. "Have you spoken to him in a while? Since the day he was supposed to come over?" I ask.

"No. And I'm not going to. He's slime. He's dogshit. He's an ass-hole."

"So why are you crying over him?" I ask.

"I don't know." This makes her cry more. In the street-lamp glow I see that her lovely, slender face is swollen and red. Strands of her hair are stuck to her tears. There may be nothing worse in the world than being a teenager, I think.

"Would you like to write him a letter and tell him what a jerk he is? You know, just to get it off your chest. You won't mail it. Just write it. I sometimes find that helpful."

She screws up her mouth in that way only my girls can.

"I'd rather take out a contract on him," she says.

"There you go again, killing people off," I say lightly, but she doesn't smile.

"Write the letter. Then go to sleep."

"I don't have paper," she says.

"Come upstairs. I have some in my printer."

"Why do I want to write him if I'm not going to mail it?" she asks.

"To get it down, so you can let go of it. To have a chance to look at your own anger. It's a healthy thing to do."

"It is?"

I nod.

"Okay," she says. "I may just mail it. I may. He deserves it."

"I wouldn't suggest it. But by all means write it."

She comes to my room and takes the paper.

"Good night, Mommy," she says, then dutifully shuffles off to write her letter. The taming of a teen. So mysterious. I try to go back to sleep, but I find that my head's now spinning. I feel rest-less. So I get up and go into my study. I'll go on-line for a while, I think. Lose myself in antiques on eBay, or books on Amazon. I'm surprised when I discover I have mail. Even more surprised when I see the letter's from Jack. Jack's mail has been sporadic since

Laine's been in the hospital, so I'm thrilled that there's a new letter from him. But I don't feel quite so happy when I read it.

Dear Jane,

Laine is doing well, the doctor says. I'm not sure how much longer they want to hold her. The really upsetting thing is that they keep asking her questions, as though she might have been abused. And of course, the suspicion is certainly cast on me. She told me that one of the doctors asked her if her daddy hits her. Or hurts her. You can't imagine how awful this feels. I'd lie down in the road for her, I swear. And there's all that guilt I've felt all those years from not monitoring Suzanne and her drugs. I live with that every day. And then to be accused. It hurts.

The boys are missing my presence at home, and though I'm doing as much work as I can here at the hospital, my office is certainly feeling my absence. I feel torn and tired. My back aches from hours in this straight chair.

Last night, after Laine was asleep, Claire came in to check on her. I told her I wanted to go out with her. She said she's been hoping I'd ask her. She was very sweet. She even blushed. I kissed her, Jane. It was pretty exciting after all this time to touch someone. If you hadn't suggested it, maybe I wouldn't have done it. She smelled so good. Her lips were soft. I mean, I feel like I've really opened up my heart to you in these last few months of letters. All my fantasies have been about touching you. But maybe you're right. Maybe our lives are too far apart, and will never come together. What was it the old song said? "Love the one you're with."

I wake up Friday morning in a perfect rage. The girls have fortunately already left for school. I'm all alone with a lethal feeling. I have the urge to break something, or throw something against the wall. But any bad behavior that I might inflict would be inflicted on myself, since I'm the one who has to clean it up. Instead, I just lie on the bed and kick my feet like a baby. Wildly. About ten minutes of this and I'm exhausted. My heels ache. And I feel rather stupid. Of course I'm upset about Jack kissing the nurse instead of me. Furious. I feel betrayed. How could he? Why would he? Ah, but after the anger passes, I'm just sad. Because I was the one who told him to. Sad because he's so far away. Sure, there are benefits to technology like E-mail. Without it, I would never have discovered what happened to Jack. Never again have heard his thoughts, been able to tell him what he meant to me, enjoyed his lovely letters. But as small as the world's become, it's not yet small enough to throw my molecules in his direction and allow me to reconstruct myself at his front door.

Lying in bed, exhausted, achy, miserable, I decide that I'm going to swear off men altogether. I don't need Jack. I don't need Hank. I was happy before them. Fine. Relaxed. Life was predictable. My biggest concerns were about my girls and my job. Bills and baths. Pains and pleasures. I could deal. It was fine. That's the way it's going to be again, I tell myself.

Still, come Friday afternoon, after a day spent shuffling and tweaking the rooms of Hank's house-to-be, I can't help wrestling with the temptation to get dressed and take the train into Manhattan for Hank's opening. I just want to tell him the design is going well, and share some of the ideas I've had for his house. Of course I know he'll be busy schmoozing rich Park Avenue matrons or stroking the press. Especially since the artist himself won't be there, he'll have to make himself the center of attention. I realize I'll probably be ignored or end up lingering awkwardly with a glass of bad white wine in front of paintings that appall me.

Still, come six P.M., the girls announce that they're spending the night at two different friends', and left alone, I find myself pulling out a black dress that slenderizes, and a shade of red lipstick I save for special occasions when I want to look far more exotic than Jane Larsen from Chicago. I don't want to arrive too early. I know that would look foolish. Yet I don't want to miss the most social part of the night. I take one last look in the mirror. "I yam what I yam," I say, not in the least appeased.

I don't know about you, but parties like this generally make me feel as inadequate as cheerleading tryouts did in high school. Why does this metaphor seem to encompass all that our generation remembers about failed popularity? There are very few of us, I suspect, who don't have it written on our desperate souls. I can't help always being certain that in a new social situation the room will be packed with people far hipper, sexier, better connected, thinner, and more attractive than I can ever be. I imagine rooms full of people with dyed black hair and clunky shoes, clones of the kids who worked at Paris, Washburn, and Green. Flat bellies and wrist-thin hips wearing size-two dresses that hang on them. Meanwhile, as I walk from the Broadway-Lafayette station, my stockings bind my middle-aged thighs and my feet hurt in the hippest clunky shoes I could find in my closet. I can compete in the housekeeping, decorating, quiche-making world. But at a gallery opening, I feel like Cait and Abby's mom, June Cleaver.

Still, when I walk into the Marsh Gallery, I try to be brave and smile like someone's just told me the most unforgettable joke. The room is darker than I expected, and filled with cheerful, glass-clinking people. Somehow, I had imagined the room would be blazing with harsh light, that there'd be nothing but white walls, huge, frightening paintings, and cold people far more worthy of living than I. Instead, the ambient lighting is soft and soothing and halo-gen pinpoints pick out the paintings like jewels on the manila walls. The paintings are small, none of them bigger than two by three feet, and many much smaller. And they are not ugly, or even brutal, really. At least, not nearly as bad as I'd come to imagine from Hank's description. I see instantly that they are sad and deep and affect-ing. Like love letters to a dead person. I can see in each painting a homesickness for what was. The horrible beauty of broken, no longer attainable things. A little girl casts a green shadow as she stares at the chaos of what was once a simple farmyard. A man stands over a dead, sprawled, broken-necked woman with his palms facing heavenward. Each of the paintings shows the sense-less ruin of war. Houses melted and broken like cardboard cartons left in the rain. Images of fire. People in shock. I am so drawn into the paintings, for a moment I forget all about the opening, the hoopla, the crowd, and stare and feel. The colors are faded, like the colors of cereal boxes left for too many months in a sunny store window. Pale robin's-egg blue and magenta and cream. Softened browns and grays. And the faces. The faces of despair. There are so many paintings they cover the walls from top to bottom. Hundreds and hundreds. How did this man manage to be so prolific in the midst of war?

"I wondered if you'd come." I look around, and Hank is standing at my side. I didn't know if he'd even greet me. He is dressed beau-tifully in a silk tweed jacket and gray flannel pants. His eyes are as blue as the robin's-egg tint in the art.

"These are really wonderful," I say. "I didn't think from your de-scription . . ."

"I wasn't sure you'd like them. I'm not sure the crowd does, though a few of the critics have already looked very interested in-deed. One guy even called them extraordinary. They're not pretty, though, you know. I don't expect to sell many, really. But, like I said, the press is fine. I really brought them here because when I saw two of them in Paris, I was so moved."

"I thought you brought them here for the press alone."

"The gallery has my name on it. I don't do things just for publicity. Of course, I want publicity if I can get it. How else can I make people come here?"

"I guess I misunderstood."

"You look great tonight," he says. I can't help feeling flattered, though I have a feeling he has spent the evening saying this to everybody.

"You too," I say.

"This old thing?" He does a funky, charming pirouette. The room is indeed filled with baby monsters with dyed Goth hair and wooden shoes. A few older, arty-looking men with ponytails, older women with gray hair halfway down their backs. A few matronly women with headbands and cheekbones that could wound. And babes. Real babes. Blondes, brunettes. Far too many in sheath dresses or boatneck tops and Capri pants and flats like Audrey Hepburn. I can't imagine why he is looking at me and not at them.

"Will you let me introduce you to some people?" he asks.

"Yes. If you'd like to. You don't have to feel obligated."

"Damn right I don't." He smiles and takes my elbow. His touch. His dangerous, electric touch. It should be illegal.

"David. Hey. Come over here. You've got to meet someone." Another middle-aged, reddish-haired man walks over. A little paunchy, not particularly handsome, but very kind-faced and appealing.

"This is Jane Larsen," Hank tells him.

"No kidding," the man says. "*The* Jane Larsen?"

"The very one."

"Wow, I didn't know I was so famous," I say coyly.

"I told him about you. He's my closest friend. See, men do talk about women behind their backs, though they don't believe it. They think we just talk about football and 'Did you see those tits?' and 'Wuz new?' 'I dunno. Wuz new wit chew?' "

I laugh. God. He's so cute. And he told his best friend about me. I suddenly feel at least 80 percent more attractive. Isn't it criminal how we rely on men to make us feel good about ourselves? My only hope is that men do the same.

"So you're the architect," David says.

"Yes. I'm really excited about designing Hank's house."

"It's on my property, you know. Well, it's his property now, but it was mine."

"Oh. So you're the one with the beautiful house. Hank said it's incredible inside."

"You'll have to come see it, especially since you're someone who would appreciate it. I love showing it off. I'm ridiculously fond of it." I can see that he is gay, or at least very effeminate. I'm not sure how I feel about Hank having a gay best friend. I guess that means he's comfortable with himself. I mean, it couldn't mean anything else, could it?

"I'd love to see it," I tell him. "I often pay good money to look into historic houses. I'm the first one on any house tour."

"Well, I won't charge."

David goes on to describe the house to me in detail, something I thoroughly enjoy. We talk about houses, about how they have souls, about surprises we have found in each of our homes. I tell him about the tintype I discovered up in the crown moldings of my back parlor. I've often wondered who put it there, this tiny photo of a triangular-faced little girl with big almond eyes like a cat's. She can't be more than seven. Her hair is pulled severely from her brow. Her hands are folded perfectly in her lap. After the housepainter found the photo lying in the trough of the crown molding, I put it in the drawer by my bed, and look at it often. But when I leave my brownstone, surely I'll put it back where it was found. It belongs to the house, not me.

David tells me about a slender gold bangle he found caught deep in the molding along the staircase in his house. He was having the stairs rebuilt and the carpenter pulled away the molding to reset the step. Inside the bangle, he told me, was engraved the sentence, "For Eleanor, so far away." David gets a soft, sad gleam in his eye. "I imagine somehow it was sent on a ship in a brown paper package wrapped in string. I've often wondered how they parted. I've often wondered how she lost it down into the molding, or maybe if she put it there."

I'm having such a fine time I almost don't mind the plain fact that Hank has pawned me off on David. Truthfully, I don't expect Hank to come back at all. And why should he? To hang out with his architect? But suddenly I see him weaving through a tangle of people toward us, and I find, against my will, that my heart is pounding somewhat louder than I wish it would.

"This crowd is great. I'm so happy we've been such a draw tonight. Did you see the letter I posted on the wall over there from the artist about his not being able to come? The English is outrageously bad, but the letter is wonderful nonetheless. It talks about his feelings about war. It's wrenching. The rest of the world is so much more serious than we are."

"Maybe because we can afford to take the world lightly," I tell him. "Maybe humor is a privilege."

"Hear, hear," David says. "Let's drink to our good and humorous fortune. You don't have a drink. Shall I get you one?" he asks.

"I haven't done the tour of the room yet," I tell him. "I want to see every painting. I don't know about everyone else, but I'm very bad at juggling wine and having deep thoughts simultaneously."

"Will you let me walk around with you?" Hank says. "Point out some of my favorites? Or would you find that intrusive?"

"I'd love it. It would make it more fun for me."

"Well, that's my cue," David says. "I'm going to walk around and find my wife. Have you seen her?" he asks Hank. Hank shrugs. His wife?

David leaves us and Hank leans close to me. "Any chance you'll have dinner with me when things wind down?"

"You want to talk about the house?" I ask dubiously.

"It wasn't the chief topic on my mind. I'd just enjoy the time with you."

"Hank . . ."

"C'mon. You want to. I can tell."

I nod. "Okay. If you behave yourself."

"Clients are so trying, aren't they?" he says to me. "Come on. Take my arm and let me show you around." He holds out his arm gallantly, and I take it. Are people looking at him, wondering why he's hanging out with me? Who's she? they're saying. The old broad with the big hips? But God, I feel like Cinderella at the ball. I love his touch, his commentary. I like to turn and look at him. I think of Jack kissing his lovely Claire and am even more free to lust after Hank. Still, inside me echoes a sort of emptiness, an uncertainty I can't shake.

Stop stop stop and enjoy it, I hiss at myself. Stop right now!

The rest of the opening I spend with Hank. He introduces me to David's wife, Anna, who is Russian, and has perfect teeth and a nose so thin and aquiline it would be envied by thousands of plastic surgery patients. She is very cold, distant even from David. She gazes at the paintings with a look that's as despairing as the people depicted inside the frames. Despite my earlier assessment that he's gay—and he may well be—he clearly is mad for her. He follows her around, adjusts her shawl around her shoulders. Kisses her cheek.

Calls her "sweet one." She ignores him imperiously. She seems to refuse to acknowledge he's there. It's rather heartbreaking to watch. But so curious.

"How did the two of you meet?" I ask him when Anna has gone off to the ladies' room, her head held as high as an eighteenth-century portrait sitter.

"Well, Hank thinks it's mortifying, but I met her through an on-line catalog of Russian women who want to marry. You have no idea how beautiful the women are there. It's mind numbing. And how many are desperate to marry a man who isn't in the midst of a love affair with vodka. I wrote a number of women for quite a few months. Anna wrote back the most often. Her English was excellent. She had things to say for herself. She was a hotel clerk, even though she had a college degree. You see, there were no jobs there. Her dream was to go to graduate school to study law. She said the concept of right and wrong intrigued her. I loved that. Nobody thinks about right and wrong anymore. They think about 'Does it feel good?' 'Is it what I want?' And here was a woman who wanted to study right and wrong. She was the front-runner from the start."

"But why did you do it?" I ask him. "Go so far away to find someone?"

He moves closer to me and takes hold of my wrist. "Look at me," he whispers. "Do I look like a man who could attract a woman like that? In America, a woman that beautiful wouldn't look twice at me."

I shake my head. Why does a man want a woman that beautiful anyway? It offends me. Maybe because I don't have the power of beauty anymore. I wonder if there's a chance in hell that the marriage will last.

"Well, I think you undersell yourself," I tell him. "You no doubt have a lot to offer. Hank said you were just in Europe. You have that lovely house . . . And you're not bad-looking. You're very appealing."

"Thank you. You're just being kind." And then he turns and looks at me squarely. His eyes look rather desperate. "Sometimes it's as if she sees right through me. Sometimes I think I was better off alone," he whispers.

My mouth fills with saliva, as though I'm going to cry. I don't know why.

"Hey," I say. Not another word comes out. I squeeze his shoulder. "You deserve good things," I say a good three minutes later. I can tell that he doesn't believe it for a second. He looks down. Shakes his head. Then looks up again, brightly.

"Hank likes you a lot," David says. "He'd kill me for telling you. I like you too, Jane."

"There are probably thousands of women just like me who would be attracted to you, right here in New York. Don't you know the odds favor men here?" Of course, I wonder if I would ever be drawn to him myself. He's certainly not my type. But like I said, he's appealing. I wonder randomly, given his effeminate nature, if he even sleeps with Anna.

"If it comes to that, if Anna and I don't make it, will you introduce me to a few?" he says

"Absolutely." I go to pull a business card out of my purse, and then look over at Anna. She's back and glaring at me. "My property," her eyes say. Well, maybe it will make her treat her property better. I scratch out the office number and write my home phone number on the front of the card.

"God," David says. "It's so nice actually talking to someone."

Hank takes me to a small restaurant in Noho. It's owned by Australians and has a twenty-foot-long hollowed-out bamboo cane in which a running river flows across the room. I am ravenous by the time we arrive. It's nine-forty-five and I normally eat at seven. I should have eaten the hors d'oeuvres at the opening, fabulous little canapés that were being dispensed on doily-bedecked trays. But I didn't want Hank to see me stuffing my face. Besides, as I said, I'm lousy at juggling food, drink, and art. I'm really longing for something filling. Steak au poivre with mashed garlic potatoes, for instance. But I don't want to eat garlic if I'm going to be near him. Fish seems more ladylike and acceptable. "With seasonal vegetables," sounds virtuous. And what does he order? Steak au poivre with garlic mashed potatoes. Life stinks.

"So, how are the designs going?" he says right off the bat. Even though he denied it, I still wonder, is this why he asked me to dinner—simply to get an update on the state of his house project? Fortunately, I can't wait to tell him about my ideas: a split staircase that descends into two separate rooms. Window seats in every room. Unique ceiling moldings that flow into Doric columns on either side of all the windows. I start to sketch on the napkins to show him, and he seems very pleased.

"This will be a house like no one else's," he says, looking proud.

"That's what I would like to give you," I say.

I look around the room. It is once again filled with the young and the hip. Women with arms toned enough to show them off, with lipstick dark enough to appear black in the low light. How happy they look to me, easy with themselves, white teeth showing often between their black lips. When I was young and hip, I had no idea that older people were looking at or envying me. I felt awkward and nascent and just hoped that someday I would be settled and happy like they appeared to be. I believed in "happily ever after" back then. I thought by now I'd look something like Barbara Bush and be glad of it. My husband would adore me for my warm, soft familiarity. My children would find comfort in my presence. My house would be a shelter for the lonely, lost, or disenfranchised.

Hank is staring at me.

"What?" I ask.

"I'm just wondering if I can hold out from kissing you tonight."

"Are you going to start again?" I say. "What is wrong with you?"

"I'm attracted to you," he says. "Is that a crime?"

"The way you're going about it, it certainly comes close." I mean it too. I don't know if in all my dating years I've ever met a single other man who runs so hot and cold. It's annoying. And I can't help reading it as his uncertainty about me and my faults.

He surely can see he's upset me. He changes the subject.

"Did you enjoy the show?" he asks me.

"Enormously."

"Me too. I can't remember enjoying an opening so much in years. It wasn't just art. It was commentary. It was life. Death too. And yet . . . I don't know if I can explain this, but it was actually life affirming."

"I agree," I say.

"You do? Good. Why then? I was trying to explain it to myself. 'What makes it life affirming?' I've asked myself. Can you put your finger on it?"

"It was about survival. That's always life affirming. The human spirit goes on amid all the destruction."

He nods. He's pleased.

"Do you like sex?" he asks me.

"Pardon?"

"Do you like sex? I mean, I'm asking because I'm trying very hard to figure out what's wrong with you. It must be something."

I laugh. "I like sex," I say softly. Do I? It's been so long, I really don't know. "Do you?" I ask.

"I could live without it," he says, very dryly.

"What?"

"A joke. That was a joke. Just wanted to make sure you were listening." If he was any closer, I'd punch him.

"You really mess with my head," I say.

"I wish you'd mess with both of mine," he says.

I gasp. "Hank!"

"Good. You got the joke. I was just testing."

"Listen carefully," I say, in my best Mr. Rogers voice. "I . . . am . . . the . . . architect. You . . . are . . . the . . . client. Repeat after me."

"Nope," he says. "It would be redundant. Besides, tonight, we are just friends having dinner. Go ahead. Eat," he says.

I barely eat anything, of course. I really wanted steak au poivre. And I'm too nervous. Too stirred up. I study his face and try to compare it to famous faces I know. He looks like a cross between the father on *Family Ties* and Harrison Ford. No, he looks like a young but gray-haired Alan Alda and that other guy on *M*A*S*H*, Mike Farrell. No, he looks like . . .

He looks like someone I would like to sleep with. Tonight. Immediately. Now. Why do I let him have this effect on me?

I insist we split the bill. He says if I'm so interested in paying, he'll let me pay next time. He puts his arm around me when we walk out of the restaurant. I like the way he smells, like cinnamon and citrus. I like the smooth hardness of his back as I put my arm around him too. I think, He's everything I've wanted. All rolled into one. Right down the very center of me is a charge as hot and extreme as lightning.

In the cab, we begin to kiss. His kisses are even hungrier than the other night. He awakens a longing in me that actually hurts; it's been neglected for years. It is a wild, long-denied coil. It stretches. It breathes. It becomes tangled in all my feelings.

"Oh, Jane. Oh God," he whispers. He presses himself against me. Here is a man who never needs to take Viagra, I think. Or already did when I went to the ladies' room.

He pays for the taxi and I walk ahead to my door. Tonight, we will set this straight, I think. Tonight, I will break this miserable streak of aloneness. I unlock the gate and the door, but when I turn, he's still standing outside.

"Aren't you coming in?" I ask.

"No," he says.

"*No?*"

"I can't do it," he says.

"You *what?*" I see the cab is still waiting for him.

"I can't do it. It's not right. I shouldn't have started it."

"You don't mean that," I say.

"Well, I'm trying to mean it," he says. He sounds like a little boy.

"Come on in." I hold out my hand to him. How did I get into the position of the seductress?

"I shouldn't."

"Of course you shouldn't. Come on anyway."

He waves the cab away, reluctantly, I can tell, and steps in. Then, of course, I don't have a clue as to what to do. If I were practiced at this, I'd take his hand and walk him right upstairs, light a candle, and change into my best nightgown. Or I'd never turn the lights on in the house at all and would make love to him in the hall. Right there by the door. Two bodies burning up right here on the hard-wood. There'd be a sweet wild silent understanding. My breasts, his chest, his hands. The rich, cool dark. We'd never forget it. The power of this postponed longing.

But damn it, I'm rusty. I haven't been romantic or sexual in so long, I can't remember how. With Dan, I'd put my hand somewhere in the vicinity of his crotch, and nine times out of ten he'd roll away. So maybe I've never had the drill down.

And to top off the confusion, there's the old angel/devil thing. On my left shoulder, I've got me in a choir robe wearing a halo whispering, "Is this meaningful, Jane Larsen? Really, dear, is it? Is this a valuable use of your time and commitment? Or could you be

working in a soup kitchen right now? And of course there's Jack."
On the other shoulder sits me wearing a glowing set of horns, red
teddy with black lace, garters, and thigh-high stockings. "You
waaaaaaant him. You neeeeeeed him. You're human. You're hungry.
And don't, for one second, think he doesn't want to do dirty things
to you. Go! Go for it, kid."

But, of course, wavering, I don't go for it. I don't take him upstairs. I don't strip him naked in the hall. I turn on the light and
hang up our coats. I lead him into the back parlor and sit him down
on the sofa.

"Can I get you something to drink?" I ask, ever the polite sixteen-
year-old bringing her date into the parlor after the dance.

"Scotch?"

"Sure. I even have single malt. Do you want single malt?"

He laughs at me. "I don't know what I want, Jane. I'm sitting
here all perplexed." I look into his eyes. I should go get the scotch,
I suppose. But I just don't know how to do this.

"Why are you perplexed?" I ask. I sit down next to him.

"Because I . . . don't just want to go to bed. And I don't want you
seducing me."

"You don't?" I say, mortified. Really mortified. He doesn't want
me. How have I misread him?

"No. I said that all wrong. I'm desperate to sleep with you. You
can tell. You have to be able to tell. But . . . oh . . . Jesus . . . It's all
my fault." He blushes so red, I don't think I've seen that shade
since sixth grade.

"What?" I coax.

"It's not you. It's me."

"Okay," I say. I have no idea what he's talking about. Fear? Im-
potence? Venereal disease?

"You were all ready at the picnic."

"Yeah. That was before I . . ."

"Before you . . . ?"

"I've got to go," he says, something resembling panic in his voice. He stands up. His rejection stings and inflames me at the same time. I want him and I want to hit him.

"Are you going to explain *anything* before you go? 'Cause, three strikes and you're out," I say. "I mean, really."

"I know. I know. I've been awful to you. And it kills me too."

"I'm not seeing it kill you," I say. "I'm seeing you flee into the forest."

He presses his lips together. Takes out a handkerchief and wipes his mouth. What's he wiping off? My kisses?

"Look. Look, Jane. Give me a little time to sort out some personal things. It has nothing to do with anything you've done, or with you at all. It's something I've done."

"You've ordered a Russian bride?"

He laughs. "No. Only David would do that. Isn't she arctic?"

"Yes. The perfect word for her," I say. " 'Arctic.' "

He takes my hand. "Please understand. I'm very attracted to you. I enjoy you. It's just . . ." He pinches the bridge of his nose. "I'm involved in a relationship—I'm mistakenly involved in another relationship."

"*Oh*. Oh, I see. Mistakenly?"

"I shouldn't have started it. It's something I have to end. Quickly."

"I see."

The disappointment tastes like bitter almonds. I sit back on the sofa and find myself crossing my arms. My door is closed. *Slam.* The lock is clicked closed. The key is swallowed. No visitors allowed. When did it begin? Before the picnic?

"No. You can't see. You can't imagine . . . it's more complicated than you know. If you knew . . ."

"So, are you going to tell me?"

"No. I can't tell you."

"Hmmm. That doesn't leave us with much to talk about. Okay," I tell him, "let me get that scotch for you. Ice?"

"Yes, sure." I head down to the kitchen, where at least without him nearby, I can clear my head. Of course, the good news is that I'm thinking, Aha! The problem isn't that he doesn't like me. Thank God! It's something else! But then of course it sinks in that it's some*one* else. And I don't know how I feel about that. I don't feel jealous, exactly. What I feel is curious. Detached. I'm reading a book about a character with a secret that he is not prepared to reveal. The fact is, I hardly know this man. The fact is, I can take him or leave him. The fact is, if he walked out this door today, in five years I might have a hard time remembering that I was *ever* attracted to him. What I *would* remember was that I built him a beautiful house, and if you were visiting me, I'd have you sit on my sofa and I'd pull out my book of houses and show it to you and say, "I built this one in Dutchess County on the most beautiful tract of land. It has a sleeping porch with a fireplace, just like the owner had as a child." And I'd show you the picture of the river stone I'd chosen for the fireplace, and the casement windows opened to the breeze above a monastic line of single beds tightly swaddled in Beacon blankets. And for a brief moment, I'd remember Hank Marsh, and his cousin Lonnie who wet the bed, but inherited the "cottage," and I would wonder, Gee. Whatever happened to him?

When I come back upstairs, he is my client again, and I am happy to have him be just that. It stuns me how close I came to giving such a vital piece of myself to a complete stranger.

He sips his scotch. "I'm trying to think about how to explain all this to you . . . but I just don't think I can right now."

"No. Don't," I tell him. "You don't need to. I was just beginning to believe that you'd been reading a book called *The Rules for Men*. I'm glad you weren't saving yourself just to tease me."

He laughs. "There are no rules at our age," he says. "Are there?"

"Human decency, I guess," I say.

"Ah, if only that were so clear-cut," he says.

I wake in the night and I'm so hungry, I could eat a freight train. I get up in the dark and go downstairs. I realize how big a brownstone can feel when it's got only one person in it. I turn the light on in the kitchen and see myself in the kitchen window. Hollow-eyed. Wild-haired. Alone. And so hungry.

I start with some beautiful red cherries I bought the other day at the farmers' market. There's real poetry in the way they look in the colander as I wash them, as the water runs blue over their shiny heart-shaped rose perfection. I must eat ten of the cherries, standing right at the kitchen sink, yanking the stems away as I bite, spitting the pits into the garbage. They are as fleshy as peaches and twice as sweet. But they're cherries. Fruit. Virtuous food. I don't feel so bad.

Ah, but I open the refrigerator now and come upon the roast beef we had two nights ago for dinner—why, for a moment, did I think the girls might eat it? Iron, I told myself at the market. They need iron. Maybe I needed iron. There's enough left for two whole meals. I eat at least one of those meals right at the sink, cutting slivers off the carcass with a sharp knife and putting them right into my mouth. Sliver after rich sliver. Half pound after quarter pound. Ah, but it's not enough. I then yank out leftover rice pilaf, and eat it with a spoon, right out of the container. The butter it was made with has congealed in the refrigerator. It sticks to the roof of my mouth, but that doesn't stop me. I eat more. And more yet. And then, I top off the whole nauseating feast with yet another slice of roast beef, and one of the Dove ice cream bars I bought for the girls. I could go on. And on.

At this point, however, I teeter annoyingly between my longing to eat more and my need to throw up. I go into the powder room off the kitchen and sit on the cold blue-and-white tile floor. I sit there for so long, the tiny squares bite patterns into my thighs. I debate, should I put my finger down my throat like so many of those young girls with the dyed black hair and clunky shoes do? No. I'm too old. Too conservative. Too intractable. Why is it that the young have all the options?

When I wake the next morning, despite a mega bellyache I don't feel even vaguely fazed about the near miss with Hank. I'm happy, I realize. I'm free. I don't have to reveal my aging body to him. I don't have to expose my heart. I don't have to feel panic when he doesn't call. I don't want any of that. I can't believe that I did even for a moment.

I think that there is actually something amoral about mating when you're too old to have children. Not immoral, of course. No. I'm not trying to be judgmental about this. No one can claim it's wrong. But amoral. There is no meaning to it. It is outside nature's need to procreate. And there are no rules. There is no necessity. It is indulgence and nothing more. It's cruel that nature leaves us with memories and longing. Sometimes more longing than we had when we had babies at our breasts. When our kids are old enough to be set free, to lead lives of their own, suddenly we're the ones who are hungry. We finally have time to notice what's missing. We have more depth in our souls, which calls for companionship.

Yet at this time, look at us. We are flabby, stiff, lined, and tired. Whose joke is this? I just can't make sense of it. You know, when you get down to it, age is a bitter price to pay for maturity.

Dear Jack,

I'm awfully happy that you've found someone you like, although I admit it stings a little, even if it was me who suggested it. Especially when you described your kiss. Still, how can I deny you happiness? God knows, after all you've been through, you certainly deserve it. I hope Claire will grow to appreciate you fully, if she doesn't already. I hope she will love your eyes, as I have. And your hands. And your voice. I hope that she will cherish your inherent goodness. Your Jimmy Stewartness. And your ability to be vulnerable. I hope too that you will hold a tiny place in your heart for me, even if you fall madly in love. I know that's selfish, but there you are. I'm human. And I don't want you to completely forget me.

Jane,

For heaven's sake. I'm not walking down the aisle tomorrow or anything. I just kissed someone else. And at your behest. We'll still write, you and I. I'll still lie in bed and think of you—yes, nearly every damn night you come creeping into my head. I still would give anything to see you. Anything. And there are many nights when eight hundred miles doesn't seem so far away at all.

Eight

$\mathcal{M}$onday morning, I wake to my alarm clock and hardly know where I am. It's been days since I've had to hear its nasty, insistent buzz. But I've got an appointment this morning at Robert D. Stockman's office, thanks to Nancy Kangol, and I want to be very alert and properly dressed for it. My girls are downstairs arguing. I hear them in their bathroom hissing at each other. The sibilance rises like steam, up the staircase. These last two weeks I have slept through their morning ritual most days, and have spent more time with them at night, when they are somewhat kinder to each other. They don't seem to want me around in the morning. They rarely address me. And frankly, I'd much rather stay up late, working on the house plans, and then sleep late in the morning. I sigh as I listen to them now, trying not to hear what they're saying. Sisters have to fight, I guess. Getting between them now would do none of us any good.

I wash my face, apply makeup, hoping it makes me look younger than I am, and dress in a chic little navy suit I bought a few months before the end of my days at Paris, Washburn, and Green. I haven't dressed in anything but floppy T-shirts and pants in days, except for the gallery opening, and I'm surprised that the silk-lined tropic-weight wool pants feel sexy against my legs, the camisole top caresses my shoulders.

Downstairs, the girls are still squabbling but they grow silent as I come into the kitchen.

"Well, look who's here," Abigail says. "Our mother who art not in heaven. Where are you going?"

"I have an interview."

"For a good job or a city-worker job?" Cait asks.

"For a good job which this time doesn't happen to be a city-worker job."

"You look nice," she says.

"You do," says Abby. "Really. Do you want this job?"

"I don't know," I say.

"Will it make us rich?" Cait says.

"Being an architect will never make us rich," I tell her.

"Lola's mother's an investment banker," Cait says. "Just think how rich we'd be if Mom was an investment banker."

"And stressed," I say. "I'd come home and scream at you every night. Everything has a price."

"Oh, you scream at us anyway," Abby says.

"I do not."

"I'm going to be a newscaster." She clears her throat. "Good evening. In tonight's headlines, a headless nun was found still running around in Central Park last night . . ."

"Abby, that's horrible."

"It's a violent world," says Abby.

"I'm going to be a newscaster on the other channel," Cait says. "We have an interview with the teacher who shot all her students at Fairview High, and we have a close-up picture of the headless nun still running. Stay tuned."

"God, you girls are frightening me."

"Toughen up, Mom," Abby says. "The world is a hard place. You gotta toughen up."

Tattoos. Tough girls. At their age, I was drawing sixties psychedelic flowers with the word PEACE emblazoned on them.

It feels odd taking the F train into the city at this hour again, wedged into the rush-hour crowd. It's a funny thing about New York, but you can't get anywhere without being touched by other people. It's not true in other cities. But here, your space is always being violated. I feel a woman's hip against my hip, a man's arm against mine. Half the people are sleeping, the other half standing up. I'm standing, holding on to the bar, wondering how I really feel about this interview. I love Robert D. Stockman's work. He appreciates the inherent beauty of houses and creates exceptional ones. He understands their sacred place in architecture. Most likely at his office, I'd have a chance to use my real skills. But is this what I want? A large office? More politics, more big, noisy bullpen rooms?

I get off at Rockefeller Center and walk the four blocks to Stockman's. His office is in a vanilla marble building with elevators that speak the numbers of the floors as you pass them. The lobby of his suite is cool and simple and adorned with his tasteful wood furniture. I try to imagine coming here every day. No Rodney to deal with. No receptionist with a spike in her ear. Still.

I'm seeing a woman named Ann Lee. She comes out to greet me, and I'm stunned to see she's wearing a suit almost identical to mine. She's an Asian woman. Slender and long-haired. Young, but not too young. She shakes my hand vigorously; her hand is cool and small-boned.

"I've heard good things about you," she says when we meet.

I'm excited to be here. I like her immediately. She has a separate office, small but neat. There are framed drawings of furniture on the wall. Antiques, it seems. A Gothic chair with a trefoil carved in the back. A heavy, simple table in the same idiom. Ann isn't an architect, she explains, "merely an office director," she says. But she asks to see my house portfolio and seems excited about it. "These are wonderful," she says. And then she talks about Rodney Paris. I don't know where she met him, but she hasn't enough bad things to say about him. "How do people stand him there?" she asks me.

"He's awful, isn't he?" I say.

She laughs. "He gives architecture a bad name." She then goes on to tell me about Stockman's, a little bit about the people I'd be working with. She talks about Bob Stockman as though he's her favorite person there, a treat to have around. A genius, she says. "Of course, a good deal of the time he's at Yale," she says. "And we miss him." I find this stunning and heartening.

Yet, when she walks me around, I see that just as I suspected, everyone works in a big studio room, just like at Paris. Noisy. Crowded. Maybe more energetic than at Paris. Better lit. Still . . .

Ann introduces me to two of the senior architects—Joe Sherman, a kind older man with a beard, and a woman named Sally Hans. I like them both. I try to imagine being here, having a corner of my own: "Good morning, Sally. Good morning, Joe. How was the concert last night?" I just don't know . . .

When I leave, I nevertheless feel encouraged. There are two more people they want me to meet another day. Ann says she'll call to set it up at their convenience. I can't help feeling hopeful that I have a good chance of getting the job. I hadn't expected that it would be like this. I thought all my interviews would be more like the one at Kohn Pederson Fox. That I would feel too old wherever I went. It's nice to know that some people see experience in a good light, that just because you've been around, it doesn't mean you shouldn't be around much longer.

Dearest Jane,

Laine is home and feeling just fine, though they want her to take it easy for two weeks. It's difficult making her understand why. She is a little girl full of bustle. She likes to do things. And even though I often don't understand exactly what she's doing, she's as focused as you or I are at our favorite tasks.

The boys are happy to have us both back with them. Well, Ned is, anyway. I think Clark is in love. He keeps getting phone calls from a girl with a Marilyn Monroe voice and he takes the cordless phone in his room and shuts the door and doesn't come out for hours. He's hardly said a word to me since I've been back. But when I look at him, I see there's this color in his skin, this glow in his eyes. Oh boy. I envy him. I try to remember when the last time was that I felt like that.

Ned sat on my bed last night and said, "Dad, you mind if I stay here for a while and talk?" Then he said, "You would never leave us, would you?" "Good Lord, no," I told him. "Whatever made you ask?" He didn't talk for a long time. "Well," he finally said, "Mom left, and I thought she'd never leave, either." And then he started to cry. It's been a long time since I've heard him cry. I guess it was all that worry that got pent up while Laine was in the hospital, and I was away tending to her. Do you remember when your kids were babies and they'd be just fine with a baby-sitter, but the minute you got home they'd cry and act out because they felt safe at last? Well,

I guess that's what Ned was doing in a slightly more mature way. It just broke my heart.

And once he'd gone off to bed, I lay in bed and felt the oddest mixture of triumphant relief (having Laine safely home) and real loneliness. I'm looking forward to my date with Claire, as much for the companionship as anything. I realized how many, many years it's been since I've had anyone to really talk to. And I thought of you. And how I love following the story of your life in your letters. I thought about how warm I feel toward you. And how I never want anything to hurt you, ever. So please don't let my going out with Claire hurt you. You will always be my special one.

Dear Jack,

I've had a perfectly lovely interview at Robert D. Stockman's this morning. I think I really have a chance of being hired. It's rather exciting. I admit, I never expected they'd be interested in me. I have to go back and meet more people there before anything would become official, of course. And I don't like counting chickens before hatching season. Still. It gets the blood going.

Oh, and don't mind me on this whole Claire thing. I've been in a maudlin mood lately. I hope you have a great time with Claire tonight. I hope you see stars.

Love,
Jane

Dear Jane,

As I recall, in cartoons, seeing stars often refers to being rather painfully knocked unconscious. Perhaps you are trying to tell me something subconsciously? I want you to examine your heart carefully for kinks!

It's great that you had a good interview at Robert D. Stockman's. God knows, I've admired him for years. He was the one who really made neo-classicism happen. I always wondered if he and I met, if he'd feel like a kindred spirit. But is a job at Stockman's what you want right now? I thought you were interested in going out on your own, exclusively designing houses. If fear is keeping you from pursuing a dream that matters to you, don't let it.

Oh, I know. I haven't done much of a job over-coming fear myself. (I should have left Suzanne long before I did. I should have confronted her about her drugs. I should have moved from this house of bad memories. Maybe I should even have left Nashville.) So, I suppose that my word is hardly law here, but it just seems that things have fallen into place so perfectly for you to finally do what really matters to you. I remem-ber that day in Iowa when I showed you that beautiful Greek Revival. Your eyes lit up and I knew you'd fallen in love with it, with archi-tecture, with houses. The way you describe the houses you've designed is magical. You deserve a career that brings you that kind of joy, every day, Jane. Perhaps because I don't really have it, it makes me want that much more for you to find it.

I lie awake all night. I toss. I turn. I try not to think about Jack making love to Claire. He wouldn't, would he? If he really liked and respected her, he wouldn't. Not on a first date. He'd get to know her. He'd ask her a thousand questions. They'd laugh together. If she didn't really matter to him, maybe he would sleep with her. If he liked her, he wouldn't. The irony is so sharp it makes me laugh.

I finally get up and sit in my pink chair in the study, in the dark. I am nearly forty-seven years old. And it's been fine all these years being alone, after Daniel moved out. Funny how the prospect of re-turning to my aloneness, now that Hank has acted so weirdly, now that Jack might well fall in love, feels bitter after all. Have I been lying to myself that I've enjoyed being alone? Or was I just shutting off a part of myself? Not fully living. Even Gloria Steinem's gotten married. Should I rethink my position?

Hank calls me. "Will you see me?" he asks.

"I'm probably going to have something to show you in a week. I'll call you when I do," I tell him.

"It's not to see plans for the house," he says.

"No?"

"It's personal."

"I thought we didn't want to be personal. I thought we finally got it straight."

"I didn't say that. I said there were things I needed to work out. And I think I have . . . Will you give me a chance to explain?"

"Should I?" I ask. I really don't want to see him. I don't want to be exposed to his Ken-doll prettiness, his hot/cold longing, his power to upset me. "I gotta tell you, I'm pretty fed up. I'm definitely over you."

"If we can't clear things up today, I won't try again," he says. "Just give me one chance. I'll explain everything."

The opportunity to sort out the past is the draw here. He'll ex-plain everything? That should be interesting, I tell myself.

"Okay. One chance," I tell him.

We agree to meet in Bryant Park the next day for lunch. He says he'll bring a picnic.

"It won't be like the last picnic, will it?" I ask.

"You mean where I try to seduce you and then I'm furious when you don't respond? No. It won't be like that." He laughs, but I can tell he doesn't think any of this is funny.

> Dearest Jane,
>
> Well, I'm no longer a recluse. I had my date with Claire last night and it was very nice. We had dinner and talked until very late. She's a kind woman. Divorced once. No children, though obviously, as a pediatric nurse, she loves children. She's thirty-five. Young for me, I guess. She wants to have children, she told me. That's what matters to her most.
>
> I tried to remember to do all the things I used to do: open car doors, ask her if the temperature was right in the car, drop her off in front of the restaurant while I parked. But I had to relearn it all. Like a stroke victim who has to learn how to walk all over again.
>
> It was very nice. Really. But, Jane, you're the one I want to see. You're the one I want to open a car door for. You're the one I want to kiss good night. You're the one I've come to trust. Maybe we're eight hundred miles apart. But you might be surprised to learn that there are airlines that can breach the gap. Should we stop being cowards?

I sit on one of the little movable French park chairs that fill Bryant Park. They're very pretty but uncomfortable as hell for anyone over 110 pounds (no doubt, the top of the weight chart in France). I wedge myself into it. And feel sorry for anyone who has to see me from behind. Still, I enjoy the autumn flowers, the chrysanthemums and asters and the last of the zinnias, and the breeze, which is a rarity in Manhattan. But most of all, I enjoy the fact that when my lunch with Hank is over, I don't have to go back to a miserable communal office. This morning, I got a call from the lady at Stockman's office. She wanted to set up my meeting with another tier of people. I agreed to go in next Wednesday. I look forward to going there again. Maybe I'll get the chance to meet Robert D. Stockman himself. But I wonder if Jack is right. Maybe I don't want another job like Paris, Washburn, and Green. Maybe now is the time to be brave. Can I be?

The trees are already beginning to turn—the London plane trees first with their floppy, maplelike leaves. Tonight they say will be the first frost. And then all the leaves will change and fall. I see Hank across the park, clutching a white bag, looking for me. We promised we'd meet at the northeast corner, near the restaurant. But he's peering all around as though he's forgotten our plan. Even across the park, he looks striking in his tweed jacket and jeans. If I saw him and didn't know him, I'd be tempted to stare for a moment and wish I did. I've tried ever since we spoke to guess what he's going to reveal today, and frankly, I can't imagine. In fact, part of me isn't even interested. I keep thinking about Jack's letter. He went out with Claire, but he wished it was me.

I wave my arms, trying to capture Hank's attention, but maybe I'm invisible. I should get up and go tell him where I am, and if I wasn't wedged so solidly in this horrible chair, I might. Fortunately, he finally spots me, and crosses the park smiling, holding up the Balducci's bag like a peace offering.

"God, I'm sorry. I couldn't remember where we said we'd meet," he says. "But I've got lunch."

"It's okay."

"I think my memory's shot, you know? You pass fifty and it just goes to hell. I don't have a blanket. But the grass is decent here."

I nod and finally squirm my way out of the evil pincer chair. We find a spot on the grass and sit down. As he spreads out his small feast, I can't help but feel I'm caught in some strange déjà vu.

"How are you?" he asks.

"Fine."

"Lovely day. Love this weather."

"Me too." Okay, I think. I'm ready to hear why we're here.

"I'm putting up a new show," he says. "I told you I had a few of the old abstract expressionist artists, or in some cases their families, as clients?"

"Yes."

"Well, everyone's bringing in the work in the next two days. I think it will be a great show. I can already tell."

"Are you going to tell me why I'm here?" I ask, rather rudely, I suppose.

He nods gravely. "I guess I was trying to work up to it," he says. "Okay." He takes a deep breath. He looks rather pale. "Remember I said I was involved in a . . . relationship?"

"Yes." I nod.

"Well, it's over. I ended it."

"Oh," I say. What else can I say? Good? I don't care enough to say good.

"It was Peggy," he says.

"What?"

"I was sleeping with Peggy."

"You . . . How . . . Why . . ." I look at him. A perfectly ordinary, handsome man. A rat. A jerk. A fiend. A bat from hell.

"I know. It wasn't a good thing."

"But she was the one who set us up. Why would she do that?"

"Because we didn't start sleeping together until after she set us up. I think she set us up, and then thought better of it. She's the one who started . . . well . . . she wanted . . . well . . . it doesn't matter, does it?"

I am so stunned, I feel perfectly numb. If a freight train came roaring right through the middle of Bryant Park, I wouldn't be surprised, nor would I move. Peggy? So happy with S.D., she said. And Hank's been sleeping with her? I remember when she was married to Sam, she said that even if he was cheating on her, she could never, ever cheat on her husband. It was immoral, she said. It was wrong. God, middle age stinks. You lose all your idealism and fall back on failing desire.

"It was a terrible mistake from the beginning," he says. "I was just plain weak. I mean, not only is she married, but we're a terrible match, she and I."

"I don't think so," I say.

"You don't?"

"I think you're just the right guy for her. The only guy who ever really made her happy was Sam. You're quite a bit like Sam."

"Do you think so?" he asks, clearly flattered. "Well, it doesn't matter because I broke it off."

"Was she upset?" I ask.

"She was furious. With you," he says.

"With me? She was furious with me?" I can't imagine what I'm going to say to Peggy when I call her. First she tries to set me up with a guy and then she sleeps with him. And now she's furious with me? Everything becomes clear. That night she came over and tried to talk me out of liking Hank. The weird, disjointed phone call when I told her how excited I was about him.

"I wasn't going to tell you it was Peggy. But then I realized it would always be between us, this lie. This unspoken thing. And it wouldn't surprise me if Peggy told you about it . . ."

"So, let me get this straight. Is it fear of living with a lie between us that motivated you, or the thought that Peggy might expose you at an inopportune time?"

He doesn't like my questioning. "It shouldn't have happened. Period," is all he says.

"So why is she furious with me?"

"Because you're single. Because I like you. Because I broke it off with her because of you."

I have nothing to say to him. Nothing. When we went out to dinner after his show, he was already sleeping with Peggy. When he kissed me so hungrily in the cab, was he comparing me to Peggy? Peggy is beautiful. Peggy is still thin. When I invited him in, he was already sleeping with Peggy.

"I picked you," he reiterates, as though he's reading my mind.

"I didn't know it was a contest," I say dryly. "I didn't ask to be picked. I don't want to be *picked*."

"Forgive me, okay? I didn't have to be honest about this," he says. He holds out a sandwich.

"Didn't you?" I ask.

"It's smoked turkey and Brie," he says.

"I don't want it."

"Or you could have this. It's smoked salmon, capers, and chive cream cheese. I get it all the time. It's delicious."

"No," I say. He looks downhearted.

"I was going to bring various things like I took to the picnic up in Dutchess, but I thought this would be easier, sandwiches. Oh, I also brought a three-bean salad." He wrestles around with the bag, looking for it.

"Hank, I don't want your fucking three-bean salad."

"Oh," he says. "I forgot forks, anyway."

I realize as I sit there on the grass in Bryant Park, across from a fifty-something-year-old man, that this is the sort of thing that happened to me when I was in my late teens or twenties. I'd fall for a guy. I'd find out he'd been sleeping with someone else. This isn't something I expected to be experiencing at the ripe old age of forty-six. I want to be June Cleaver, Barbara Bush. I want to be part of a family. I get up. My legs are already asleep, endlessly buzzing like my alarm clock on a too early morning.

"Don't go," he says. "I thought you'd be pleased. I ended things with Peggy for you."

"Look. I'll call you when I've got house plans to show you."

"Jane." He stands up beside me. "Just sit down and have lunch. Let's be grown up about this."

"Grown up?" I say. I wonder what that means. I used to feel grown up when I had small children and responsibilities and was too tired to put my eyeliner on straight in the morning. But I'm a butterfly about to come out of my chrysalis now. My girls are nearly grown. I have no husband to worry about, dress, or love. Does grown up mean sitting down on damp grass to have lunch with a man who's sleeping with my best friend?

"I'll call you when I have your plans drawn," I say. I walk away, trying to look tall and thinner. Feeling giddy and pleased. I was never the sort of woman who walked away before. I like knowing I can be one now.

Dear Jack,

I have thought a good deal about your letter. I've read it so many times, if it were on paper, I would have worn it out. It thrilled me. It scared me. I'm afraid to see you, you know. You remember me when I was at my best. When I was young enough to enjoy removing my clothes in front of another human being. Young enough to be impressed forever by you and the things we shared. Young enough to believe in true and end-less love. Remember me like that. Don't spoil it.

I'm forty-six years old now. I'm imperfect. I'm cynical. And even with my cynicism, it's easier these days to like who I am inside than to like who I am outside. I sometimes think that would be the ultimate thing. The thing I would wish for if a genie popped up from a bottle. To look on the outside how I feel inside. Still young. Still strong and slender. Still lovable. Still a size six.

You see, when you finally saw me, you'd be disappointed that I didn't look eighteen anymore. And I have such a Prince Charming memory of you, how can anyone live up to that?

But, Jack, I just want to be clear: if I could change who I am, if I could feel beautiful again, I'd see you in a minute. You've been the fantasy that got me through everything. Maybe that's why I'm so afraid. I still need that fantasy. I'm afraid to lose it.

It's eleven o'clock at night. The girls are in bed. I finish the last page of a novel, close the book, and sigh. It's been good to lose myself in the story, to forget what I'm feeling. But now that it's over, I'm restless and tired all at once. I need to go to sleep soon anyway since I have that interview at Stockman's again tomorrow. I lean against the headboard. I feel miserable. The incident with Hank has shaken me. Peggy is a quirky person. I've known that for years. But how could she so purposely do something that had the potential to hurt me? And Hank. I can never forgive him for this. I'll create a house for him, and then I'll be done with him for good. I'm ashamed that I wanted him so much, that he stirred up so much feeling in me. I'm ashamed that I was so clueless about what was going on.

And then, of course, there's Jack. If only I had the courage to see him. If only I could feel better about who I am. It's easy to feel romantic about him, to imagine he and I coming together with flaming passion, but only if I substitute the old Jane. The one with the long hair and long hippie dresses and innocence. How thrilling it would be to touch him again. To lie in his arms again. To feel him inside me. To know he loves me. For the first time, really loves me. It's impossible to hold that thought. Impossible.

I turn out the light and try to sleep. I think about my interview tomorrow. I want it to go well. I'd be proud to say I worked at Stockman's, surrounded by his careful, wise furniture. Among people he's hand-chosen. I want to see if I can make the grade, pass the test, see if I stack up at my late age. But is working at Stockman's what I want, ultimately? I ask myself. Does prestige matter to me? Or does fulfillment? What would my life be like if I really had the courage to go out on my own?

These have been good weeks, I think, some of the best weeks I've known. What a sweet realization, that something like being fired could bring a new perspective into my life. That now, a few weeks later, I can see this as time off with pay or a chance to design a house while being cushioned financially, instead of as a horrible insult. Once, I needed to play hooky. That's because my life wasn't filled with my own choices. It was controlled so totally by others. Now the choices dance like sugarplums all around my bed. Maybe when your worst fears are realized, you realize there's less to be afraid of than you thought. Do I want to limit my choices again?

When the phone rings, I assume it's Peggy. I left a message for her, saying merely that we needed to speak. No doubt she knew why I was calling. Or maybe not. Maybe she can't imagine that Hank would tell me. Do I have the energy to talk to her now? I almost don't answer it. And then it occurs to me that it might be Barney. I have to be available for Barney. My heart clenches as I pick up the receiver.

"Hello."

"Jane."

The startlingly deep voice is instantly familiar.

"It's you," I say. "Jack." How astonishing that an ear can recognize a voice in a single word after so many years.

"Can you talk? I tried to figure out when would be a good time to call."

"It's a fine time. I just turned out the light. Jack. My God."

"It's me," he says. "I thought it was time we talked."

"It's amazing to hear your voice." That voice. So deep, so dusky . . . I hear a hint of Tennessee creeping through.

"I tried three J. Larsens before I found you. Woke a few people up, I guess."

"You found me." The immediacy of his voice thrills me in a way I didn't know I could be thrilled anymore.

"Your letters have meant so much to me," he says.

"And yours to me." I realize I'm actually shaking. This is the man who for nearly thirty years has populated my dreams, has haunted me.

"You did a wonderful thing contacting me," he says. "Sometimes when I think about it, it feels as though I was lost and you found me."

The tenderness I feel for him grows with the sound of his voice. Until now, even with his letters, he's been a fantasy I could keep at bay. Now, with his voice in my ear, I know I didn't make him up. I know he's real, and in my life again.

"You said you're reluctant to see me," he says.

"It's not that I don't want to see you. I'd love to see you. It seems almost unimaginable," I say.

"I think it's most imaginable."

"You won't like me, Jack."

"Jane. It's not like I don't know who you are. I like you immensely. More than you know."

"But you don't know who I am now. You can't. Inside and out I've changed. Daniel really hurt me. Just like Suzanne hurt you. I'm not sure I'm much for relationships anymore. And I'm so damn old. And I'm not thin. I'm not thin at all. Maybe we just like the idea of this long-distance romance because it's safe. You must still see me as an eighteen-year-old. It's great to be in love with an eighteen-year-old."

"I have a pretty clear picture of you in my head. And the last thing I want is to be in love with an eighteen-year-old. How boring would that be?" He sighs. I can just imagine him. How he must look now. How he must have changed.

"I guess it sounds like a cliché, but it's who you are inside that makes me want to see you. It's this woman I've remembered all these years all grown up. Look. I'm not expecting perfection. You as you really are. That's all I'm expecting. And it will be enough for me."

Will it? I wonder. Could it be? What will I feel when I see Jack changed? I've rediscovered in his letters a kinder person than I knew before. A more vulnerable one. It's true. I don't care how he looks.

"Let's do it, Jane," he says. "Let's see each other. Think about it. Tell me, what's the worst thing that can happen if we see each other?"

I pause and wonder what's been holding me back. "I guess that my fantasy about you will implode. And that you'll be disappointed in me."

He laughs softly. "So it's better to keep it a fantasy, to miss out on making it real than to risk losing it altogether?" he asks.

"Yes. Then it's always mine."

"And, as your fantasy, you can completely control it?" he says. Yes. That's exactly how I feel.

I am ashamed to say so, but I tell him this.

"I won't be disappointed in you. I haven't trusted any woman in so long. I feel like I can trust you. You can't imagine how much weight that carries for me. I don't care how you look. Just be the best you. And I'll be the best me."

"Do you think?" I ask. Could it really be so easy?

"I think."

"Jack . . ."

"It's up to you, Jane," he says, his voice sounding suddenly weary. "I just want to be with you again. I feel like you've . . . I don't know . . . awakened something in me that was dead for a long time. I'm happy to get up in the morning, for a change. I could sleep with Claire, I suppose. She likes me. I like her. But you, Jane. You're the one who's made me feel sexual for the first time in so long . . . I want you . . . I really want you . . . Do you remember how I used to call you 'little girl'? 'Little girl.' I was such an asshole."

"I liked it. I'd forgotten till now that you did."

"Do you remember making love with me at all?"

I do remember, but only vaguely. "It was so long ago," I say, "and I was so young and inexperienced. But what I remember most, Jack, is lying in bed with you afterward and talking. Like friends. Real friends."

"I'm glad you remember that," he says. "I remember that too. I remember your innocence."

"I've lost that," I say.

"Oh, I'm not so sure that's true."

"No?"

"I imagine there's still uncharted territory," he says.

"Really," I say skeptically.

"Well, for one, I wonder how intimate you've really let yourself be."

"Oh . . ."

"Have you?"

.

"I'm not sure what you mean by 'intimate,'" I say.

"I mean letting yourself be open, be seen as you are, being vulnerable."

I sit silent for a moment, thinking through what he's asked me. I believed I was intimate with Daniel, but he was lying to me from the start. How well could I possibly have known him? How much did I ever reveal to him? And other men meant so little to me all those years after Jack and before Daniel. There was sex, but no real intimacy. That's probably what would have happened had I slept with Hank.

"Maybe you're right," I say.

"Christ, Jane. I want to see you again. I want us to try."

"But we're eight hundred miles apart."

"Who cares? We won't be when we're actually together. Negative distance. That's what we'll have."

"Negative distance." I shiver. We are silent for a moment. I lean back against my pillow and close my eyes. "How would we ever . . . work things out?" I ask. "I mean, if we fell in love again . . ."

"I'm already falling in love again. Or maybe for the first time. I never gave you a real chance before. Give me a chance now. If it's right, we'll find a way."

Something quickens in me. Something that I haven't felt in so long. Even when I kissed Hank, even when I found that hunger for him, it wasn't this. This is much deeper, more precious, closer to pain. More full of pleasure.

"Okay," I say. "How do we do it?"

"Shall I come there?"

"Yes."

"On a weekend when you don't have your girls?"

"Yes."

"Shall I stay with you?" he asks. His voice has never been sweeter or more seductive all at once.

"Yes," I say. "But what will you do with your children?"

"Oh," his voice is full of sunshine. Lighter. "I'll find a way," he says. "Don't worry, I'll find a way. Jane?"

"Yes?"

"It'll be worth it. I promise you." I smile. I hear the old confidence in Jack's voice again. It warms me like brandy.

In the morning, at Stockman's office, I'm taken in to meet Brad McDougall. He's the senior architect under Stockman. He's younger than I thought he'd be. Younger than me, for certain. He has an intense face. Dark, bruised-looking circles beneath his eyes.

"Jane Larsen?" he asks. He looks puzzled.

"I'm here for an interview," I say hesitantly.

"Oh, I know that. It's just . . . I thought maybe we'd met before, but you're not the person I remembered as Jane Larsen."

"Oh." Great start, I think. He probably thought I was some young hot thing he met at an industry party with a similar name. Jane Lawson. Jan Lerman. And now he's face-to-face with me. Ouch. I can read it on his face.

"So, what are you looking for in a job here?" he asks. His question throws me. I had expected to meet him and let him do most of the talking. I haven't done that many interviews in my lifetime, but I know that letting the interviewer do most of the talking is the surest way into his heart.

"I'm looking for a job where I can use my best skill . . . my skill for designing houses."

"Well, we do a lot of houses here. But you know, Bob does most of the initial designs . . ."

"Wouldn't there be opportunities, though, to create some of my own? Lesser projects?"

"People come for Bob's talent. We're here to implement it. He

sketches things out. We make it come to life. Ron Danke does all
the fine, detailed design. He's designed fabrics for Bob. Furniture,
things like that, then Bob approves it."

"Okay," I say. "Well, what would I do?"

"Work with Bob to make things come to life, as I said. He'll say,
'I see clerestory windows in the living room. Sleek doors. Interesting knobs. Silver.' Then you design the doors, the knobs. The room,
more or less. You spec out the options on windows. Things like that.
And of course, someone's got to design the plumbing, wiring."

"Me?" I ask.

"Perhaps," he says. "Do you have a problem with that?"

"Maybe so," I say. "I've been an architect for twenty-three years.
I've designed dozens of houses. I don't want to design only plumb-
ing. Sure. If I design the house, I'm happy to design the plumbing.
But I'm too experienced to be siloed."

He nods. Probably, I shouldn't have told him that I've been doing
this for twenty-three years, shouldn't have admitted how old I am.
Bad form, I guess. Surely I've been doing this longer than he has.
Will that intimidate him?

And maybe I shouldn't have told him I have limits to what I'm
willing to do, but I just don't want to do grunt work anymore. I've
graduated. I don't want to ride the subway to work one day and
stand outside my office, not wanting to go in. Jack, I think, would
be proud. When Brad McDougall shakes hands with me, I no
longer believe I have a chance of being offered the job.

Still, I ask Ann Lee if I'm going to get the opportunity to meet
Stockman. At least I would have that as a memory, meeting the
great man.

"No," she says. "If we hire you, you'll meet him. He's here so
rarely. His time is so precious." I guess that means he's here, but he
won't see me.

I'm introduced to one more person, a man named Lyle Cross. He's the money man. The CFO, I guess.

"What are you looking for money-wise?" he asks me point-blank. He stares across his desk, over his silver-rimmed half glasses.

I feel utterly unprepared. I haven't thought about this: What should I ask for? Should I ask for what I was making at Paris? No. I was being underpaid at Paris for years and years. I don't even know what senior people are supposed to make anymore. I press my lips together and blurt out a figure.

"Oh," he says, and seems pleased. I immediately know I should have asked for more.

"Well," Ann says as she escorts me to the elevator, "we'll let you know, one way or the other, within the next two weeks." I shake her tiny, cool hand.

"That would be great," I tell her. All the way down in the elevator, I think, Well, that's that. I now have no expectations for a job offer. And I'm even more uncertain about whether I would take it, even if it was offered. I ride the subway home, dispirited. And then once up in the dappled comfort of my bedroom, with the breeze blowing through the curtains, I happily tear off my suit, my stockings, and pull on soft old jeans and a huge old button-down shirt. I walk into my study and sit down at my computer table. Hank's house is nearly done. It's the best thing I've ever designed. Designing it has been delicious, despite the personal torment surrounding it. Designing houses is the pleasure I live for. Screw Brad McDougall. Screw Stockman's. This is what I was born to do.

Dear Sweet Jane,
 Would the weekend of the twenty-fifth be okay?
I know that's only ten days from now. My house-

keeper can stay with the children that weekend. Laine is comfortable with her, and when I've had to travel on business, she's the only person Laine would ever accept taking my place.

Don't think I'm not scared to have you see me too. I'm changed. I've aged. I'm not the boy with the long black hair and beard and bravado any- more. And I haven't been with a woman in so many years, you may have to teach me how. From scratch. So let us approach this as friends, old and trusted friends. You said that's what you re- member. Us lying in bed afterward, as friends. You help me. I'll help you. Whatever happens after that, happens. Oh, Jane. I am so hungry to see you. So hungry.

Love,
Jack

P<small>eggy</small> answers her phone on the first ring.

"Jane!" she says when she finds out it's me. "How *are* you?"

"Well, I . . . I think we have something to talk about," I tell her.

"We do?"

"Hank."

She is silent for a moment. I hear her brain toting up what she should say.

"What about Hank?" She coughs in the falsest way imaginable. Peg's never been very good at lying. Ohio girls can put on New York airs, but that doesn't make them good at subterfuge.

"Let's see. Could I . . . be upset because you're sleeping with him?"

"Where did you hear that?" she asks.

"I've heard that and more. I hear you're mad at me too."

"Jesus. What did he do? Tell you everything? I can't believe he did that. I mean, adding insult to injury."

"Wait. Who's insulted here and who's injured?" I ask. "Gosh, I think it's been me."

She is silent for a few moments. Silence is not something I often associate with Peggy. "I'm sorry," she says. "I couldn't help it. We went out for a drink. To talk about you. Really. I didn't know what was going on with the way he was treating you after your trip to the country, and I wanted to talk it out. I've always been attracted to him. Ever since the first time I met him years ago."

"Great. So you set him up with me."

"After two drinks, the next thing I knew . . . well, we were at the Algonquin. I still love the Blue Bar. And I said I was going to the ladies', and instead I went up to the desk . . ."

"I don't want details. You always want to give me details when I don't want them."

"I'm trying to be big about this. I'm trying to tell you it was my fault. I went and got the room . . . Look. I love S.D. I really do. But he's been ignoring me. I know it's no excuse. I know I had no right after fixing up the two of you. But you never seem to appreciate men the way I do. I really got into Hank, Jane. He's so sexy . . . He's so . . ."

"*Don't* tell me."

"Okay. Okay. I tried to warn you away from him. To tell you he was a bad choice."

"Did it happen again?" I ask softly. "After the time at the Algonquin?"

"I thought you didn't want details."

"I'm just trying to understand the way he was acting. I'm just trying to understand."

"I pushed it. He resisted. At least a little. He really likes you, Jane. He's made that infinitely clear. He told me it was a mistake from the start and that he wants to make a go of it with you, since I'm not even available. The thing is . . . I really fell for him, Jane. I felt more than I wanted to. And now things feel all screwed up with S.D. I mean, *I* feel screwed up with him. He hasn't even noticed. Oh, Janie . . ." Peggy's voice has melted into tears. Though I don't want to, I can't help feeling sympathy for her. It reminds me of the way she was when she discovered Sam was cheating on her. But of course now, she's doing the cheating.

"How many times, Peg?"

"Why do you want to know?"

"I just do." I grit my teeth and wait.

"Three times. We met three times. He was always resistant."

"Showing up at a hotel is not being resistant."

"Yeah . . . But he kept saying, 'This is the last time.'"

"Right."

"Jane, do you hate me?"

"Hate. Ummm. Yes. At the moment, that might sum it up." It's funny. I don't hate her, exactly. But I'm mad enough to let her think I do.

"Can I . . . Is it possible to . . . repair our friendship?"

"Do you want to?" I ask.

"Yes." I wait for her to say she's sorry, or that hurting me was the last thing she wanted to do. But she says nothing of the sort. She just sobs softly into the phone like the cheated-on wife.

"Anyway, just for the record," I tell her, "I'm not going out with him again. You can have him. I am simply his architect. I don't want anything more to do with him."

"No. He wants to go out with you. He says he felt like you and he were a great intellectual match."

"Great." Yeah. I'm the intellectual match. Peg is the physical match. "No way. I'm designing his house and that's it. I've got to go."

"Jane, say you forgive me."

"I'll call you when I do," I say.

"We've been friends for twenty years," she says.

"Well, you should have thought of that when you pulled down your pants," I say, and hang up on her.

My, my. I am a woman who can walk away. Still, walking away from Peggy hurts more than walking away from Hank. I barely knew Hank. Peggy and I know everything about each other. When I found out I was pregnant, she was the very first person I called. When the twins got their first periods—on the very same day—she was the first person I called. When I knew I had to leave Dan for good, she was the first person I called. And I can't tell you exactly why we're friends. We're not alike. She is mercurial, manipulative. A little crazy. And very entertaining. I am quieter, safer, far too predictable. Ah yes. I see the attraction. Opposites who have come to vaguely understand, and normally tolerate, each other. Of course, this time, she's gone too far.

Still, at my age, new friendships are rare. I know that I have lost something precious. Flawed, like all things. But very precious.

Nine

It's beginning to get dark early these days. Late October. And there's an icy coolness in the air, a delicious relief from the miserable, hot summer we had. Still, I'm burning up and turning inside out. It's October 25, and in a few minutes Jack will be here. I can't seem to understand that it's true. I feel as though I am watching a made-for-TV movie. What will happen to the old college lovers now?

But some part of me has been clued in, because while it all seems remote and unreal, I'm literally quaking with nervous energy. I've dressed in my favorite black-flecked knit dress, a belt with a silver buckle, a cashmere sweater, new black-lace underwear. In the last few days, I've perfectly plucked my eyebrows, applied cherry-red toenail polish, remembered to put lotion on my legs and arms every single day so they no longer feel like sandpaper. I look in the mirror and see a middle-aged woman all dressed up. And it's amazing, but I like what I see. Maybe because I'm so excited. Maybe because I'm used to myself. I'm larger than I want to be, but there is something still so strongly feminine about my curves. Will Jack feel that? My eyes are dark and purposeful. My lips are lined and sensual. I look like a woman who's seen things, who knows things. A woman you would trust. He told me to be the best me that I can be. And that's what I've done. And now, all I have to do is wait.

Wait. It's never been so difficult. The meal is cooked. The house arranged just so. I come into the front parlor and sit on the love seat by the window, and watch the sky turn slate, and then that taffeta blue of early dusk. The skies over New York City rarely have much depth. They always seem painted on somehow, like a mediocre high school set. But tonight, the electric blue is punctuated by a golden light glinting under the clouds.

Under this sky, Jack is coming my way. Probably he's in a taxi right now, sliding down the Brooklyn-Queens Expressway, nervous too. If he really does learn to love me, if he actually can accept me as I am right now, how extraordinary that will be. The good thing about falling in love when you're middle aged is that you don't have to ask your beloved if they'll still love you when you're old and gray. You're already old and gray. To have someone love me now, love who I actually am, would feel more extraordinary than winning the lottery.

I hear a car door slam and stretch up to see. Down below in the soft, dusky light, a wiry figure is stepping out of a taxi. Jack. His dark hair gleams in that last soft light. I watch him help the driver pull a gray suitcase out of the trunk. I know those movements. I know him all these years later as intimately as I did back then. I feel my whole body grip, for a moment. Clench. It isn't a good feeling. It is somewhere between nausea and giving birth. It is pain and lack of control. It's fear. Like a spasm, it passes, and then I go to the front door, only pausing for a moment before I open it. I step out on the stoop and look down at him still paying the driver, not yet cognizant that I'm there. I watch, hyperaware. It must be the adrenaline. Every detail is clear and notable. The way he shuffles through his wallet, the way he looks up as he hands the driver his money. I know, no matter what happens, that I'll remember this.

The cabdriver slams his door and starts to drive away, and then Jack sees me. When he smiles, a heat rises in me like a thermometer in the sun. I can't help smiling back. He comes up the steps, grinning, pulling his suitcase behind him. "I'm here," he says softly. I take it all in: the gray tweed jacket, the khaki pants, the black T-shirt. The strong, manly neck. He's still slender, but he's always had a broad chest, a muscular neck. A wrestler's body. Still I'd forgotten that he's not tall like Daniel or Hank. In my mind, he's always seemed big, so impressive.

"Jack."

He lets go of his suitcase and takes my face in his hands. This is it, I think. The inspection. His smile doesn't change at all, just broadens. His eyes fill with warmth. Maybe he really does like what he sees? His face, so close to me, is more dear to me than I could ever have imagined. The man who gave me a career, a vocation, is standing with me, looking into me. Mirth comes into his hazel eyes. I note the flecks of silver in his sideburns. The lines in his face, and the softness beneath his chin; every change seems somehow magical, beautiful. Age has somehow lost its sting in his familiar face.

"My Jane," he says. "All grown up. I'm not disappointed. I'm not disappointed at all."

There is nothing in this world Jack could have said to me that would have been as compelling. He's not disappointed. My whole being seems to lift. Breathless, thrilled, my mind racing, I take his hand and draw him into the house. With the door locked behind us, he sees none of the beauty I've worked so hard to create in the house. He seems to see only me.

"You look exactly as I imagined you would. Better," he says.

"You look so . . . familiar to me. As though we saw each other last week."

He laughs. "Twenty-eight years ago last week."

He takes my face in his hands again and kisses me. It is liquid and longing. It is nothing less than extraordinary. It's then I realize that I hadn't expected this meeting to be good. That I have told myself it will be a disappointment, a travesty, a mistake. For ten days now, ever since we agreed to see each other again, I've hardly had a hopeful thought. Never once, in those days and nights of worry and waiting, have I imagined how familiar he would seem to me, yet how new and extraordinary my feelings would be. Never once have I imagined he'd be pleased with the person I've become.

I take him into the back parlor, where the sofas are deep and welcoming, where the marble mantel is aglow with pillar candles I lit, blew out, and relit a half hour ago, trying to decide whether they seemed too self-conscious, a seduction, or welcoming, making this a celebration. They flicker and reflect in the mirror above the mantel.

"Beautiful," he says, regarding the candles. "God, Janie, what a house."

"I do love it," I say.

"I won't even let you see mine. It's so sad compared with this."

There is a soft, distant look that enfolds him for a moment. An old sourness that comes and leaves just as quickly. "Later, you'll have to give me the tour," he says. "And show me the portfolio of your houses."

"And I want to see pictures of your children, and show you pictures of mine."

He gets up and goes to the mantel, where a photo of the twins sits, framed in a simple silver rectangle. He shakes his head. "This is Abigail and Caitlin?" he asks. "They look nothing like you," he says.

"No. They are exact copies of Daniel. I merely carried them."

"No mean feat, I'm sure," he says, looking up, smiling.

"They were as small as pigeons. Together, they weighed hardly more than a large baby."

"They're beautiful. I mean, really extraordinary. But I somehow imagined I'd see a picture of them and find the young you all over again."

I shake my head. "The young me has to stay in your head, I guess."

He nods. "It's here," he says. "So all these years that I've been miserable, you've been living in a palace?"

"You should have seen it when I bought it," I tell him. And for a few minutes I talk about the years of work, the way it used to look. Cut up, unappreciated. Covered over. It is comforting to talk about houses with Jack. Jack is the man who made me love houses in the first place. We laugh. We are easy with each other. Easier than I'd ever guessed we could be.

Down in the kitchen is the meal I've already cooked. A romaine salad with oranges and slivered almonds in the refrigerator. Salmon with a brown-sugar glaze waiting in its pan on the stovetop. French green beans as tiny as threads. Couscous with herbs. In the dining room are two place settings carefully laid, the napkins tucked in silver rings, red gerbera daisies and purple salvia arranged in a round blue bowl in the middle of the table.

Everything beautiful, planned, waiting. Yet a part of me just wants to stop all this. A part of me would love to walk out the door and not expose myself to the flood of feelings, or even the flashes of numbness, that touch me when I look at him and think, He's here. A part of me freezes when I consider that tonight, after we eat, we will most likely make love. It has been so many years since

I've made love. Jack says I will have to remind him. No. He will
have to remind me. A part of me would never like to expose myself again: not physically, not emotionally, to the shock and thrill
of lovemaking, to that moment when losing yourself is the goal. It
is so much easier to dream about it, and lose nothing. So much
less dangerous to keep myself separate. I loved making love once.
I was insatiable once. And then it all became ugly. A burden. A
painful longing Daniel wouldn't fulfill. Can I learn to embrace it
again?

I give the tour of the house and Jack notes all the things that
make the house unique, the beautiful hardware and moldings.
The arrangement of each room. We carry Jack's suitcase up to my
room. He marvels at the beautiful bed alcove with the plaster pi-
laster marking its enclosure. He loves the moldings and knots in
the floors, which remind him of the floors in the English Building we helped save. He touches the marble mantels and likes
their cool, smooth bite. "Like a glass of cold cream," he tells me.
"I can't think of anything finer than living in a house like this," he
says.

"You can wash up while I get the dinner all ready," I tell him. "It's
cooked. I just have to reheat everything. Come down in a few minutes," I say, hoping for a few minutes to gather my wits.

"It's almost too much, isn't it?" he asks.

"What?"

"Being together like this. It's almost too rich. It'll be good to have
a minute apart to breathe, won't it?"

I nod. He's read my mind. I'd forgotten how it feels to have
someone understand me.

In the kitchen, I am so remarkably happy assembling the plates
and putting them in the microwave. Like a bride, I think. For once,
I'm not cooking for someone who thinks everything I like to cook is
gross or inedible or an insult to the senses.

Reasons why I'm thrilled that Jack is here:

1. He accepts me as I am . . . at least so far.
2. He understands my silent thoughts.
3. He loves my house the way I do, for the reasons I do.
4. Tonight, I can tell him I'm afraid and he won't laugh.

At dinner, we talk and laugh. He likes my cooking. He likes being with me. That's something that words don't have to tell you. You just know. I can barely eat, don't need to eat. Maybe ever again, I think.

After the plates are pushed away, Jack pulls out his wallet and shares pictures of his children. Clark is so much like him, it startles me. I can hardly put the picture down.

"It's you," I say.

"I know. Even I see it. It's like looking in a mirror."

Ned is a funny little boy with glasses, just as I imagined he'd be, but his face is softer and younger than I expected, and his eyes are large, dark and sad. He looks less like Jack used to, and somewhat more like he does now. Wounded, I think.

"He looks like a professor," I say.

"A theologian. The man who makes you regret your sins just by being in the same room with you. He doesn't want to project that, I don't think. He just does. My little minister." He takes back the picture and looks at it for a minute, bemused. "He's the one who's been hurt the most, I sometimes think. Laine doesn't remember Suzanne, but Ned does. Someday, I suspect he's going to make a therapist's day."

Jack hesitates before he pulls out the picture of Laine.

"And this is Laine," he says. "I have to warn you. She does not look like a normal child." He says this somewhat formally, as though it's rehearsed, something he's had to say many times. "I love her anyway. I love her for who she is."

I take the picture from him and see a horribly lopsided face. Eyes too popped and large. A mouth like a smear, and yet that mouth is smiling. And that smiles makes her face beautiful in its crooked way. I find myself getting choked up. Tears come right into my eyes. He's watching me.

"Does she frighten you?" he asks.

"No. She breaks my heart."

"She has no concept of pity," he says. "She thinks she's lucky. She doesn't really know that she's different. Not really. Or if she knows, it just doesn't matter to her. I love her, and she's more grateful for love than my other two children."

"Children don't show gratitude for being loved. They expect it. Mine expect everything from me."

"Most children don't. But she's happy to have us as her family. I think that for a long time I've considered my job in life making sure she's happy. Her first few years were so rough . . ." His eyes look far away for a moment and I see pain there. Pain I can only imagine, never really know.

I put my hand on his and he looks up at me and smiles.

"I'm glad I'm here," he says. "More than you can know."

"Are you scared?" I ask.

"Terrified," he says. "Thrilled too."

"I'm terrified too."

"Good. We're even, then." He leans over and kisses my brow. "There's no rush with this," he says. "We do what we want to do. We stop if it feels wrong." I nod.

After the kitchen is cleaned up—Jack helps, drying the pots, talking—we turn off all the lights downstairs, put on the alarm, and go up to the bedroom. I remember briefly how it used to feel with Daniel there, closing up the house for the night. Knowing that I would lie in bed and feel lonely—in this very bed—Daniel turned away from me. I feel sad just remembering.

While Jack is in the bathroom, washing up, I go to the dressing room between my bedroom and the study and change into a black silk nightgown I bought last week. The gown is beautiful, but uncomfortable. I know I will be aware of it all night. Still, it shows off my breasts, whittles my waist. I had found it irresistible, now I wonder if I should change. It reminds me of the silk gown I wore on my wedding night. White silk with scads of lace and spaghetti straps. Bias cut and tight. It looked blissful in the store. I wore it once, and could never bear to sleep in it again. Maybe because even on our wedding night, Daniel didn't seem very interested. We'd already been living together for a year. He had already been sleeping with many other people. Of course, I didn't know that then. I just knew that when we made love, it felt as though he was merely indulging me.

I wash my face at the sink in the dressing room. I hate to take off the makeup, to expose the late-forties woman beneath the paint. But there she is. Fresh. Not so bad. Glowing. Jack comes out of the bathroom in an open robe. Beneath it, I can see boxer shorts, a T-shirt. It's so odd. We haven't been together in all these decades, and here we are getting ready for bed like old partners. Roommates, I think with a smile.

"Can I light a candle?" he asks.

"Yes. I guess." There is a votive on the mantelpiece. How many years has it been since it glowed? I find a book of matches in the button box on my dresser. Again, that quaking feeling begins. He lights the candle and we turn off the rest of the lights.

I start walking toward the bed. "Come here near the candle so I can look at you," he says.

"I don't have any makeup on."

"It doesn't matter. Let me see you as you really are."

We stand by the mantel. So close to each other the electricity arcs between us.

"You're shaking, aren't you?" he asks.

"Yes."

"We don't have to make love tonight."

"We don't?" I ask. I realize I'm not at all relieved. In fact, I feel miserable. His saying we don't have to make love reminds me far too well of all those nights when Daniel made excuses. We climb into bed, and I turn away from him.

"What's wrong?" Jack asks.

"You don't want me," I say.

He laughs. "Oh, Jane."

"You don't."

"Are you joking? I was trying to be sensitive."

"Well, stop being so fucking sensitive," I say. We laugh in the dark. We're friends again. He takes me in his arms and kisses me. His kisses are wet, deep, absolutely tropical. I never want them to end. He admires the nightgown in the candlelight, then asks if he can take it off without ripping it.

"Probably not," I say. "Do I have to take it off?"

"No. We also don't have to make love."

"Do I have to take it off to make love?" I ask.

"I see you, Jane. And nothing I see makes me love you any less. I like what I see. I like who you are now."

"I'm lumpy. I'm old."

"I'm a guy who hasn't made love in so many years, who knows if I still can?" he says. "Will you laugh at me if I can't?"

"Of course not."

"Then take your nightgown off. Love is all about exposure, isn't it?"

"What makes you so brave?" I whisper.

"I've lived too long with the alternative."

Making love with Jack is nothing like lovemaking before. Not even with Jack. Because tonight, he's so present. And it's all about curiosity and discovery: the peach-round shape of a shoulder, the touch of skin, the pressure of hips against hips. Somehow, we hold our connection through it all. I've never known lovemaking like this. I lost touch with Daniel every time we made love. But Jack. We talk, we whisper. We feel everything together. And when I freeze, when for a moment I feel nothing but a desire to run, he knows that too.

"What?"

"I don't know."

"You having trouble?"

I nod. "I'm numb, almost. It's fear, I guess."

"It's okay," he says. "Let's just talk for a while." But the talking turns to touching, and I come alive again. I am ready now. Ready for him.

He looks into my eyes as he enters me. We move as one. Like music. Like singing a cappella. One tune. He touches me when I need to be touched. He helps me feel everything. He looks afraid sometimes, and we slow down. He cries when I come.

There are few moments in your life that alter you. Few moments that act as a curtain between then and now. The past and the future. Few moments that are better in real life than in memory. If I tell you that tonight is one of those moments, you might groan. You might say that it's too romantic. Too idealized. Supplied by my longing. You'd be wrong. I am here. I am feeling this. I know. Pleasure is fleeting. Love is uncertain. But at this very moment, lying in his arms after we've made love, I am happier than I've ever been. Ecstatic. I feel suddenly certain that ecstasy has eluded me all my life, until now. And now, I never want to lose it.

It doesn't matter that the nightgown isn't made for sleeping because we sleep naked. At least for a while. About four in the morning, I wake shivering and go to the closet for my favorite pink knit gown. The one that feels like an old friend. I put it on and climb back into bed. Jack is fast asleep on his stomach, his head turned toward me. In the streetlight, I cherish the soft glow of his face. Childlike, trusting. His nose is pushed so hard against the pillow, it pugs up. His dark, silky hair is cowlicked like a little boy's. I have two emotions at once: (1) a feeling that I never want him to leave, (2) terror. He will leave, I know. And then what? Our lives are so different. We are each responsible for children who are used to the places they have always lived. And in my case, daughters who need to be near their father. And what about my house? I could never leave New York. I can't imagine it. And Jack, would he ever leave Nashville? He has his own firm there. In some ways, he's much more established than I am. His boys and Laine have been through so much. Laine's school is there. Jack's whole life is there . . .

I lean back on the pillow and try to sleep. This naked man next to me has opened my heart. But I feel it closing. Because what good will it do?

He wakes before I do, and when I roll over, he's gone. I listen for him in the bathroom, but he isn't there. I brush my teeth and put on a robe. I've slept relatively well for having shared my bed, and yet I look like I've been up all night. I can't help putting on a bit of makeup: some blush and some concealer on the dark crescents beneath my eyes. But the concealer won't stick. I can't hide the darkness I feel. It's a dull morning. There won't be any sun today. Most likely, rain. I look out and see that the trees are turning at the tops. Autumn. I've never liked the heat of summer, and I love the autumn here. But New York winters are sad.

Jack's in the kitchen with a bowl of cereal. He found the bowl, the cereal, the milk, all of which strikes me as extraordinary.

"I was hungry," he says.

"Did you find what you need?"

He takes my hand. "I have now," he says.

Oh, brother, I think. Is he going to get all romantic again? It's not what I want. I feel oddly angry. Huffy. I turn away from him, and pull the orange juice out of the refrigerator, then shove it back in.

"Hey, Jane?" he says. "What's going on?"

How did he read me so quickly? I could get away with a week of anger before Daniel realized it.

"I don't know."

"You don't know or you don't want to tell me?"

"I don't know. I just feel crabby. I don't know why."

"Let's see, does it have anything to do with the terrible time we had together last night?" He smiles softly.

I shake my head, can't help smiling back. I swallow some tears that have risen unexpectedly into my eyes.

"I guess I just don't want to feel this much," I whisper.

He nods. "I know exactly what you mean. Let's see if raising your blood sugar helps. You want some cereal?" I nod.

"Okay." He walks to the cabinet. "Smart Start, Honey Nut Cheerios, Life."

"Life."

"Good choice. Always choose Life."

He takes a bowl from the cabinet, a spoon from the drawer. He wants to take care of me. It's amazing. Someone wants to take care of me!

"I should be waiting on you," I say.

"You did last night," he says. "My turn to cook. And let me warn you, this is about it when it comes to cooking. I know how to make quiche, hamburgers, and salad. And cereal, of course. I'm excellent at dishing out cereal." He throws the dish towel over his arm as he serves the cereal, suddenly the snobby waiter about to serve the bouillabaisse.

"Quiche?" I ask him. "You make quiche?"

"Suzanne taught me. And lemme tell you, I make a mean quiche. Broccoli, ham, tons of cheese . . . as dense as a brick. But the buck stops there. Once Laine said, 'Daddy, no more quiche. It smells like rubber bands.' But the boys like it."

"I can imagine you as a father," I say. "Easily."

I eat my cereal in silence for a while. He watches me.

"What?" I ask.

He shakes his head. "I'm just taking it all in," he says. "So I can remember you when I go home."

"Will we ever see each other again?" I ask.

"Jane. For God's sake, I'm in love with you. Of course we'll see each other again. A lot."

"You're in love with me?"

"I think I am."

We laugh. Our uncertainty is so mutual.

"It will be expensive," I say.

"Who the hell cares? Pawn the diamonds. This is worth it . . . Is that why you're crabby?"

"I guess I want to know what will happen."

"Look," he says, "if I lived next door, we wouldn't know what would happen. Let's just play it out. I just told you I love you . . . Is it . . . is it mutual?" he asks. He looks so vulnerable sitting there. "I mean, I'm sitting here with Crabby Appleton. Maybe you just want to get rid of me."

"Crabby Appleton from *Captain Kangaroo*!" I say. " 'Rotten to the core.' "

"Yes."

"And Mighty Manfred the Wonder Dog. And Tom Terrific!"

"Yup."

"That was 1956, 1957. God, are we old! Ancient," I say.

He looks glum.

"What?" I ask him.

"I was waiting to see if you love me," he says. He sounds about nine.

"I'm crazy about you," I say. "But it feels like having a third arm, at the moment. I don't know what to do with it."

"A third arm. Interesting analogy," he says. "Okay. I'll take it. As long as you're crazy about me. Does that mean you love me?"

"You want to hear the word 'love'?"

"Yes."

"I have so many feelings. And it's scary as hell." I wish I could give him what he wants, but it's the best I can do for now.

"Ah, I know what you mean," he says softly. "But the good part is, we're in it together."

Jack and I spend three days learning to touch. To sleep together like spoons. To give each other silence sometimes. I see in him occasionally a restiveness, a squelched fury, and it makes me step back, hold back. It comes out unexpectedly, when we have to wait in line for nearly ten minutes to pick up our checked coats at the Metropolitan Museum of Art, or when I get so caught up in a conversation with him, I forget to make us get off at the West Fourth Street subway stop and we have to walk back from Fourteenth Street.

For the briefest moment, here or there, I witness the anger and impatience of an unhappy man. Such a quiet flicker, yet I think, This will never work. It's bound to go wrong. Someday, he's going to turn that on me. I find myself looking for problems, or searching his eyes to see boredom or distaste. I don't see it. But I search and search. Sometimes, I think I'm almost disappointed not to find it.

On the last night, Sunday night, we make love while it's still light out, and as sort of a joke, I tie a silk scarf over his eyes, so he can't see me in all my cellulitic glory. But I find with him blindfolded, I can tease him, play with him, not let him know what I'm going to do to him until I do it.

"I'm going to touch you," I tell him.

"Okay."

"Ah, but where do you think?"

"I don't know." He shivers. He's thrilled. We're playing in a way that says he has to trust me.

"Can you feel my hand near you?"

"Yes."

"Where?"

"Near my thigh."

"Wrong."

"Your hand isn't near my thigh?"

"No. My breast is near your thigh. My hand is here." I grab his instep and he jumps. "And here." I touch his neck. "And here." I tease his cock. Then we are laughing, wrestling, taunting each other. But I'm in charge. By the time I straddle him, and take him into me, it's dark. The streetlights have gone on. I ride him sweetly, insistently. And I feel beautiful. Fluid. And young. Then, I reach down and pull the blindfold from his eyes. And the pleasure we feel together, looking at each other the whole time in the semidark, is extraordinary. I'm sure that when I was eighteen we never made love like this. The pleasure is like a peony that starts as a tight, simple bud and blooms into something blowsy and huge and saturated with color. Always, before, he's been the elder, the leader. But tonight, when I take over and tease him, and control our fun, we become equals.

As we lie there afterward, I nestle into his shoulder, smell the sweetness of his skin, feel his hard, smooth chest and experience satisfaction deep enough to last me. Tomorrow, he'll be gone, I think. We feel like adjoining pieces of a jigsaw puzzle, creating a bigger picture, but tomorrow we break back into two.

"What time do you have to leave?" I ask him.

"Tomorrow?"

"Yes."

He sighs. "Never," he says. "I'm just staying. You don't mind, do you?"

"We'll have to buy you a whole new wardrobe."

"And a full-time father for my kids. And someone to take over my position at Jack Crashin and Associates. Can I find that at Bloomingdale's?"

I am silent. I taste tears before I know I'm crying. I look over at Jack and he's peering at the ceiling. He has a sudden drawn look. He's shaking his head. He looks over, maybe noting my silence, and sees I'm sad, pulls me closer to him. In the morning, he will go.

"We could look at this two ways," Jack says.

"What do you mean?"

"We could say, 'What a fine mess. Now we have all these feelings for each other and we're eight hundred miles apart.' Or we could realize how lucky we are, that despite eight hundred miles between us, we've found each other again. I prefer the second way," Jack says.

"What will happen?" I ask him.

"We'll make it up as we go along."

"It's scary," I say, noting that I sound like a child.

"I'm scared too," he says. "But it's so much better than what I've had for so long. It's worth wading through the fear."

I lie in his arms, swim in the warm strength of his hold on me, wish I could memorize every breath, every altered molecule of this

moment. But I can't. In a few hours, it will be gone, relinquished
to four or five mental images, poorly rendered, weaker each time I
visit them.

"You know what this feels like?" I ask him.

"No. What?"

"The night before you went away to Yale."

"No," he says. "It's nothing like that." His grip is suddenly tighter.
I hear the catch in his breath. He wonders if I'm right. "No," he
says again. "This is a beginning. That was an end."

"It wasn't an end for me. We wrote. We stayed in touch for a
while. I always hoped . . . that someday . . . I never let go of the relationship."

"Well, this time, neither of us will let go. We'll write, we'll talk,
I'll come here again, you'll come to Nashville."

"And in the end, what?"

"We can't see it from here. That doesn't mean an answer isn't
there."

"You're more patient than I am."

"Yes," he whispers. "When it comes to things like this, I suppose
I am." He knows it too. I've never had the grace of patience. The
certainty that patience requires. "You wait and see," is all he says.
"You wait and see."

He's scheduled for an eight o'clock plane. The alarm clock goes
off at six. His car to the airport is to come at seven. We are quiet
this morning. Tired. He eats his cereal in silence. He doesn't look
up at me. I sit quietly in my chair, eating nothing. This weekend has
felt like a time out of time. It has no relationship with my daily life.
Today is Monday, and when he is gone, my life resumes. This week,
perhaps I will hear from Stockman, or decide that I don't care. This
week, I will show the first drawings to Hank. This week, I must de-

cide if I care about making up with Peggy. And nothing that happened this weekend will change any of it. If I never see Jack again, this weekend will feel like a Fabergé egg. Perfect and useless. Something I can take out and examine when I am sad, or hungry for beauty. I feel indescribably deflated.

The car honks its horn outside. In the distance, I hear fire engines. I think about how when he is gone, I will sink into a hot bath and cry. We go up to the entrance hall and he pulls his suitcase from the corner where he's set it.

"I'll call you tonight," he says.

"I'm not sure people can have relationships from afar," I say.

"I don't know about other people. But I'd like to try."

He pulls me to him and kisses me. His kiss is far too slow for the car outside, which honks again. He's in New York. Things must move much more slowly in Nashville.

"I love you," he says.

I don't answer him. I don't know how I feel. I'm jangled. Confused. He smiles softly.

"It's okay," he says. "I know this is hard. I know it's confusing." I shake my head in wonder as he goes out the door. Standing on the stoop, I watch him lift his suitcase into the trunk, then open the car door and get in. His usual wiry energy seems gone. He looks tired. Funny how you can read that from up here. The door shuts, and in a moment, the car slips down the street, stops at the light, then disappears down the slope of Park Slope.

When he is gone, I shut him out like a window being slammed closed. I don't think of him at all. I don't take a bath and cry. I step into a shower and lather furiously. Then I go to my study and work hard on Hank's house. In the middle of the afternoon, I am distracted by pangs of longing for Jack. This is no Fabergé egg. I can't let it be. This is something I must *make* happen. This is the beginning of my new life, if I choose it to be. I have choices now, and I must make them. I have choices, and I want to make them.

Barney calls.

"Jane. I have something to tell you," he says.

Oh no. I've been waiting for this and pushing it out of my mind day after day. I call every three days now, more if she's on my mind. Barney has patiently kept me informed. But I've been waiting. I've known that time is running out.

"The prognosis isn't good," he says.

"How bad is it?" I ask him.

"She's in the hospital again. It won't be long . . . a few weeks. She may be in the hospital the whole time. Or a hospice." His voice cracks. I imagine that he's crying.

"Barney." His words have hit me like a cannonball in the stomach. I've been standing but I sit right down on one of the dining room chairs. I can hear my next-door neighbors arguing. Through the dining room windows, I watch a family pass on the street, the woman holding a pale bald baby in a carrier. Life is going on all around me. But in my head, everything's stopped.

"There's no hope?"

"Nothing short of a miracle," he says.

"Does Aggie know?"

"I told her that we have a lot to fight. I didn't see the point of telling her she has no time to fight it."

"You did the right thing," I tell him. "I'm coming down there," I say.

"No. Not yet. If you come, she'll know she's dying."

"I can't not see her," I say. "I have to see her before she . . ."

"Before she dies. I've learned to say it, Jane. It's better to say it. It helps me. Okay, come. Maybe you should." He sounds very tired, and for the first time, I think, he sounds old. "God, Jane, I love her," he whispers to me.

"Me too, Barney," I say. "We'll survive this together. I'll call to tell you when I can be there. I love you," I tell him. "I love you."

When the girls come home from school, I talk to them about Aunt Aggie. They sit in their respective chairs, each clutching at some part of herself. Cait is holding on to her elbows. Abby is pulling her knees up to her chin.

"They're sure they can't do anything?" Abby says.

"It doesn't seem so. I thought you guys should know."

"It's a good thing Barney's there with her," says Abby. "She'd be all alone if he wasn't there." I nod.

"I'm going down," I tell them. "In two days. I've talked to Dad. You'll stay with him."

"Shouldn't we go?" Abby asks.

I shake my head. "No. You have school. Dad will put you on a plane for the funeral." I can hardly say the word. I remember my mother's funeral. I was in so much pain, it was all a blur to me.

"Barney's going to be a mess when she dies," Caitlin says. She has tears in her eyes. She's always the first to cry. "Will he still come for Christmas dinner?" she asks.

"If he's up to it. He'll always be welcome."

"They're so cute together," Abby says. "Like they just fell in love. The way they hold hands and everything. The way he can make her blush."

We all look at each other in silence. There are tears in all of our eyes.

"When you or Dad is sick or anything, you'll take care of each other, won't you?" Abby asks.

"You don't have to worry about that now, thank God," I say.

"We're both young and fine." But I wonder. What would happen if I was truly ill, or Dan? How alone the thought makes me feel.

"If you say one more word about Mom dying, I'm leaving the room," Cait says. "You're going to live until we're old ladies. Right, Mom?"

"I'll do my best," I tell her.

That night, I call Hank.

"I'm ready to see you," I say.

"You've forgiven me?" he asks breathlessly.

"About the house. I've finished my drawings. I want to show you."

"Oh."

"I think you'll be pleased. I've given you options. I've got a good sense of costs."

"Jane. What about us?" he says.

"No," I say. "It's not going to happen. Look, I need to get together with you soon. I have to fly to South Carolina. My aunt is dying."

"I'm sorry," he says. "Are you close to her?"

"Very."

"Why won't it happen, with us, I mean?"

"Because . . ." I take a deep breath. "Because I'm in love with someone else."

"What? Come on. You can't be."

"I am."

"But you said nothing earlier." I know he doesn't believe me. He thinks I've made it up to hurt him. But telling him has made it even more real to me. I am in love with Jack. I can't close him out. He's right here in my heart. Someone knows me. Someone understands me. Someone accepts me as I am. And I love who he is. I wouldn't change a hair on his head. Could there be any more cause for love?

"So, can you come over and see the plans tonight?" I ask.

"Okay," he says. "Can we talk about us some more then?" he asks.

"No," I tell him. "I know you don't believe me, but no."

At nine-thirty, he comes over. His eyes are bright. I sense he still believes he can seduce me. Instead, it is the drawings that seduce him. Presenting them to him is thrilling. He is so excited about the house, the details, he makes me go over the plans again and again, asking endless questions. Later, leaving, he tries to put his arms around me to thank me and I step away.

"No. I really am in love. You'll find out from Peggy. He was my college sweetheart. He just spent the weekend with me. You're too late, Hank." We weren't right for each other, anyway, I think. But I don't say it.

Just as I'm getting ready for bed, Jack calls.

"Hi there," he says. His voice sounds so welcome to me. "I can't believe I'm here and you're there."

"I know."

"I had a wonderful time with you," he says. "It was much more than I could have imagined."

"Yes. I'd feel so happy . . . except . . . My Aunt Aggie is dying."

"Oh no. Jane. Jesus. You said she was ill."

"I didn't know it was this bad. I'm going down there on Wednesday. I wish you were here."

"Do you want me to be there?" he asks.

"You mean in Charleston?"

"Yes."

"You can't leave your children."

"Maybe not immediately."

"Barney said it could be a few weeks. I don't know how long I'll stay down there. Daniel said he'd be happy to take the girls until I come back."

"Where will you sleep?"

"On the couch at Barney and Aggie's apartment."

"I could talk to my housekeeper. I could see about coming in a week or so."

"Jack," I say. The thought of his presence warms me. "Maybe after I get there. Maybe after I see how long . . ." I start to really weep. I hate feeling so weak.

"If you need me, I'll come," he says.

Two days later, I am in South Carolina, standing by Aunt Aggie's hospital bed. She seems so small, so lost in her bed. Even her face seems shrunken, childlike, lost in the swollen maw of the white hospital pillow. In sleep, her lids are as blue and translucent as a baby's.

"Aggie?" I whisper. She stirs, and then opens her eyes. When she sees me, it's as though her whole being smiles. As though the faint wattage that's left in her musters a sudden glow.

"Janie," she says. Her voice is hoarse. Barney warned me it would be. Some drug, maybe, or illness, has taken away the sweetness, the remarkable youthfulness of her voice. "I was hoping you'd come soon."

"I'm right here."

"Sit down," she says, as though she's inviting me into her parlor. "Hold my hand," she tells me. Her hand is light and birdlike and pale on the sheets. I lift it into mine. Enclose it. Warm it.

"Are you afraid to be here?" she asks me.

"No. I'm glad to be here."

"Are you afraid of death?" she asks.

"Are you?"

She smiles. A saint, I think. She's always been a saint. "Only for Barney," she says. "Will you look out for him?"

I nod. "Yes. Of course."

"Will you tell Bess and Charlie and Peter I love them?"

"Yes."

"And Abby and Cait, of course."

"You're not going to die right now?" I ask. "Are you?"

She laughs. It's astonishing to me that she can still laugh. "Not right now. But soon enough. I want . . . I want to tell you these things while I still can."

"I'll remember all of them."

"Most of all, watch out for Barney. Most of all."

"Yes. He's here. In the corner right there, you know." I look over at him, sitting in the only extra chair near the other now empty bed.

"It's okay. He knows I worry about him."

"I'll look after him. I promise."

She closes her eyes. She'll sleep for a while, I think. I can't help remembering my mother's death. How I sat by her bed for a whole month, day after day, watching her die. When she was awake, she was always fighting it: a demon wrestling with her sense of who she was. In the end, my mother got so bitter, it was as though with every encroachment of the cancer, any kindness left was forced from her. How angry she seemed. How unhappy I realized she was, and had been for years and years. Aggie is the opposite. In her bed, she exudes a serenity. There's peace lighting her face. A quietness my mother never knew. This is how I want to die, I think. At one with my life. Ready.

Barney and I take a walk. It is warm and breezy. Swimming weather. I've packed summer clothes, but too serious for South Carolina: all of them black or gray. I don't own appropriate warm-weather clothes. I think of these last years. How Aggie's always come to New York wearing pink or salmon or turquoise. Tropical colors that hit me right between the eyes. Tropical colors that feel right only here in the South. Now, I feel equally inappropriate. Hot in my dark clothes. Self-conscious.

"I'm glad you've come," Barney says. He looks very tired. And shorter than I recall. His hair is nearly white now. And there are pale lines cupping his perfect smile, the one that garnered him the name "the Cheerful Weatherman" many, many years ago.

"The doctor told me this morning she has only a day or two left. She's going much faster than he thought she would. Aggie says that when she's gone, you might stay on, or come back soon and help me sort through her things. I have a list of things she wants to give to you kids. And to some of her friends. She said if you were there, it would be easier for me to go through them."

Barney is saying this very dutifully, like a child, but I can tell that he barely comprehends what he's telling me. He's saying it without any emotion. It's clear that just beneath the surface, he is dangerously liquid. I take his arm.

"I guess I've been lucky to have had her as long as I have," he says. "Lucky that I've had a wife who made me so happy." His voice is very high, very thin.

"Did you know you loved her right away?" I ask. "When you first met her?"

"Oh no. My first wife and I had an awful divorce. I didn't want to date anyone. A friend sat Aggie next to me at a dinner party. She was the first person who made me laugh. I thought, Well, I have no real interest in her, but if I go out with her once, everyone will leave me alone. See, people were always trying to set me up with women back then. So I took her to a movie. And after the movie we took a walk and she said, 'Barney, I know you can't believe it right now, but someday you and I are going to get married.' "

"She said that?" I'm shocked. It doesn't sound a thing like Aunt Aggie.

"Yup. She later told me it was the bravest and best thing she ever did. But that night I was thinking, Marry me? Sure, Toots, in your dreams. Still, I thought about how pretty she was, and funny too, and decided, well, it wouldn't hurt if I went out with her a few times. You know, just enjoyed myself. What harm could it do? And I kept saying that same thing to myself every day for two whole years. She was just as patient as could be. Never said a word about her expectations. Never seemed unhappy that we were always sort of casual. And then one day, I got real sick. I had the mumps. It's not a big deal when kids get it, but when grown-ups do, you just want to die. She came over and took care of me. And while I laid around with a fever of a hundred and four point five, I realized, right here in my life was the real thing. Wonderful. Beautiful. Loving. What the hell was wrong with me?"

We stop at a wooden park bench and Barney sits down. He leans forward, putting his hands between his knees. He looks off into the distance. As though he can see it all again.

"When I was better, I went to see her. She was living at your house at the time. That was a beautiful house Ed bought. I loved to go there. There were big elms in the yard. And that stream that ran out back. It was so peaceful. And then all you kids were always giggling and running around. I remember it like a picture. Just like a picture."

"Me too," I say softly.

"I always used to tell you that I really came over to date you. You were my own secret true love. Do you remember?"

I nod. I'd forgotten about that. I loved Barney. I loved how he made Aunt Aggie so happy. How she used to spray perfume into her hair before he came, and check herself a hundred times in the mirror, asking me, "Do you like this dress? It's not too too, is it? Does my petticoat show? Do you think he'll like it?"

"Well, I came over to pick her up that night. We were going to take the train into Chicago for a play at the Goodman Theatre. I was still pretty woozy. Pretty weak from the mumps. She was all dressed in pale yellow. A sweater, a skirt. Even pale-yellow shoes, I think. I got down on one knee right in your living room and asked her to marry me. And she looked at me, all soft and pretty in that pale yellow with her black hair. And you know what she said?"

"No. Tell me."

"She said, 'Told you so.' I laughed so hard I couldn't stop. She did too. I guess we've been laughing . . . ever since."

I'm crying. I don't know why Barney's story has touched me. I scrabble through my purse looking for a tissue, sponge off my tears and turn to him, expect that he's crying too. But he's not. He's just sitting on the park bench smiling. Smiling as sweet and big as you'd expect the Cheerful Weatherman to smile. And I just have to stop crying and smile with him. The two of us sit for a long time in silence, smiling, waiting for Aggie to die.

That night, I speak to Jack after Barney is asleep. And I am astonished how quickly Barney falls asleep. How can he rest so easily, I wonder, with Aggie so close to death? Perhaps Barney's tie to her is so strong, he will be the first of us to be able to let her go.

"It won't be long now," I tell Jack. "A day or two at most, the doctor said."

"Much faster than you thought," Jack says.

"Maybe it's better. Maybe it's just as well. It hurts to see her so tiny, so frail. She was always the strongest, the most vibrant. She'll always . . . always have my heart."

"I know she will," Jack says. His voice is like a lullaby.

"I told Cait and Abby I'd like them to come to the funeral. They want to come. Dan is ready to send them."

"I want to come too. I didn't realize it would be so soon. But I've called everyone to see who could stay with my kids. If it was just one night, I could leave Clark in charge. But more . . . My housekeeper's in Arkansas right now, through next week, visiting her mother. I don't know how quickly I can get away."

"You don't have to come," I tell him. "I don't expect it."

"I want you to expect it," he says.

"I don't want to expect too much from you," I say. I know I sound cold. Or bitter. I sound like my mother. But what's the good of putting my heart into something that can never come to pass?

"What's wrong?" he asks.

"We'll never really be together, will we?" I ask.

He is silent for a while. "I think anything can happen if we want it to."

"What are you going to do? Give up your firm? Drag your kids up to New York? Laine. How would she take it? And Ned? Because I can't come there. Not until the girls are in college. They need to be near Dan. And what am I talking about, anyway? We've only seen each other once in twenty-eight years . . ."

"I think we know what we want," he says. I don't understand him. I don't know how he can be so sure. But he was always like that. More confident than me in everything. More certain than I ever could be. "We just have to be brave enough. To take the risk of being wrong," he says. "At our age, haven't we learned that everything is repairable?"

"I can't believe you're saying that," I say. "You. After Suzanne. How could you say that?"

"Because here I am. Alive. Fine. It was awful for a while. It's been hard on everyone. It took me far too long to heal. But here I am. My life has been safe now for far too long."

"So, what will happen?" I ask.

"Nothing right away. We both need more time. The children

have to get used to us as 'us.' And we have to meet each other's kids. Laine may scare you. She will always be with me. With us. She will never grow up, you know. When we are old, she will still be a child. You'll have to see if you can stand that. If you can stand her. I love her, but she's mine."

"I know," I say. "I don't know how I'll feel."

"Thank you for being honest," he says. "There will be plenty of time for you to find out how you feel. Clark and your girls maybe should go off to college before we decide. But if we want to be together, we'll be together. Because life is short. And people die. And you only get a few chances to be happy." I think of Aggie. I think of my mother. And I know he's right.

"I love you, Jane," he says. "I don't need to see you again to know. I don't need another year to pass."

I haven't said "I love you" to a man in so long the words feel thick in my throat. I've danced around it too long. The time is now. My heart starts to gallop. I wonder if I have the courage to tell him. Through Barney's window, I can hear the rush of the ocean. The breeze blows the curtains, and in the next room, Barney snores evenly. With each breath, his life moves closer to being alone, and yet he sleeps.

"I love you too," I say. "I do."

"I know you do," he says.

Aggie dies the next morning. We are sitting by her bed. We have just arrived, as early as they would let us in: eight A.M. Aggie is paler, tinier. Perhaps rather than dying, I think, she is shrinking to nothing. She reminds me of the tiny Japanese show doll that she brought back for me many years ago from Japan. The tiny, chalky-white face. The feverish red lips—so blushed she almost appears to be wearing makeup. Her still-black hair glows dark against the pillowcase, just as the doll's lacquered black hair once glowed in its white pillowed show box.

Last night, or perhaps this morning, another patient was moved into the other bed in this two-bedded room, a heavyset woman with purplish-red hair.

"I told the last nurse a half hour ago that I want fruit," she tells the nurse now in a shrill voice. "Bananas. Apples. I don't give a damn. Any kind of fruit. What the hell is wrong with everybody around here? I'm a patient. I deserve what I want. I want fruit. I WANT FRUIT!"

"Your doctor says you can't have fruit. None. He says there's concern about your blood sugar levels."

"I am not a fucking baby. I want fruit."

"I'm sorry. Not today."

"An orange?"

"No."

"Prunes?"

"No."

"I want to see the administrator."

"I'm sorry, ma'am. I'll find your doctor."

"I don't want the asshole doctor. I want to see the administrator. I'm not asking for desserts. I am not asking for cherry cheese-cake . . . I'm not asking for chocolate éclairs." I'm wondering if she's delirious or just incredibly crabby. "I'm not asking for a man. I *want* a man. But I'm not asking for a man—except for the administrator. I just want some FUCKING FRUIT!"

Barney looks upset. He squirms in his seat, looking over at Aggie now and then as though she is a child he wishes to protect from the tirade. She sleeps quietly, so quietly I keep watching her chest, just to make sure it's rising and falling.

"Maybe we should talk to the desk about moving Aunt Aggie somewhere quieter," I whisper to him.

He nods enthusiastically. "Maybe," he says. "I want the last sounds she hears to be us, to be happy, kind sounds."

"I'll go ask them," I say. I get up and start toward the hall. But for some reason, I turn back and look at Aggie. And the minute I see her again, I know she's gone. I can't explain it. I'll relive it a thousand times, I'm sure. She was silent and emotionless before, but now it is so clear, she's emptied like an eggshell that's already hatched.

I look at Barney. He looks at me. There is no panic. There is no reaching out for a wrist or listening to her chest. There is no need for the call button. I shake my head. He shakes his. Our faces don't change. There are no tears. Just shock. There are no words of pain. Just silence. We are listening for her soul rising, and hearing nothing. We are looking into each other's eyes having lost what matters.

The woman in the next bed says to herself, "All I want is fruit."

I call the rest of the family that night: Bess and Pete and Charlie. They all agree to come for the funeral. I call my mother's and Aggie's one surviving brother, Uncle Stan, and Barney's sister.

And then I call Ed.

"Aggie gone? Oh, Jane." His voice is thick.

"She went faster than we thought. I wanted to know if you want to come to the funeral."

"I wish I could come," he says. "I owe her."

"Owe her?" I ask.

"I can't afford it, though. Especially now. I don't have a suit . . ."

"I could lend you the money. You could wear a sports jacket . . . You have one, don't you?"

"Yes, but . . . I'd better not. It would be hard for me, with the walker."

"Bess said you were having trouble getting around. She didn't tell me you have a walker."

"Had it a few months. Hate the way it looks." I'm silent for a moment. How little I've stayed in touch with him. How little I've given him. Though once, he gave me everything. He gave me a lavender room and a cherry tree and a father.

"What if I come to Chicago and get you?" I ask him. "I could carry your luggage, help you on the plane and off."

"You would do that?" he asks. I think about the money. I don't have a job now. But the other kids can pitch in. Together we can afford it.

"I want to. If you want to come. All of us kids would be there. I want you to come, Dad." I haven't called him "Dad" in a very long time. It feels good to say it. Wonderful.

"Jane, I couldn't ask you . . ."

"I'm asking you."

"I'd . . . If you really think you wouldn't mind . . ." I hear real excitement in his voice. "I owe it to her," he says, "I really do. And to see all of you kids . . ."

"I'll call you back and tell you when I'll be there," I say.

At two o'clock the next afternoon, I am locking and lifting his luggage, a beautiful old leather suitcase with sewn handles, the very one he used to carry for business trips when he was the king of Velveeta. His hair is perfectly combed, his long cheeks shaven. He is wearing an old tweed jacket that is too large on him now. Yet, he is still a handsome man. He still has dignity, though when I turn to close the door to his nearly empty room, I am saddened that it seems to be all he has.

At four, we are sitting on the plane to Charleston. His kind old face is lit with happiness.

"I've never been to Charleston," he says. "I'm just sorry it has to be at a time like this."

"What did you mean when you said you 'owe Aggie'?" I ask him.

"Oh," he says. He bites his lip. He struggles, I can see, for a moment about whether he should tell me.

"Aggie sent me money. I knew it was her. Every month for years."

"Aggie sent you money?"

"Yes. For ten, fifteen years. She didn't say it was from her. But it was. It had a South Carolina cancellation stamp on the envelope. I was pretty sure it was her handwriting on the envelope. There was only one letter—the first time she sent it. It said, 'Spend this as you need it.' I wrote her and thanked her, but said I would send it back, if it was from her. She never answered. I don't know . . . I guess if the money stops now, I'll know for sure."

I squeeze his hand. I imagine what it's been like for Ed in his little room on Clark Street, just barely living, with his walker and his single bed, his hot plate and his money from Aggie. How odd that a life could go so wrong. A life that was, for a while, so joyous and full. It was just like Aggie not to let him know for sure that the money was from her—it was the only way she could get him to keep it.

"Would you ever consider living near me?" I ask him.

He turns to me. I can see surprise in his eyes. Distrust too.

"Do you mean that?" he asks.

I nod.

"I wouldn't live with you," he says. "I don't think that's right."

"No. Of course not. Anyway, you'd never be able to negotiate all the steps. I'd find you a little place nearby. Maybe one of those places where older people live in apartments, if that's what you wanted. You know, where there are sometimes concerts or lectures or classes. And meals, if you want them. There's one right on Prospect Park. It overlooks the trees. I've never been in, but . . ."

"I couldn't afford it, probably," he says.

"I think we'd find a way," I tell him.

"A way?"

"Leave it to me," I say.

After the funeral, I will talk to Bess and Charlie and Pete, I think. Maybe even Barney. We all owe him something. We've ignored him for too long.

At the Charleston airport, I push Ed in a prearranged wheelchair to the gate where my girls are arriving. I arranged it so that we only have to wait a half hour for them, but our plane was late and within minutes they are coming through the jetway door. I stand in the airport air-conditioning, shivering as I watch them walk toward us. They are at the pinnacle of their beauty, at the beginning of their lives. Cait looks intimidated by the crowd, tries to spot me. Abigail struts with more purpose as though it wouldn't matter if anyone arrived to pick her up. But, I can see that even she is feeling fragile, that it is bravado. At this time of death, they are an elixir. I never noticed before, in their slender grace, in the tilt of their heads, how much they remind me of Aggie.

Ed stands up from the wheelchair to hug each of them. "I don't really use a wheelchair," he tells them. "Just here at the airport, with all the walking . . ."

"Okay," Abby says. "I'll ride in the wheelchair, and you push me." She plops down in the chair. "C'mon," she says.

Ed laughs. I can't remember the last time I saw Ed laugh. I've forgotten how wonderful and baritone his happiness sounds.

After the funeral, I come back to New York with the girls. Bess has agreed to take Ed back to his apartment in Chicago, then take a puddle jumper to Indianapolis. She volunteered. She and Ed spent a lot of time talking after the funeral. Maybe it's the closest she's ever been to him. And maybe it's the most open Ed has been with any of us in a long time. Mother is gone now. Aggie too. Perhaps it makes us realize how precious we all are to each other. Charlie and Pete readily agreed to share in a fund for Ed, to help pay for his move near me, for his rent. Even the twins seem excited that he might move close to us.

All through the funeral, they've been angels, but by the plane trip home, they've started to chip away at each other and now they are close to fisticuffs as we enter the taxicab.

I lean my head back against the taxi seat and realize how truly fatigued I feel. "I'm going to kill you," Abby says.

"After I murder you," Cait says.

"Stop it. Both of you. One more word and I'm getting out and walking!" I say. Surprisingly, they grow quiet, maybe out of respect for all they've seen in the last few days. The taxi driver is playing some Arab music, singing along vaguely. The girls start making faces at each other as they listen. The sound of the tires plays a different and more inevitable rhythm. The traffic slows as we near home. It is after four P.M. Rush hour.

And then it hits me. Surrounded by family, I never felt it so keenly: I cannot believe that Aggie is no longer alive. Though I stood at her graveside and shoveled a tablespoon of dirt onto her coffin. Though I helped Barney separate her jewelry and other effects, and now am wearing a beautiful diamond-and-sapphire band she inherited from her mother. Though I have cried many tears. I cannot believe that now I am the eldest. Of all of us. Except for Ed. And Barney.

The cab exits the Brooklyn-Queens Expressway, and slides through the crush of Flatbush Avenue, narrowly avoiding bicyclists, pushcarts, and other careening cars. And then in a few minutes, we are driving down Seventh Street accompanied by the red-gold confetti of falling maple leaves. Our house sits quietly among its brown neighbors, indistinguishable, stately. We are home. Humbled and tired. But home.

I don't see him until we start to climb the stairs. He is hidden by the dogwood tree. But he's there, sitting quietly on the top step, waiting. Jack. He stands now and comes down to help me with my suitcase.

"Jack!"

"Hello," he says, as though I should be expecting him. The girls look at each other querulously.

"This is Jack Crashin," I tell them. "My very old friend." They each say hello, looking back and forth between Jack and me. He doesn't kiss me in front of them. I'm relieved. Wise Jack. I hand Abby the key and they go on ahead, to open the door and turn off the alarm. When the door closes behind them, I turn to Jack, set everything down, and throw my arms around him. I am aging. I am no longer pretty. My bones ache and my scale warns me. My children fight and my friend Peggy and I are only now just beginning to speak again. But I feel more loved than I ever have. I feel blessed.

There are no immediate happily-ever-afters. I am surprised and thrilled to be offered the job at Stockman's, but I don't take it. I risk finding work building houses on my own. A bad risk at first, it turns out. So bad, Daniel finally gets to support the girls alone, for a month anyway. It makes him jubilant. He glows every time I see him. But then, all at once, when my money is low, and my spirits lower, I am offered more opportunities than I can handle. And I stay up late, drawing house after house. Creating places where people can find solace from the world, make their dreams come true, fall in and out of love, and pass many years.

Hank's house is built and published in *Country Living*. He was not so wrong about the siting. The house is after all even more beautiful close to the pond than where I wanted to set it. I stand on the sleeping porch one night, hands squeezed tight, rocking on my toes, as Hank lights his first fire, and the flames roar up and paint the river stones and the room a glorious shade of gold. I look out, and the firelight ripples on the pond, like sun on silk.

Hank is dating Peggy, since S.D. left her, but I hear he's cheating on her. David told me. Anna went back to Russia, so David calls me often, mostly to ask if I know any women I might set him up with.

Ed has moved to a studio apartment for seniors just ten blocks from our house. They give him decent meals in a downstairs dining room (boring, he says, because they add no salt since almost everyone else has blood pressure problems). Still, he's put on weight and has made friends with a woman named Jodi who's wild about canasta and Johnny Mathis. I secretly think she's in love with him. At first when I visited him, he and I would sit in the common room that overlooks the park and talk about the good old days. He seemed to like that too. But lately, he talks more about these days. Or about the future.

Soon Cait and Abby will go off to college. And then perhaps, Jack and Ned and Laine will move in. Sometimes Jack and I fight. Distance is hard. I fall in love with him more and more, each time we are together, and sending him off on a plane or getting on one myself often seems terribly cruel. Sometimes I think Jack's confidence crushes me. Sometimes I am strained by Laine's need for him, her resistance to me. By my girls' distrust of Jack and the whole situation. By Ned's piousness, and his teenage silence.

But there are many nights when I lie in bed and think about how lucky I am to be starting again. To still have challenges to meet. Sometimes I lie in bed and dream of a house. It sits by a pond or a lake or an ocean. There are plenty of rooms for visiting children. Rooms for grandchildren and friends. Rooms to grow old in. But best of all, there's a long, sunny dining room with French doors, a fireplace, and a simple Federal mantel. In the middle of the old pine floor sits an enormous table where we are all gathered: Cait and Abby, Jack, Clark, Ned, Laine, Bess, Pete, Charlie, and of course, Ed and Barney. Everyone is eating and laughing. I come in from the kitchen with a renewed platter of roast beef for people to take seconds. I set it on the sideboard, and in the firelight, I take the chair at the head of the table. I look around at each and every face, pausing at last on Jack's, and feel a fullness in my heart, wondering, How could things ever get any better?